DEADLY BONDS

Books by L.J. Sellers

DEADLY BONDS

A DETECTIVE JACKSON MYSTERY

L.J. SELLERS

THOMAS & MERCER

Published by Thomas & Mercer, Seattle
www.apub.com

Amazon, the Amazon logo, and Thomas & Mercer are trademarks of Amazon.com, Inc., or its affiliates.

ISBN-13: 9781477824306
ISBN-10: 1477824308

Cover design by Paul Barrett

Library of Congress Control Number: 2014902951

Printed in the United States of America

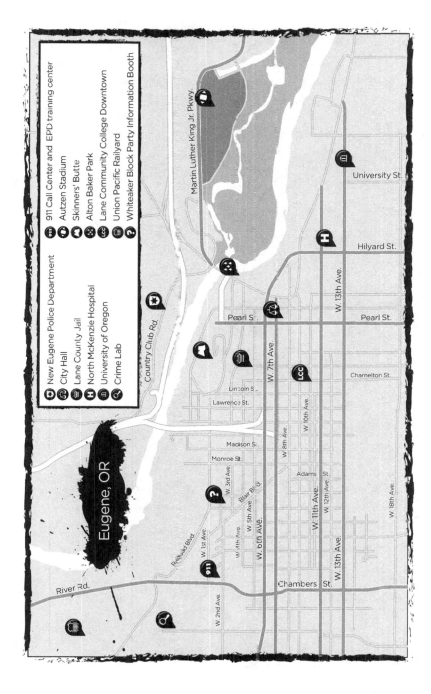

Eugene, OR

New Eugene Police Department
City Hall
Lane County Jail
North McKenzie Hospital
University of Oregon
Crime Lab

911 Call Center and EPD training center
Autzen Stadium
Skinners' Butte
Alton Baker Park
Lane Community College Downtown
Union Pacific Railyard
Whiteaker Block Party Information Booth

Martin Luther King Jr. Pkwy.

University St.

Hilyard St.

W. 13th Ave.

Pearl St.

Pearl St.

Charnelton St.

LCC

Country Club Rd.

Lincoln St.

Lawrence St.

W. 7th Ave.

Madison St.

Monroe St.

W. 8th Ave.

W. 10th Ave.

Adams St.

W. 3rd Ave.

Blair Blvd.

W. 5th Ave.

W. 4th Ave.

W. 11th Ave.

W. 12th Ave.

W. 18th Ave.

Railroad Blvd.

W. 1st Ave.

W. 6th Ave.

River Rd.

Chambers St.

W. 13th Ave.

W. 2nd Ave.

Cast of Characters

Det. Wade Jackson: Violent Crimes Unit / task force leader
Katie Jackson: Jackson's daughter
Derrick Jackson: Jackson's brother
Kera Kollmorgan: Jackson's girlfriend / nurse
Danette Blake: Kera's daughter-in-law
Det. Lara Evans: task force member
Det. Rob Schakowski (Schak): task force member
Det. Michael Quince: task force member
Ed McCray: ex-detective / private investigator
Sgt. Denise Lammers: Jackson's supervisor
Sophie Speranza: newspaper reporter
Rich Gunderson: medical examiner (attends crime scenes)
Rudolph Konrad: pathologist (performs autopsies)
Jasmine Parker: evidence technician
Joe Berloni: evidence technician
Victor Slonecker: district attorney
Jim Trang: assistant district attorney
Amanda Carter: young mother / homicide victim
Benjie: Amanda's toddler son
Dylan Gilmore: Amanda's neighbor
Lucille Caiden: Amanda's grandmother
Christy Blesser Chadwell: Amanda's best friend
Carl Wagner: Amanda's benefactor
Logan Grayson: football player
Jake Keener: Logan's roommate
Danica Mercado: Logan's girlfriend
Trey Sandoval: Danette's boyfriend / football player

DEADLY BONDS

CHAPTER 1

Tuesday, September 3, 1:15 p.m.

"How much cash did you log into the evidence system?" The state detective was thirty-something and eager.

Too young for this investigation, Wade Jackson thought. "$125,540."

A flicker of disbelief. "Who took possession of the money?" The man asking questions sat across from him in a conference room at the Eugene Police Department. At least they'd come to him.

"Ethan Young." One of three officers at the evidence lab under investigation for *misplacing* thousands of items of evidence— including drugs, guns, and money. Jackson shifted, not used to being on this side of an interrogation.

"The evidence log says only $100,540 in cash was submitted."

Thieves and idiots! "The log was altered. You can ask my partner, Rob Schakowski. He was with me when we logged it." The money had been recovered from an old robbery case, and they'd taken it in together to avoid this exact scenario. He hated the pall of suspicion, but he expected to be cleared. His phone beeped, and the other man nodded. The state detective understood the nature of Jackson's job.

The text was from Kera: *I need you at the hospital. There's been a car accident.*

A shiver shot up Jackson's spine. Had she been hurt? Even if she hadn't, his girlfriend was a strong woman who rarely asked for anything. This had to be bad. "I have to go." He didn't bother to explain.

Jackson charged from the room and almost bumped into Lara Evans.

"What's wrong?" Evans, the only female detective in the Violent Crimes Unit, grabbed his arm.

"Family emergency." Jackson paused. "An accident."

"Is it Katie?"

No one else in the department knew his fifteen-year-old daughter had run away from home months earlier. "The text was from Kera. I have to go to the hospital."

"Is she okay?" Evans' blue eyes filled with compassion, and her heart-shaped face pulled him in. She was often the best part of his workday.

"I think so." He trotted down the wide hallway and out the door leading to the back parking lot.

Twenty minutes later, he found Kera pacing the emergency waiting room. Even from a distance, she was striking—tall and broad-shouldered, with wide cheekbones, full lips, and a long copper braid. Micah, her toddler grandson, played nearby with colorful blocks. Another family huddled in the opposite corner, but most of the seats were empty.

She heard his footsteps and turned. Wordlessly, she fell into his arms and he held her tight. When she was ready, she would tell him. After a long moment, Kera pulled back and glanced at the boy on the floor. Micah grinned, drool running down his chin.

"It's Danette. She and Trey crossed the center line on Highway 58 and smashed into a truck. Trey was driving and he's critical, but"—Kera choked back a sob—"Danette might die. They've given her six pints of blood, and she's still in shock."

Jackson wanted to comfort her, but his cop mode kicked in instead. "Why were they on Highway 58?" It was a dangerous road, even in daylight.

"They were coming back from the Cougar Hot Spring." Kera's eyes flooded with tears.

They'd probably been drinking. If Danette died and the driver was drunk . . . "Is Trey conscious?"

"I don't know. They said he was critical but would probably pull through."

"Are his parents here?"

Kera shook her head. "He's a UO football player. I didn't want Danette to date him, but what could I say?" Danette wasn't Kera's daughter, but she was the mother of her grandson. Kera's son, Tate, had been killed in Iraq and had never known he was a father. Danette and the baby lived with Kera, one of the reasons Jackson and his girlfriend hadn't moved in together yet. A new worry wormed into his gut. If Danette died, Kera would become the baby's full-time parent. They'd faced this before, and he was no more ready now. He squeezed Kera's hand. "It's gonna be okay."

Jackson felt a tug on his pant leg and picked up Micah. The boy hugged him, and little pangs of joy—or maybe pain—tingled in Jackson's chest. He'd always wanted a boy, someone to share his love of muscle cars and rebuilding engines, the way he and his own father had. A few years earlier, his daughter had helped him build a three-wheeled motorcycle, but she'd only been humoring him.

He turned to Kera. "Have you eaten? Should we head to the cafeteria?"

"I need to stay here. A doctor said he would be back soon with an update."

The worry in her eyes made him feel helpless. Jackson sat, keeping the boy in his lap. "Then I guess we wait."

While they talked about the young people in their lives, his phone rang. He glanced and saw that the call was from his boss. Sergeant Lammers only called when she had a new assignment; otherwise she texted or e-mailed. He let the phone ring. Kera needed him. But how long could he sit in the hospital with her? What good would it do? He felt Kera staring to see if he would answer. He couldn't meet her eyes.

"Take it if you need to," she finally said, her voice resigned.

Guilt stabbed at his gut. Little Micah reached for the phone, and as Jackson pulled it away, the call connected. Lammers' voice boomed even with the cell at a distance. "Jackson? Are you there?"

He stood. "Yes, hold on." The waiting room had filled in the last hour, and there wasn't anywhere private. Jackson looked back at Kera, mouthed *I'm sorry,* and headed outside. "What's going on?"

"Possible homicide. A young female in a house in the Bethel area. Probably dead since yesterday."

Damn. Why had he answered? Dead young women triggered emotions he'd rather not feel. "I'm at the hospital with Kera. Her daughter-in-law was in an accident. Can someone else take the lead? I'll join the task force when I can."

An exasperated sigh. "I can't spare you. Schak is in court, and Evans is still too green for this kind of case."

Jackson was silent. Budget cuts had shrunk their division, and his boss didn't have many options.

Lammers pressed. "If Katie was in the hospital, that would be different, and we'd find a work-around."

He couldn't argue. He also hated hospitals and dreaded the possibility of being here for days. "Who called it in?"

"We're tracking the cell phone now. The caller refused to give his name."

A guy. The killer? "What's the location?"

She gave him the street address and he cringed. Pershing Street was in a pocket of low-rent houses near the railroad tracks, where transients came into town on boxcars, hopped off when they slowed in the train yard, then trotted down Roosevelt on their way to the Catholic social service center. The victim could have been killed by a drifter. But the area was also filled with drug houses and addicts, so her death could just as easily have been an overdose.

"I'm on my way. I want Evans out there too. And Schak on the task force as soon as he's out of court."

"I'll make the calls."

Jackson went back inside to apologize to Kera, but she and Micah weren't in the waiting room. Had they been taken to see Danette? That could be a good sign. He called, but Kera didn't answer, so he left a message instead: "I'm sorry, but I was called out to a homicide. Please keep me posted. I love you."

Back outside, the late summer sun beat down, so he pulled off his jacket for the trip across town. He was ready for the cooler weather that was coming. His girlfriend and daughter both loved summer and would be sad to see it go. An unexpected loneliness made his ribs ache. He missed Katie and her silly sense of humor. Would his daughter ever come home? The longer she stayed out there on her own, the less likely it seemed. And now he'd hurt Kera's feelings as well. No matter how hard he tried to be supportive, he kept disappointing the women in his life.

CHAPTER 2

The drive to the crime scene was short, as were most trips in Eugene, Oregon. The small city spread out around the Willamette River, lush with tree-lined streets and busy with bicycles. It was also the only home he'd ever had, and protecting it his only real job.

Jackson parked behind one of the patrol cars already at the scene, climbed out of his city-issued sedan, and started up the walkway. The house was larger than most in the neighborhood, which had been built in the forties to house railroad workers. But the building still had the faded paint, dried-up landscaping, and dirty windows that marked it as a low-end rental. A green Ford Focus sat in the driveway. To the left, a uniformed officer interviewed a neighbor, and a second officer stood on the cement front step. Jackson didn't know him.

"We cleared the house," the officer said, "but I needed to come out for a minute."

"Anything I need to know?" Jackson hated surprises—like loose dogs or unexpected objects in the corpse.

The officer shifted, uncertain. "No suspects or obvious weapons, but I had to bust open one of the bedroom doors because it was locked. And it was empty."

Weird. Why would someone lock an empty room? "We'll see what that means."

Jackson reached in his carryall for peppermint gum, in case the body had started to decompose. He pulled on latex gloves and slipped a camera out of his carryall. Photos would be his first order of business. The patrol officers had likely taken some, but he needed his own set.

Bracing himself, he pulled on paper booties and stepped inside. A glance at the dirty gray carpet revealed no blood and little hope of a footprint. He crossed the living room, noting it was minimally furnished: only a couch, coffee table, TV, and crate of books. *Had she just moved in?* Across a short hallway, the bedroom door stood open and feet hung off the end of a thin mattress. Jackson's stomach felt heavy, and a flash of pain tweaked his intestines, surprising him. His last CAT scan had showed the fibrosis shrinking. *Was it growing again?* He shoved the thought aside. It was more likely an ulcer from worrying about his daughter.

From the foot of the bed, he snapped several photos of the body, noting the details through the buffer of the camera lens. A small, lean woman, younger than twenty-five, with reddish-blonde hair and a butterfly tattoo on her left hip. A tank top covered her upper body, but her shorts were on the floor. No obvious wounds or blood. *A life cut far too short.* The sight of her shaved pubic area made him turn away to take photos of the room. Also minimalist: a thin foam mattress, three crates of clothes stacked against the wall, and a shelf with a few personal items. She obviously hadn't lived here long and had traveled light. *Who was she?* He pocketed her cell phone from the shelf, planning to search it soon.

Before he could spend time locating her ID, he had to mentally process the scene and try to visualize what had happened here, before everyone else crowded into the space. That meant getting up close and searching for bruises and obvious trace evidence. The medical examiner and evidence technicians would soon take over the detailed extraction of hairs, fibers, and fluids, so this was his chance to view the scene as the killer had left it.

He reminded himself that she could have overdosed, or died of a snakebite for all he knew, but instinct—and a half-naked body—told him this girl had been victimized. His brain filled with an image of his own teenage daughter dead in some seedy hotel. Another flare of pain in his gut. He shut down the thought and knelt on the sheet-covered foam. Jackson lifted her left hand. No wedding ring and no defense wounds he could see. But her arm was stiff, so full rigor mortis had set in, and she'd been dead for at least twelve hours, possibly longer. It took up to three days for the muscles to relax again after death. But by then, her corpse would have begun to smell, so she'd probably died the night before.

Taking photos as he went along, Jackson searched her body, finding no obvious abrasions. Tiny broken blood vessels under her eyes signaled his first real clue. He reached for the hair draped across her neck and pushed it aside, expecting to find bruises or red marks. They weren't there.

Footsteps in the hall made him turn. Evans had arrived.

"What have we got?" She pulled on gloves as she moved toward the mattress and knelt on the other side. Her dress pants and light-blue blazer looked out of place in the dingy room with stained curtains.

"I'm not sure. There are no obvious signs of trauma, except broken blood vessels under her eyes."

"You can get those from a dental appointment." Evans reached out and touched a faint line on the victim's hip. "A stretch mark, probably from gaining weight. But the cast-aside shorts indicate—"

"What the hell are you doing with the body?" Rich Gunderson yelled from the doorway. The medical examiner was fifty-something and had barely survived a recent round of budget cuts. Barely clinging to his job hadn't motivated him to cut off his gray ponytail or wear anything but his usual black-on-black. It hadn't improved his crime-scene attitude either.

"Just doing our job." Evans stood and looked at Jackson. "Where do you want me to start?"

"Find her ID. I need to check out the rest of the house. Something isn't right here."

Another glance around the bedroom told him there wasn't an adjoining master bath, only a closet with no doors. No surprise in a rental like this. A few dresses and shirts hung in the recessed space. Jackson headed into the hallway and noticed three other doors. Likely a bathroom and two more bedrooms. Where were her roommates?

The smaller bedroom gave him pause. Clothes and toys belonging to a young child, likely a boy, covered the floor, and a small foam mattress lay in a corner. Where was the kid? His pulse picked up as he rushed into the third bedroom.

Empty, except for the faint smell of cigarette smoke and mold. His mind jumped from one thought to another. Why would she rent a three-bedroom house if she had so few possessions? Or had she not finished moving in? And where the hell was the kid? Maybe someone else with a child had planned to move in, then changed their mind. Or the killer had fled with the child after assaulting his new roommate. Or maybe the boy had wandered off.

Jackson hurried back to the small bedroom and glanced at the closet. The doors were missing there too, and the closet was empty, including the overhead shelf. He grabbed his cell phone and called dispatch. "Detective Jackson here. Have you had any reports of a lost or found child? Maybe a boy, about three or four years old, picked up in the Bethel Trainsong area?"

"Do you have a description?"

Jackson looked around for a photo. "Not yet. Will you alert officers to be on the lookout?"

"Right away. Call back if you get more information."

"Thanks."

Maybe there was a photo of the child somewhere. Jackson took a step toward the hallway, but a small sound caught his attention. He spun around, listening hard. Had that been a thump? A dog or something brushing against the house? Another small sound from below. A whimper? He followed it toward the closet and kicked a cardboard box of shoes out of the way. Maybe a dog or animal was stuck under the house. Or a frightened little boy.

Jackson knelt in the closet doorway and spotted a seam in the carpet. A plastic handle pressed against the dirty fabric, blending in. He lifted the access door, letting it rest against the closet's back wall. Cool, dusty air rose from the dark space below. Jackson dug in his carryall for a flashlight and softly called, "I'm a police officer. I'm here to help."

Silence for a moment, then another whimper. He shone the light into the dirt under the house. "Can you crawl toward the light? Don't be scared. I'm here to help."

A little sob made his heart lurch. The boy was down there! "You must be hungry. Come out and I'll get you something to eat." Evans would have a protein bar in her shoulder bag. She prepared for everything.

Something moved directly under him, so Jackson froze. The top of a small head came into view, then the boy looked up. His eyes widened and he quickly retreated out of sight.

What had scared him? Jackson was a big man with a rugged face and nearly black eyes, but he'd never frightened a child before—that he knew of. "Hey. Don't be scared. I'm a police officer." Then it hit him. No uniform. Jackson pulled out his badge and held it down into the hole with the light on it. "Here's my badge. I don't wear a uniform because I'm a detective."

Should he call in one of the patrol officers? Maybe the boy would respond better to a woman.

The little head came into view again and his hand reached for the badge.

"I'll let you hold it if you come out."

The boy crawled into the space under the access hole and stood, his head sticking above the opening. Tear-streaked dirt covered his sweet face, and curly ash-brown hair hung in his eyes.

"I'm Jackson. What's your name?"

The boy silently reached for the badge again. Jackson reluctantly let go, and the kid clutched it like a security blanket.

"I'm going to help you out of there now."

More silence. But the kid didn't retreat, so he lifted him out of the hole. Before he could set him down on the carpet, the child threw his arms around Jackson's neck in a tight grip. The sweetness of the gesture soon gave way to a mild sense of panic. He had a job to do.

"This must be Benjie." Evans came into the room. "Where was he? The patrol officers should have found him."

"Under the house."

Evans stayed near the door. "His mother's name is Amanda Carter. I found this little guy's picture in her wallet with his name on the back."

"Do you have anything to eat in your bag? I promised him something." Jackson hoped to trade the food for his badge.

"I have half a protein bar."

While Evans rummaged in her bag for it, Jackson negotiated with the boy, whose head now rested against his shoulder. "Evans is a detective too. She's going to give you a snack, and I need you to give me my badge."

Benjie took the snack but held firmly to the badge.

"Evans, will you call social services while I try to get some information from Benjie?" Jackson wasn't optimistic the boy would answer questions yet, but he had to try. "After you call, search the house for personal documents. A computer, family contacts, a rental agreement. Our victim hasn't lived here long."

"I'm on it."

They both headed out of the room.

"What have you got for me?" Rob Schakowski was in the hall. The barrel-shaped detective with a buzz cut had been his partner at crime scenes for two decades.

Jackson was relieved to see him. "How was court?"

"The usual. The defense lawyer tried to make me look incompetent."

They both hated testifying in court even more than filling out reports. "I'm glad you're here. I need you to find out who owns this house, then search the car out there."

"Will do." Schak headed back to the living room.

His arms started to ache, so Jackson sat down against a wall, the boy still gripping him tightly. The weight of the small body, the tiny hands locked behind his neck, the absolute dependence— he couldn't remember the last time he'd held a child this way. A decade had passed since Katie had clung to him like this after a nightmare. What had the poor boy witnessed? How long had he been under the house?

"You're safe now," Jackson whispered against Benjie's soft hair. "You'll be fine." The boy's mother would not, but he'd leave that difficult conversation to a social worker with the right skills.

The memory of having to tell Katie her mother was dead made his eyes grow warm. The worst day of his life. This one was shaping up to give it some competition.

"Why don't you sit and relax?" He encouraged the boy to loosen his grip, and the kid finally let go, sliding into Jackson's lap. "You're a brave boy. It must have been hard to crawl into that dark space."

The boy glanced up with a tiny smile but didn't speak.

The trapdoor would have been heavy for him to lift. Or had his mother put him down there to keep him safe? "How old are you, Benjie?" The boy looked tall enough to be four, but his dimpled face made Jackson think he might be younger.

The boy held up three fingers, then took a bite of the protein bar.

"What made you go under the house? Did your mother tell you to?"

Benjie shook his head.

"Can you tell me what happened?"

The boy buried his face in Jackson's chest.

He stroked Benjie's hair and told him not to worry, that everything would be okay. *Liar.* His mother was dead, and his life was about to radically change. But at least he was young enough to bond with a new care provider. Losing a parent at age three was less devastating than losing a parent at fifteen. Just ask his daughter.

Evans came back into the hall. "Social services can't send anyone for a few hours. They suggested taking him to the department."

"Typical." He wanted to curse the devastating budget cuts that had affected every office of city and state government—but he wouldn't do it in front of the boy. Still, it was time to do his job and process the crime scene. Jackson stood, knowing better than to ask Evans to take the child.

He carried Benjie through the house, hoping to hand him over to a patrol officer. Jasmine Parker, a crime scene tech, was taking fingerprints from the front doorknob. Her work was too important to interrupt. They nodded at each other as Jackson stepped outside. The patrol officer who'd been on the porch was knocking on a door across the street. No one answered, and the officer turned and headed down the walk. Jackson gestured for him to come back over.

As he waited, he tried to reassure the boy. "Another policeman will take you to our office. You'll be safe there. I need to work."

Benjie whimpered and clung more tightly. *Damn.* This wouldn't be easy.

When the officer approached, Jackson asked his name.

"Terry Valenciano. We worked a scene together about five years ago. But I was new then and we didn't actually meet."

"I need you to take this child into the department and wait with him until a social worker shows up. His name's Benjie and he's pretty scared."

"Uh, okay." The officer couldn't hide his discomfort.

Jackson pried the little fingers from their grip on his neck. "Terry is a nice policeman. He'll let you push some buttons in his car." He tried to hand over the boy, but Benjie let out a shriek and grabbed for him again.

"Hey, you're safe now. You'll be fine," Jackson pleaded. The boy cried and fought to hang on.

Officer Valenciano mumbled, "I'm really not good with kids."

Jackson gave up. "Never mind. I'll keep him with me."

Still carrying the boy, he went back inside and stopped in the hallway. About six people were in the house now, all doing their jobs, and he felt rather useless. He could still direct the investigation and process information, but he had to protect the child from hearing anything disturbing.

"Benjie, I need to put you down so I can get something. You can hang onto my leg. I'm not leaving you."

After more negotiation, he was able to set the boy on the floor, but Benjie instantly grabbed a fistful of pant leg. Jackson searched his carryall for earplugs, one of the many useful items he carried on the job. After a bit of cajoling, he persuaded the boy to wear the earplugs, and in exchange, he let Benjie play with his flashlight. The boy held it with one hand, still clutching Jackson's pant leg with the other.

Jackson removed an earplug and said, "You can sit in the hall and see me no matter which room I'm in. I'm not leaving you. I just need to work."

The boy still wouldn't let go. Jackson put the earplug back in and stroked his hair. Poor kid. He vowed to find out what had happened here, no matter how challenging.

He stuck his head into the bedroom, where the medical examiner was extracting fluid from the victim's vagina.

"Was she raped?"

"There's swollen tissue and evidence of a sexual encounter, but we may never know the exact circumstances."

"Any idea how she died?"

Gunderson rolled his eyes. "We usually do an autopsy before giving a finding."

Jackson ignored the sarcasm. "What about when she died? Have you taken her temperature?"

"Most likely between eight and ten last night. Now let me do my job."

Jackson glanced over at Evans. She had dug through the victim's plastic crates—a poor person's stackable dresser—and pulled out everything but the clothing. Now she was squatting next to a crate, glancing at a folder of papers. Just witnessing that made his knees hurt. He loved working with Evans, but sometimes her stamina and flexibility made him feel old. More often, she kept him upbeat. Whenever he considered taking a less-stressful job, the thought of never again seeing Evans and his other teammates made him want to stay.

"Find anything?" he called from the hallway.

"She has immunization records for the boy, but there's no birth certificate for either of them." Evans riffled through the stack of papers. "This is mostly the kid's drawings, recipes for gluten-free food, and coupons. No bank statements, no rental agreement, no saved mail."

That was unusual. "What about a computer?"

"There's a small tablet, but I haven't looked at it yet."

"Bring it to me. It's something I can do until the social worker gets here." He remembered he had the victim's cell phone in his pocket and hoped to find a family contact. Someone out there would want to know what had happened to Amanda. He also hoped they would take little Benjie into their lives. He hated to think the boy would end up in foster care.

His cell phone rang. It was Lammers. "We've got the owner of the phone who called in the body. Tess Gilmore. She lives right next door, on the corner."

"I thought the caller was male."

"That's what dispatch said. Talk to everyone in the house."

As much as he wanted to handle the questioning himself, Jackson relayed the information to Evans and asked her to go next door. With Amanda's tablet computer in one hand and Benjie's little fingers in the other, Jackson took a seat on the couch. He texted Lammers and asked to have Quince join the task force too. This was shaping up to be a challenging investigation.

CHAPTER 3

Lara Evans smelled cat shit on the front lawn and dreaded entering the house. Plywood covered a bedroom window, the siding had cracked from lack of paint, and the blinds in the front were broken. A long, dry August had killed the grass and withered the rhododendrons.

She knocked lightly, trying to sound more like a missionary than a cop. These people would probably not be happy to see her. A woman in a long black sweatshirt opened the door. Evans' first thought was, *It was too hot for that.* Her second, *Where were your pants?*

"Tess Gilmore?"

The woman tilted her head.

Evans held out her badge. "Detective Evans, Eugene Police. I have some questions about your neighbor."

Early thirties with cropped plum-colored hair and an eyebrow ring. Tess stared, as if trying to make up her mind. Evans braced for a door slam. "I'd like to come in."

"I'm not feeling well. Can you come back later?"

She stepped forward. "The woman next door is dead, and you called the police to report it. We have to talk about this now."

"Oh shit." Tess jerked her head in exasperation but stepped back to let Evans enter.

"I didn't make that call." The bare-legged woman gestured for her to sit.

Evans looked around at the furniture, spotted several cats, and decided to remain standing.

"My kid must have." Tess turned toward the hall and yelled, "Dylan! Get in here! A cop wants to talk to you."

The bitch! She'd warned her son on purpose. Evans started for the hallway.

A window slammed open in the back of the house.

Shit! Why did she always get the runners? Evans bolted through the kitchen and out the back door. A teenager was half-way across the small brown backyard. She sprinted after him, reaching the fence as he started to climb over. Evans grabbed his black hoodie and jerked him down.

"On the ground! Arms behind your back." She resisted the urge to pull her weapon. Shooting an unarmed teenager was not on her list of career moves. "I just want to ask some questions."

The boy cursed but complied. One knee on his back, Evans cuffed him, then helped him up. He looked young, with shoulder-length dark hair and his mother's narrow face.

"If you behave yourself, I'll take the cuffs off."

"I want a lawyer."

Evans laughed. "This isn't television." She nudged him toward the house. "Unless you killed her, you're not in trouble."

His silence as they walked back unnerved her. An innocent person would have protested the accusation. She wanted to question him without his mother present. Afterward, she would search the house. The boy's eyes were bloodshot and he smelled like pot, so, unless he had a medical card, it was within her rights.

Inside, his mother stood near the sliding glass door, watching.

"I'm going to question him in my car," Evans said, walking past her.

"No." Tess grabbed her son's arm. "Talk to him right here in front of me."

Damn. It had been worth a try. They sat at the kitchen table, and Evans tried to ignore the crusty cereal bowls, unopened mail, and cat hair. She'd seen much worse. She set her recorder on the table and she clicked it on. The mother bit her lip but didn't protest.

Evans locked eyes on the boy. "What's your name and how old are you?"

"Dylan Gilmore. I'll be fourteen next month." He slouched in his chair, trying to look defiant.

"Where were you last night between eight and ten p.m.?"

"With a friend downtown."

"What's his name and where can I find him?"

"*Her* name is April, and she hangs out at the library."

"Last name? Address?"

He shrugged. "I don't know. I just met her yesterday."

"That's not much of an alibi. Did anyone else see you downtown last night?"

"Yeah, but I don't know their names."

His mother cut in. "He wasn't home or next door. I can vouch for that."

Evans ignored her and kept her eyes on the kid. "Tell me what happened when you called 911 today."

Dylan looked down at his hands. "I accidentally threw my frisbee over the fence, so I climbed over to get it back. Then I saw her through the window."

Pure fabrication. Evans snapped her fingers, and the boy looked up. "How did you see the body through the window? You'd have to be standing right there."

"My frisbee landed next to her house."

Evans softened up to try for empathy. "So you decided to look in her window. Most boys your age would."

He hunched forward. "Well, yeah. Something wasn't right."

"What made you think that?"

"She looked dead. I mean, she was naked and not moving." His voice turned whiny. "You would have thought so too."

His mother cut in again. "Why didn't you tell me?"

They both ignored her. Evans asked, "Did you think to help your neighbor?"

Dylan's face tightened. "I called the cops, didn't I?"

"How well did you know Amanda?"

"I didn't." He shifted in his chair and drummed his fingers. "I don't want to talk about this. But I'm sorry she's dead."

Sorry sounded like guilt. Time to pry open those emotions. "Was it an accident? Maybe you were just messing around and she—"

"No! I was never in her house." The teenager swallowed hard. "She'd just moved in." He jumped to his feet. "This is why I didn't give my name! I knew you would blame me. Cops are all the same." Dylan stormed down the hall.

Evans let him go for the moment. She would check out his alibi and likely question him again.

The mother stood and pointed at the door. "I want you to leave."

Evans didn't budge. "Did you see or hear anything over there last night?"

"No. I had a friend over and we were busy." She squinted with annoyance. "I already told the other cop that."

A patrol officer must have done a canvass. "What's your friend's name?"

"Ed Quatkemeyer."

Evans started to jot it down. "How do you spell that?"

"How the hell should I know?"

Boy, was she tired of this family's attitude. Evans struggled to keep her tone friendly. "I need to know about the woman and kid next door. When did they move in?"

A big sigh as Tess sat back down. "I think it was Saturday or Sunday. The house had been vacant for a long time, so I was surprised to see all the activity."

"Who owns it?"

"Don't know. Don't care."

"Tell me about the activity."

"What do you mean?"

"When did you first see someone? Who was it? What were they driving?"

"A little light-blue pickup was parked out front Friday night when I came home from the store. But I didn't see anyone."

That didn't match the car over there now. Maybe the landlord had come by. "What next?"

"Then the woman and the kid showed up in the green Ford a day or so later. That's all I know."

"Did you talk to her?"

"Nope. I told you. I mind my own business."

"How long have you lived here?"

"Why?"

"Because I want to know." Evans had lost her patience. "A woman is dead and we need to find out why."

"I moved here in January after I left my bastard ex-husband." Tess jumped up and grabbed a pack of cigarettes from the counter.

"My ex isn't Dylan's father, in case you're wondering. I had Dylan when I was in high school."

The woman was younger than she had guessed. But still too old for an eyebrow ring. What else should she ask? "Who lived in the house next door before it was vacant?"

"Some tweakers, but they didn't last long. I swear the cops were there every other weekend."

Meth addicts. No wonder the rental looked beat-up. "I need to take a look at Dylan's room." Evans held up a hand. "I don't need a warrant. He smells like pot, so I'm entitled to search for it."

Tess crossed her arms. "What *are* you looking for?"

"I just want a feel for who he is." She really wanted to look for weapons, violent posters, or dead cats. Anything that might indicate Dylan was a psychopath.

Tess gave an exaggerated headshake. "He didn't do anything to that woman. Dylan isn't violent."

"I'd like to believe that. Just let me step in and look around."

"Fine."

Tess padded down the hall on bare feet, her sweatshirt barely covering her ass. Evans followed, thinking it must be weird for a teenage boy to have a mother who didn't wear pants.

The woman knocked briefly, then waited for a response.

"I'm not in the mood," her son shouted through the door.

"Too bad. We're coming in." Tess pushed it open, and Evans walked through.

"I just want a quick look around. Do you have any weapons in here?"

Seated on the bed, Dylan snorted with disgust. "I hate guns. I don't even play video games."

"Good to hear."

The room was small and cluttered and reeked of sweat and semen. But no weapons, and the posters were of Tony Hawk and other skateboard champions. Evans glanced in the closet and under the bed. Shoes, skateboards, and a collection of flesh magazines. But at least he wasn't reading about bomb making.

"Let me see your computer desktop."

"Why?"

"I want to see your screensaver."

"Whatever."

Dylan reached for a laptop on the floor, clicked the space bar, and turned the computer to her. An image of a pretty young girl filled the screen.

"Who is she?"

More eye rolling. "Miley Cyrus. Before she cut her hair and went crazy."

Evans assumed she was some kind of pop star. "Okay."

On her way out, she turned to the mother. "Keep your son home for a few days. We'll want to talk to him again." A request that would probably be ignored.

Tess followed her outside and stared at the house next door with all the cop cars in front. "You know, now that you asked me, I think one of the tweakers who lived there before drove a little blue truck."

CHAPTER 4

A loud voice outside caught Jackson's attention. Through the open door, he saw a short, stout woman arguing with the patrol officer guarding the entrance. Mariah Martin, a manager at Children and Family Services. She often handled emergency scenarios when she couldn't find a caseworker who wasn't already overloaded. Jackson set the victim's cell phone aside and patted Benjie's leg. The boy was snuggled up against him on the couch.

"There's a nice lady I want you to meet." Jackson stood, and the boy jumped up too, grabbing for his pants again. He was ready to pass on the childcare responsibility and get fully functional again. Jackson started toward the door, feeling like he had to drag Benjie along. Guilt forced him to pick up the child, and the little arms locked around his neck. What had this poor boy witnessed to make him so afraid? Or maybe it was the eighteen hours he'd spent in the dark under the house. That would have freaked him out too.

"Let her in," he called through the door.

The officer stepped aside, and the social worker barreled into the living room, moving fast for a round woman on short legs.

"Ms. Martin. Thanks for coming."

"You're welcome. And please call me Mariah."

They'd met on another homicide two years earlier. "This is Benjie. He's three, and he's had a rough time. He was hiding under the house since last night."

"Oh, the poor dear." Martin pulled a small stuffed toy from her oversize purse. "Would you like to hold this, Benjie?"

Snuggled against Jackson's shoulder, the boy wouldn't look at her.

"He seems quite attached to you."

"Yes. I found him and he decided he trusts me." Jackson remembered the plugs and removed them from Benjie's ears. He glanced at Martin. "I didn't want him to hear our conversations, but I had to keep working. This is my case, and the first twenty-four hours are critical."

"You did well. Would you turn around so he can see me over your shoulder? I need to make eye contact."

For ten minutes, the social worker coaxed, sweet-talked, and bribed Benjie, but he wouldn't let go of Jackson. In the end, she had to forcibly remove him and carry him out as he cried hysterically. The boy's distress crushed Jackson's heart. Another disappointed person in his life. But what choice did he have? He had to work, and that meant talking about the kid's dead mother. It was for the best.

"I'll come visit you," he called out, trying to give Benjie some comfort. Why had he done that? He didn't have time to follow through.

"Don't let it get to you." Evans came up the walk as he watched Martin buckle the sobbing child into her car.

"I don't know why he bonded with me like that."

"You're a good man." She touched his arm.

Jackson shook off his guilt. "Unless you have a suspect, your report from next door can wait until our task force meeting."

"I have a weird theory, but we need to find the homeowner first."

"Schak called county records, but we haven't heard back yet. Now, he's out in the backyard, looking for signs of an intruder." Jackson started for the bedroom, and Evans followed. He looked at his watch. "We'll meet at six in the conference room. Meanwhile, let's see what Gunderson has to say."

As they entered, Parker was vacuuming trace evidence from the bedsheet while the medical examiner zipped Amanda's body into a black plastic bag. Jackson hoped her parents would never see that image. "What else can you tell us?"

"Livor mortis on her backside means she died right here and wasn't moved. Subconjunctival hemorrhages in both eyes indicate pressure was applied to her neck or face. Or that she had a coughing fit right before she died." Gunderson stood and turned to them. "She also has petechiae, indicating asphyxia, but without bruising or ligature marks on her neck, it doesn't look like strangulation. I'll know more when we cut her open."

"When's the autopsy?"

"Probably late tomorrow. I'll check with the pathologist and let you know."

Schak stepped into the crowded bedroom. "Look what I just found in the yard."

They all spun toward him. Schak held up a bloody pocket-knife.

CHAPTER 5

Tuesday, September 3, 5:45 p.m.

Evans stopped at a Dutch Brothers drive-up and ordered three cups of house coffee. The district attorney, or even their boss, might come to the task force meeting, but she only treated her detective partners. She loved Schak like a crusty old uncle who had her back no matter how much grief they gave each other. But her feelings for Jackson were complicated.

Seeing his tenderness with the little boy had stirred up a longing she'd thought she was over. But it was best to ignore it. She'd been dating a great guy—Ben Stricklyn, an Internal Affairs detective—for nearly a year and had started thinking they might have a long-term future.

Evans paid for the coffee and headed toward County Club Road and the new department headquarters. She loved the new building with its wide-open spaces and big windows that looked out onto a wall of green trees and shrubs lining the freeway and river. But still, coming here didn't feel like slipping into an old pair of jeans the way walking into the downtown location had.

The SWAT unit she hoped to join still met at the training center on Second and Chambers, so some things about the department wouldn't change. If she passed the physical test on Monday, she would become the only woman in the elite unit. Months of daily bench presses, crunches, and bicep curls had made her upper body strong. She still ran and kickboxed every day too. She'd become as strong as her five-five frame allowed her to be—and she'd done it while still holding a full-time job. But would it be enough?

In the new conference room, she sat near the dry-erase board, knowing Jackson would ask her to chart the investigation. The padded chair swiveled and reclined, making her smile. So much nicer than the metal chairs in the old building. They had also acquired an oversize, flat-screen monitor for watching videos and interrogations.

Schak lumbered in a moment later, pulling off his jacket. Sweat marks the size of footballs lined his armpits, and his shirt was wrinkled. But he was smart and tenacious and she loved working with him. "You need to start carrying one of those personal-size fans," she teased.

"Right after you stop wearing those prissy-colored blazers."

Evans laughed. "You're just jealous because men are limited to black, brown, and blue. Blah."

"Don't forget gray."

"It's not even a color." She picked up a cup. "Coffee?"

"Hell yes."

Evans took one over to him as he sat across the table. She returned to the board and wrote *Amanda Carter, 24* in big letters at the top, then drew two lines down the middle. On the left side, she noted what little they knew about the victim, starting with a brief physical description. Under it she wrote *Benjie, son, 3,* realizing they didn't know his last name, which might not be the same as his mother's. She added *hiding, afraid* after his name.

Jackson stepped in, glanced at the board and the coffee, and smiled. "This is why I want you on my team, Evans."

Six feet tall, with dark hair and a hint of gray at the temples. But it was his face that pulled her in. Rugged with a strong jaw, yet symmetrical enough to be handsome. Plus, a sexy scar above his left eye, which he'd finally admitted was the result of a dog bite.

"You're late." She'd given him shit to hide her feelings for so long, it was habit now. But his pinched brow caught her eye and she remembered his family situation.

"Sorry. I stopped at the hospital to see Kera for a minute. A family member was in a car accident."

"Not Katie, is it?" Schak asked.

"No, it's Danette, the baby mama of Kera's grandson." Jackson sat at the end of the table, as always, so they could talk in a circle.

"How's Kera doing?" Evans wouldn't let herself dislike someone she didn't even know. But Kera was tall, beautiful, and owned Jackson's heart, so they would never be friends. Evans smiled and handed him a coffee.

"She's holding strong."

A moment of quiet.

"So no pizza?" Schak asked. He winked to show he didn't really care.

"Your doctor would approve," Evans said.

"Approve of what?" Michael Quince strode into the room. An even better-looking detective and more her age. But Jackson had been her mentor when she'd transferred to Violent Crimes, and he'd captured her heart before she'd ever met Quince.

"Not feeding pizza to Schak." Jackson nodded and took out his case file. "Thanks for coming. Let's get started."

"That bloody knife is bugging the hell out of me," Schak blurted. "Our victim doesn't have a mark on her."

"We'll see what the lab reports about the fingerprints," Jackson said.

Evans added the knife to the right side of the board where they would list the evidence.

"Don't forget the broken blood vessels in her eyes," Jackson called out.

"And the victim's transient nature," Schak added.

Evans wrote *few possessions, no paperwork* under Amanda's information, then turned to the group. "What else do we know about the victim?"

The room was quiet for a moment. Then she remembered the uniform she'd found in one of the crates. "I think she works in patient care. She had yellow scrubs in her crates."

"Who takes care of the boy while she works?" Jackson pondered.

Quince broke in. "Will someone get me up to speed?"

It was Jackson's case, so he summarized the death scene and their findings so far.

After giving it a moment, Quince said, "Except for the trauma-tized boy, we don't have any solid reason to think it was murder."

"She was half naked and had probably been raped," Evans argued. "Also, the woman's lifestyle indicates that she travels light and moves frequently, so she may be on the run."

"Or she's a prostitute or drug addict." Quince gave a small smile. "Just playing devil's advocate. Without paperwork or a family connection, we don't know anything about her."

"I have her phone," Jackson said. "I only had time to glance at her recent calls and texts and didn't find anything that seemed personal, but I'll examine it thoroughly tonight. We have to find her family." He took a long pull of coffee. "What else have we got? We need a plan of action for tomorrow."

"The county called with the homeowners' names." Schak glanced at his notepad. "Dan and Julie Beckett. They live in Cottage Grove, and I called and left a message. I asked them to come into the department as soon as they could."

"Great. Anything interesting in the car?"

"Not really. Her registration lists an address near campus." Schak rubbed his bristled head. "I called the apartment complex and she moved out on Friday."

"Did she give a reason?"

"The manager said she wanted more space."

"We may question her old neighbors if nothing else breaks open." Jackson turned to her. "Give us the rundown on your conversation next door."

Evans used her fingers to tick off her main findings. "A thirteen-year-old boy named Dylan Gilmore reported the body, Amanda only moved in a few days ago, and a small light-blue truck was there on the weekend—before Amanda moved in—but not again."

"What's your gut feeling about the boy?" Jackson wanted to know.

"He seems okay on the surface. A cursory search of his room didn't turn up any weapons or violent drawings." She paused, thinking about the knife that had surfaced later. "Dylan says he saw Amanda's body through the window, so he admits being in the backyard. Maybe he dropped the knife. I'll need to question him again."

As she wrote the witness/suspect's name in the middle of the board, Jackson said, "Good idea. But without any knife wounds on the victim, a judge will never give us a subpoena for his prints or for a more thorough search."

"Damn liberals," Schak tossed out.

Everyone laughed. He was only half serious and mostly wanted to be amusing.

Evans brought up her long-shot suspect. "The neighbor, Tess Gilmore, says the previous tenant from six months ago was a meth addict who also drove a small blue truck. What if he came back and tried to take up residence? The place has been empty since he moved out, or was evicted, so maybe he has a grudge. Not to mention a drug problem."

"I like it." Jackson sounded upbeat for the first time since the meeting started. "I'll ask the homeowners about the previous tenant when I question them."

"What's my next move?" Schak asked.

"Run Amanda's name and vehicle through every database you can. We need to know more about her."

The door burst open and Sergeant Lammers charged in. "We have another possible homicide."

CHAPTER 6

Lammers locked eyes with Evans. "I need you to take this one. Schak has court again tomorrow and has to meet with the investigator for the evidence lab fiasco." Their boss was often irritated, but tonight her eyes had a wild look.

"What about me?" Quince asked. "I can take it." He'd transferred from the Vice unit and hadn't been given the lead on a homicide yet.

"You don't want this one." Lammers gave a mock shudder. "The university's star quarterback is dead, and it may be an overdose. The politics could be a pain."

"So you give it to me?" Evans loved taking the lead, but she had little use for football and even less for politics.

"You're always whining that you want more responsibility, so here's your chance."

Bullshit. She didn't whine. But she did want another solo case. "Where is the body and what happened?"

"His roommate found him on their bathroom floor with blood on his face and called paramedics. But he was dead when they got there."

Shit. They'd contaminated the scene just by showing up.

"It's worse than that," Lammers added, reading her expression. "They took him to the morgue."

And double shit. They'd also left her without a real crime scene to examine and probably lost trace evidence from the body. "Why do I always get these cases?" Her first lead assignment had been a woman who'd woken up from a coma and claimed someone had tried to kill her. Her second had been an unconscious college girl in the hospital.

Lammers flashed her a grim smile. "Because I like you."

"Who's going to assist me, since Jackson has everyone on his task force?" Evans knew the answer.

"It's probably an overdose," Lammers said, avoiding the issue. "I'm sure the case will be resolved as soon as the tox screen comes back. Quince can help, if necessary."

"What's the victim's name?"

"Logan Grayson. I'm sure you've seen him in the news." Lammers slid a thin file across the table. "Here are my notes. I suggest you start with the 911 call."

At least she had a first step. "I'm on it."

"Please keep me updated. Both of you." Lammers wagged a finger, then strode back out.

Evans turned to Jackson. "Sorry. I guess someone else will have to follow up with the kid next door."

"Quince will take it. Good luck with your case." A tight smile from Jackson this time. They were still down two detectives, and now they all worked unpaid overtime to get their jobs done.

"I guess I'm out of here."

"Let us know if you need anything," Schak said, as she walked by.
"Thanks."

Evans headed outside, relieved to feel a cool breeze as she crossed the parking lot. The days were getting shorter, and the orange ball of sun sat low on the horizon. Traffic roared on the nearby expressway—the one disquieting thing about their new location.

She climbed into her sedan, feeling a little rattled. She had to put Amanda Carter out of her head and focus on Logan Grayson, a name she realized she knew. A star player for the University of Oregon Ducks and a big deal for Eugene sports fans. He'd had a front-page write-up in the *Willamette News* after a bowl game the year before, and they'd speculated he could win the Heisman Trophy this year. His death would be devastating for a lot of people.

Lammers had suggested starting with the 911 call, but Evans wanted to see his body and talk to the roommate who'd found him. She hoped like hell another officer had called his parents. She'd never had to tell someone their loved one was dead and didn't want to start today. Opening the file, she read through Lammers' notes. Jake Keener had found Grayson and made the call. She keyed in his number and got an answering service, so she left a message, asking him to call back ASAP. According to the notes, the two young men had shared an apartment near campus on Patterson. She would head there first, put up some crime scene tape, and talk to the neighbors.

A second call, this one to the medical examiner, was almost as pointless. Gunderson picked up but sounded grumpy. "What do you want?"

"Are you still in Surgery Ten?" Their nickname for the autopsy room in the basement of the old hospital.

"I'm leaving now." A door slammed in the background. "You must have caught the campus case, and I sympathize, but you can't see the body tonight. It's been a long damn day, and he'll look the same in the morning."

"Can you tell me anything?"

"He had an abrasion on the side of his head and some bruising on his chest, but he's a football player, so I don't know what any of it means yet."

"What about the blood on his face?"

"His nose bled before he died, but there's no swelling to indicate he'd taken a blow there. It could have been drug-induced. We'll do the autopsy tomorrow. I've already taken a call from his coach."

Oh boy. "Does he want the truth or a cover-up?"

"He wants it resolved quickly," Gunderson said. "So Jackson's victim will have to sit in the cooler for a while."

He wouldn't like that. "When did Grayson die?"

"Best guess is between midnight and three a.m."

Midnight? He'd lain on the bathroom floor all day? That was a little weird. "Thanks. See you in the morning."

Driving out of the parking lot, Evans changed her mind and decided instead to stop by the dispatch center on "two and Chambers," as everyone in the department called it. Before she questioned the roommate, she wanted to hear what he'd said to the 911 operator. Picking apart little slip-ups was a good way to pry out information and sometimes elicit confessions.

Her stomach growled, reminding her that she'd missed dinner. And she'd given her protein bar to the little boy. She hated to waste time making a stop, but she needed to eat something if she had to work late. Even though a burrito sounded good, she wouldn't have the time or energy to run it off when she finally got home. Sugar-free frozen yogurt from the TCBY drive-up window would have to suffice.

The red-brick center was more attractive in the soft light of the setting sun than in bright daylight. Its L-shape wrapped around a helicopter pad, and the big blue SWAT vehicles sat in the parking lot out back. She would be testing here on Monday. The thought made her stomach clench. Failing was unacceptable. It would only reinforce the idea that women couldn't do the elite SWAT job. Only one other woman had ever made the cut, and she'd been quickly promoted out of the unit to a supervisor job. Evans didn't want that, but she'd worry about the politics later.

She keyed in her code and headed to the call center, a spacious area with plenty of windows and room to move around. Dispatchers had high-stress jobs, long hours, and quick burnout. The department tried to make their workspace as comfortable as possible. She checked in with the supervisor, an older woman who was at least five-nine and soft, with little muscle. It irritated Evans when tall people wasted their physical advantage. But Margo DuPont was competent and pleasant, so she liked her just fine.

"Lara. Good to see you." Civilian employees used first names.

"Thanks, Margo. How's the job?"

She let out a rush of air. "An eventful day."

"I picked up Logan Grayson's case, and I'd like to hear the 911 call." Evans took a seat.

The supervisor's mouth turned down. "We all prayed he would make it."

He'd never had a chance. "Grayson died late last night." The call-takers' hope was a little puzzling. "Did his roommate think he was still alive?"

"He must have. He was hysterical and kept shouting for us to save him. But I'll let you hear it." She handed Evans a headset, glanced at the clock, then clicked a few keys. Margo's desk held three monitors, and Evans didn't envy her job.

The voice on the call was obviously young and upset, but somewhat gender neutral, and he spoke with a slight Southern accent. The call lasted three minutes, but the first few moments contained all the pertinent information.

Caller: "My roommate is on the floor and not breathing. You gotta send help now!"

Dispatcher: "What's your name?"

"Jake. But who cares? Just send an ambulance. You gotta save him!"

"Where are you?"

"Near campus, 1330 Patterson. Apartment number three, on the top floor."

"Try to be calm. An ambulance is on the way."

"Under the blood, his face looks gray. We can't lose him. Our season'll be shot."

"Where is he bleeding?"

"From his nose. But it's dry now."

"Have you tried giving him mouth-to-mouth resuscitation?"

"No way. I called you. I'm not a medic."

"Does he have a pulse?"

"I don't know! You gotta get someone here. He can't die."

"Had he been drinking or using drugs? The paramedics need that information."

"Fuck if I know. But I'll bet his bitch of a girlfriend was here. If she had anything to do with this, I'll make her life hell."

"Please be calm and don't hurt anyone. Help will be there soon."

"I fucking can't believe this."

Before the call was over, Jake was crying, and Margo had choked up too. Evans was thinking about the girlfriend. Who was she? And what had she done?

Finding out couldn't wait until tomorrow. With suspicious deaths—which included any young person who died in a non-accident—detectives worked almost around the clock for the first few days. After that, witnesses disappeared, details were forgotten, and suspects fled or hid. She would question the student's neighbors this evening when they were more likely to be home than tomorrow during the day. She'd also pick up the dead man's computer and cell phone if she could find them.

The apartment building was new, one of several that had replaced blocks of old Victorian houses around campus, changing the look and demographic of the neighborhood. Despite the fresh paint and modern finishes, the structure was still student housing and not visually appealing. The trees and lawns of the older homes were gone, and the building bordered the sidewalk, leaving no room for landscaping. Even though Evans had liked the look of the older homes, she wouldn't have wanted to live with the ancient plumbing, tiny bathrooms, and leaky single-pane windows.

A blue patrol unit was parked on the street, so an officer was still at the death scene. Probably waiting for an investigator to show up. Good news. She didn't have to track down the manager.

Apartment number three occupied the top floor with only two other units, the student equivalent of a penthouse. The door was ajar, and Evans walked in without putting on booties. No point in it now that paramedics had trampled the floor. The officer sat in the dining room, texting someone. Evans walked over, noting a laptop, a stack of papers, and some personal items on the table.

"Officer Miller." She'd worked patrol with him a few years back. One of the good ones who didn't abuse arrestees or harass homeless people.

"Evans." He jumped up. "I should say 'Detective Evans.' How's Violent Crimes treating you?"

"I'm still getting assigned cases like this, but otherwise I love it." She rested her heavy shoulder bag on a chair and pulled on gloves. "What have we got?"

"None of the neighbors on this floor was home to question, but I did a thorough search and gathered what seemed important."

"Thanks. I don't see a cell phone."

"I didn't find one. It might have been on him. Maybe a pocket."

Damn. Another information delay. "Any observations I should know about?"

"The paramedics were already dealing with him when I arrived, so I can't tell you about the condition of the body." The officer's expression changed to worry. "I hope it was some kind of freak medical thing. Because Grayson is the Ducks' starting quarterback, and no one wants to hear that he overdosed. It's not good for recruitment."

"Any drugs or alcohol in the apartment?"

"Beer in the fridge. That's it."

"Did you talk to the roommate?"

"Briefly." Miller looked at his notes. "Keener came home around four thirty after football practice. But he had stayed at his girlfriend's place the night before, so he hadn't seen Grayson all day. Keener said he slept for a while, ate dinner, then went to the bathroom and found the body."

Something didn't add up. "The 911 call came in at six thirty. He was home for two hours with a dead body?"

Miller shrugged. "Men don't pee as often as women do."

Something was still wrong. "Is the roommate a football player too?"

"Running back."

"So Grayson must have missed football practice, but Keener didn't check on him?"

Miller flushed a little. "I didn't ask about that."

"Anything else?"

"Jake Keener was distressed, so he went to stay with a friend. Here's his contact information." The officer handed her a small scrap of paper, torn from his pad.

"Thanks. Send me a copy of your report too, please." The scourge of law enforcement—writing up reports about everything.

"Can I go? I'm beat."

"Of course."

Evans conducted a tour of the apartment, noting that the place was bigger and nicer than any student housing she'd ever seen. Did they have a cleaning service? And who paid for that giant flat-screen TV? She knew the football players had scholarships that paid for room and board, but now she suspected wealthy alumni made private contributions to their living expenses as well.

She trusted that Officer Miller had found anything obvious, so she didn't waste time on a detailed search of drawers for the moment. She would get to it eventually, probably the next day.

In the bathroom, she took pictures from every angle, noting the lack of grime. Total neat freaks, except for a few stray hairs. Pulling on gloves, she bagged and tagged several—some blond and some short, dark, and curly. But seeing the scene didn't give her any real information, and it was hard to visualize what had happened here. Jackson had taught her to at least try to mentally map out a scenario. All she could see was a drunk, oversize young man taking a piss, then collapsing on the floor.

A search of the medicine cabinet turned up an over-the-counter sleep aid and a prescription bottle of Nardil, a medication she wasn't familiar with. The name on the bottle was Logan Grayson. She wanted to get online right away to find out what it was prescribed for, but decided to finish her bathroom search first. The bottle went into an evidence bag before she squatted to examine the floor.

She spotted a small discoloration on one of the off-white tiles. Dried blood? Evans dropped to her knees and scraped it into a two-inch evidence bag. She leaned down with her face close to the floor and looked around. Under the edge of the vanity, she spotted an earring. A woman had been here. Maybe recently. Had she watched or helped Grayson die? Evans reached for the earring—a teardrop shape with a white pearl finish—and bagged it too.

She stood, noticing the toilet was open, the seat was up, and the water was yellow. Evans dug a small plastic bottle out of her shoulder bag and scooped up some liquid. It might not be valid evidence for court, but, if the urine wasn't too diluted, she could take it to Any Lab Test Now and for fifty bucks find out if the victim or his roommate had a drug problem.

Remembering that the medical examiner had said the corpse had a head wound, she used a small magnifying glass to examine the edges of the vanity for flesh or blood. Clean as everything else. Grayson hadn't fallen against the rounded, cultured-marble countertop.

Back in the living room, she used her tablet computer to get online. She was surprised to discover that Nardil was an antidepressant. It hadn't occurred to her that an athlete could suffer from depression. Clearly, she needed to learn more about Logan Grayson. In the foyer, she stuck crime-scene tape across the door and knocked on the opposite apartment.

A giant young man opened the door, wearing only white briefs and a big smile.

What was with the no-pants people? Yes, it was still warm, but this was Eugene, not Phoenix.

"Oops. I thought you were someone else. Just a minute." The door closed.

Two minutes later, it opened again, and he was dressed in green nylon shorts and a yellow tank top. UO Duck colors. "Who are you?"

"Detective Evans, Eugene Police. What's your name?"

"Lamar Owens. Should I come out?" He was brown skinned and big as a refrigerator.

Evans didn't want to assume he was dangerous, but she wished she had a taser. "I'd rather come in. I have a few questions."

"What's this about?"

"Logan Grayson."

"Is he in trouble?" His heavy brows almost made his eyes disappear as they furrowed.

He didn't seem to know his neighbor was dead. Oh shit. "Let's go sit down."

"No problem."

He stepped aside, and she moved cautiously into the spacious apartment. This one had clothes, books, and empty fast-food wrappers lying around. Owens yanked a backpack off an oversize chair and said, "You can sit here."

She perched on the arm, not planning to stay long. "I'm sorry to break this to you, but Logan died last night."

His eyes widened and his mouth slowly opened. After a stunned moment, he leaped up. "What the fuck!" He grabbed his head in disbelief.

Evans braced for more. "I'm sorry. The paramedics took him away earlier this evening. I thought you knew."

"I just got home." His voice was dazed.

"How well did you know Logan?"

He slammed the flat of his fist into his chest. "He's my team-mate, my friend, my brother."

Still thinking of him in the present tense. A second later, the big man spun and punched the wall with a massive fist.

Evans jumped to her feet. Was he going to spin out of control? "Please be calm. I need your help."

Owens punched the wall again, then turned back, the anger draining out of him. "What happened? How did he die?"

"That's what I'm trying to figure out. Please sit down so we can talk."

He slumped into the chair across from her, his head in his hands.

She had to ask. "Where were you between eight last night and eight this morning?"

He looked up, startled. "I was right here. I watched some TV, then went to bed at ten. Practice in this heat wipes me out." His big round face held no deceit. Only pain and anger.

"Did you hear anything unusual across the hall?"

"Sorry, but I sleep like a bear in January."

He looked like a bear too. "Did you see Logan last night or talk to him?"

"No, but I saw his car in the parking lot."

"What does he drive?"

"A red Miata." Grief bubbled under the expression on his face. "He was probably with his girlfriend."

"What's her name?"

"Danica Mercado." A flicker of distaste. "She was bad for Logan."

No one seemed to like his girlfriend. "In what way?"

"She flirted." His voice cracked. "And cheated. And made him crazy."

"Is that why he was depressed?"

The big guy blinked. "I didn't know he was."

"Why did Logan stay with a girlfriend who made him crazy?"

"She's gorgeous. And a cheerleader. And it's a social pressure thing."

"Where can I find her?"

He started to speak, then burst into tears. Owens didn't hold back or struggle for control. Grief took over his body and gushed out. The sight of his sobbing overwhelmed her. Evans squeezed his shoulder, put down a business card, and got the hell out.

CHAPTER 7

Tuesday, September 3, 7:47 p.m.

Jackson drove down Franklin Boulevard, spotting the all-glass Jaqua Center at the University of Oregon, built with money from Nike chairman Phil Knight. The water feature surrounding the seamless building glistened in the twilight. Moments later, he passed the new Matthew Knight Arena that had replaced the old, much-loved brick-and-ivy Mac Court. He hadn't been inside the new facility yet.

In addition to all the new buildings on campus, much of downtown Eugene had been transformed into massive apartment complexes to handle the influx of students coming from out of state, attracted by the UO's perennial Top Ten football team. Soon another thousand apartment units would be built. Jackson didn't feel directly affected, but on some level he didn't believe it was for the best. Eugene belonged to everyone, not just the athletes and students.

At the edge of the city, he took the freeway exit, then quickly turned right, heading for the Moon Mountain area. A few years earlier, another case had brought him up here to Mariah Martin's house, looking for a murder suspect. Now he was on his way there to see Benjie, as he'd promised. He couldn't get the boy out of his mind. The way he'd clung to him had stirred up old longings, deep commitments, and new fears.

After knocking on Martin's door, he glanced at his watch. Almost bedtime for a little boy. Maybe he shouldn't have come. But he'd called the social worker before leaving the department and she was expecting him.

Martin opened the door, and Jackson heard crying in the room behind her.

"Thank god you're here. He's been inconsolable." The social worker's eyes were stressed and her jaws clenched. She stepped back and waved him in.

A mix of feelings washed over him: dread that he'd made the wrong decision; joy that he was needed, that he could be a good parent to someone; and worry that he wasn't prepared for any of it. Jackson braced himself and walked in.

From the couch, Benjie looked up and his eyes widened. "Jackson!" The boy scrambled to the floor and ran to him. Jackson picked him up and gave him a hug. The boy hugged back with surprising gusto.

Jackson pivoted to Martin, who slumped with relief. "Has he said anything?"

"Just your name."

"Have you tried therapy toys?"

"Of course." The social worker, wearing a loose-fitting housedress, suddenly reached for a blazer she'd thrown over a chair.

What now? Visiting the boy, then leaving him, would be stressful for all three. He couldn't bear the thought of making Benjie cry again. "Should I just take him with me? I mean, until he starts to feel safe and can begin therapy?"

"That seems best."

"Do I need to fill out any forms?"

"Not yet. He has to have some family somewhere. Let's see how this goes." Martin turned to the door, ready for him to leave.

"I'll be in touch tomorrow." Jackson started to turn.

"Do you have a car seat for him?"

"No."

"I'll give you mine for now." Martin handed him the backpack of clothes and toys Jackson had gathered from the rental house earlier. She slipped on shoes and headed outside. With Benjie's little arms clenched around his neck, Jackson followed.

While she transferred the car seat, he held Benjie and told him pointless but comforting things. He buckled him in, said good night to Martin, and drove down the hill. Caring for the child would hamper his ability to investigate Amanda's death, but what better way to honor the victim than to comfort her son?

Benjie fell asleep on the drive home and didn't wake up when Jackson carried him into the house. Not wanting to pull out the sleeper couch, he put the boy in his daughter's old room. If by some miracle Katie came home, they'd figure something else out. The third bedroom belonged to Jackson's brother, Derrick, a long-haul truck driver who'd lived in the house since they were children. Their parents had lived here too . . . before they'd been murdered a decade earlier. The house now belonged to the brothers, and their plan was to fix or update everything and sell it, now that the housing market was recovering. So far, Jackson had repaired a leaky toilet and overhauled the backyard landscaping in July.

He took off his jacket and shoes, grabbed a Diet Dr Pepper, then settled into his favorite chair. His plan was to search Amanda's phone until he found someone to notify. But first, he texted Kera to let her know he was available to talk. He also texted Katie, who'd gotten him started on the silent communication: *How are you? I miss you. I have 3 yr old boy here. His mother was killed and I'm trying to find his family. I could use your help.*

He pressed Send, fully aware that he was trying to manipulate his daughter into feeling jealous, or compelled to come see the boy, or both. Whatever would bring her home. She'd run away in the spring and had been living with her boyfriend and his mother. Recently, they'd broken up and she moved in with another friend. A woman, thank god, but her new roommate was twenty-two and that worried him. At least Katie was texting and keeping him somewhat updated. He hoped his daughter was still seeing a grief counselor, but she never talked about her mother's death. Jackson suspected she was still drinking, but she hadn't been arrested lately, so he told himself she was no longer out of control. But that could change at any moment. Katie's mother had been an alcoholic, and after a decade of drunkenness and unpredictability, his love for Renee had slowly died. He'd kicked her out when Katie turned thirteen. Another of his very bad days. Now Katie seemed to have inherited the disease. It worried him sick to see her start so young. Knowing it was his fault was giving him an ulcer. Sudden stomach pain forced him to push the thoughts out of his mind.

He booted up Amanda's phone and scrolled through her list of contacts, but they were the same short list of businesses he'd seen when he glanced through earlier: H&H BBQ, Tsunami Books, and Rite Aid Pharmacy. The only prescription drug his team had found in her home were birth control pills. First thing tomorrow, he'd contact the mobile carrier, a company called

Cricket that didn't require long-term commitments. The business also sold untraceable burner phones, and if the customer paid with cash, there was no record of ownership. But he had Amanda's name, so the company should be able to provide a history of her calls and texts. Any messages on the device had been deleted, and there were no personal phone calls either. For reasons he had yet to discover, Amanda was a very cautious person.

The rental she'd just moved into was a mystery too. How had she ended up in the house on Monday without calling a rental agency or the homeowners? Was she a squatter or had she done it all online?

After twenty minutes of getting nowhere with the phone, he pulled the victim's tablet computer from his carryall to try again. His earlier search effort at the crime scene had been repeatedly interrupted, and he'd spent most of his time looking for an address book or someone to contact about her death. He'd also failed to find her e-mail provider or access her messages.

So far, Amanda seemed to be alone in the world, except for little Benjie. This time, Jackson searched Facebook but found a different Amanda Carter. The dead woman didn't seem to have a Twitter account either. Her browser history revealed that she'd been on Craigslist recently, looking at housing. That might explain how she'd found the rental. He keyed in the address on Pershing, but nothing came up. Someone had deleted the listing.

A whimper made him look up. Benjie was coming down the hall, as fast as his little legs could go. Jackson set the device aside, but before he could get out of the reclining chair, the boy had climbed into his lap.

"I'm right here," he reassured the boy. "Did you have a nightmare?"

"Bad man."

He was talking! Progress. "You're safe now. That was just a dream."

Knowing it was too soon, it took all his willpower not to ask questions. Plus, the boy's dream could have been different from what had really happened. Jackson didn't want him to confuse the two or steer him in the wrong direction. "Would you like me to read a story to you?"

Benjie nodded.

Jackson carried him to Katie's room and searched her bookshelf for something appropriate. He found a tattered Winnie-the-Pooh story. His daughter's favorite. She'd been wearing Pooh pajamas right up until the day she ran away.

He made it most of the way through the story before his phone rang in the other room. Benjie was half asleep, so he laid the book down and stepped quietly out.

Please let it be Katie!

Jackson rushed back to the living room, snatching up his phone on the sixth ring. *Schak.* "What have you got?"

"I can't find Amanda Carter in the system anywhere."

"You think it's an alias?"

"We need to consider it."

"I've learned nothing from her devices so far either." Jackson switched gears. "I'll contact the newspaper in the morning, and we'll run her photo and see if anyone recognizes her."

"Anyone I need to question tonight?"

"No, but call the homeowners again early tomorrow. We need to talk to them ASAP."

"All right then, I'm headed out."

"Thanks for checking in. I plan to work from home in the morning, calling nursing homes." He wasn't ready to tell anyone he'd taken the kid home with him. "We'll meet at noon in the conference room and update."

"Order pizza please." Schak's voice held a smile.

Jackson hung up, checked to see if he had any messages, then made himself a PBJ. As he settled back in to look at more of Amanda's browser searches, he realized he hadn't checked to see if Amanda had any voicemails. He pressed the button, held it, and prayed she hadn't set up a password. A pleasant voice informed him there were no new messages and no saved messages. Jackson started to think she hadn't had the phone for long. And had lived a very lonely life.

Time to thoroughly search her purse. He'd picked up the denim bag before leaving the crime scene and had given it a once-over, but he hadn't searched her wallet or checked for secret compartments. He dumped its meager contents in his lap and felt all around the fabric with both hands. Nothing hidden.

Her wallet had a see-through plastic pocket that held her driver's license. Issued in Oregon, it listed her address as Keeny Hill Road in Drain. A tiny town forty miles south of Eugene. Was it her hometown? Without much to do, young people probably didn't stick around Drain for long. He made a note of the address, hoping to find the owner of the house in Drain too. It seemed unlikely the victim—who moved with plastic crates—owned property. And the registration on her car had listed a Eugene apartment. The only other card in her wallet was a blue debit card, issued by Chase Bank. He'd have to access her financial information too.

He pulled the license out of the little pocket to see it was real and a slip of paper fell out. Plain white and folded in half, the paper was thick, like card stock. He unfolded it to reveal a hand-written note: *I'm coming for you, cunt. You can't steal from me and get away with it. I will find you.*

A chill went up Jackson's spine. It looked like the stalker had found her.

CHAPTER 8

Wednesday, September 4, 5:30 a.m.

The alarm blasted Evans out of sleep. She slammed it off, rolled over, and forced herself to her feet. She'd been up late working and felt groggy, but now was not the time to slack off. She had a death to investigate and a physical competency test to pass on Monday.

Once she'd made coffee, she changed into workout clothes, then checked her e-mail. A message from Ben: *Happy Wednesday, Lara! Looking forward to this weekend's hike.*

Not anymore. Unless the medical examiner ruled Grayson's death a natural cause or a suicide, she'd have to cancel plans with her boyfriend and work straight through to Monday. She didn't mind the hours, but they saw so little of each other, it didn't seem fair. His son's sports and school activities took up most of Ben's free time during the week, so their weekends were important. Would she always be on the back burner with him? Evans responded to the e-mail and let him know she might have to work.

Caffeine hitting her system, she trotted to the workout room, put in her earphones, and cranked up some techno. She had padded the walls and floor for Brazilian Jiu-Jitsu training with an earlier boyfriend, but the thick mats absorbed blows, not sound, and she tried to be a good neighbor.

Thirty minutes of kickboxing to jumpstart her day, followed by push-ups, sit-ups, and bicep curls, then out for a hard three-mile run. Typically, she ran longer and slower, but she needed to focus on strength training for now. Pounding down the bike path, she was grateful to still have morning light. In the winter, she ran in the dark, often after work at night.

Evans left the house early and drove to the Womenspace support center, a location kept as secret from the public as possible. After two years of volunteering, at times she wanted to give it up. Her job, which she loved, took so much out of her emotionally that she had little time to socialize. But this work was important. Abused women needed to hear from people like her. They needed to know they weren't stupid or worthless, that any woman could be taken advantage of if her emotions were manipulated. Having a police officer as a counselor often gave women the courage they needed to make a change.

At the center, she went straight to the volunteer office and took a seat at the desk. The coordinator wasn't in yet, and the building was quiet. Too early for most people, but this was the best time for her, so the director had been accommodating. Her client walked in moments later.

"Hi, Cindy. Thanks for coming so early."

"It's okay. I don't sleep well anyway." She was twenty-four, thin, with dark circles under her eyes.

"Give me a second." Evans skimmed the woman's file and refreshed her memory. They'd only met twice before. "How's the job search going?"

"Not great. My only experience is waiting tables, but I'm afraid Kiren will find me if I work in a public place. One of his friends will see me for sure."

"What about private clubs? Resorts?"

"I'll try."

"Have you heard from Kiren?"

Cindy looked down, her long ash-blonde hair hanging on the sides of her face.

"Did you talk to him?"

Her shoulders slumped. "He called my mother's when I was over there." A little defensive now. "Mom started freaking and yelling at him, so I took the phone. I don't want my mother to get hurt."

"You can't talk to Kiren. It opens the door and gives him hope. And leverage."

"He said he's willing to get treatment."

"Good. Maybe he won't beat his next girlfriend." Evans lightened her tone. "But he already blew his chances with you." Cindy had pressed charges after the last round of abuse, but a judge had only given her assailant thirty days because she'd refused to testify.

"How did you get so strong?" Cindy's expression pleaded for help.

At first, Evans thought she meant physically and started to mention her workout routine but realized her mistake. "I set goals. I moved away from the place I'd been victimized. I pursued a career that made me feel powerful and valued." And let her carry a gun.

"Do you think I should move?"

"Maybe for a while."

"I'll think about it."

Evans had left Alaska right after graduating from high school. A month before that, a local sheriff had taken advantage of her youth and drunkenness and forced her to give him oral sex in exchange for not arresting her and not telling her father she was in trouble again. Her dad would have beaten her, not for drinking, but for getting caught and making him look bad.

She shook off the memory. No one fucked with her now.

An hour later in the department, she turned on her desk computer and ran a search for Logan Grayson's girlfriend. Danica Mercado had been ticketed for speeding three months earlier, and all her contact information was on file. Evans keyed the information into her case file, then called Mercado's number. When she didn't answer, Evans left a message. She hoped that wasn't a mistake. Sometimes letting people know you wanted to talk to them sent them into hiding. Even those who weren't guilty often had information they didn't want to share with the police. But driving around trying to catch someone at home could be a waste of time.

Grayson's parents were the next logical call, but they weren't in town and she wanted to make sure they'd had time to process their grief. She tried the roommate, Jake Keener, again. Still no answer, so she left another message. On the university website, she tracked down the phone number of the Ducks' head coach and called it, not even sure what she would ask. The coach didn't answer either, but he would probably be easier to find. The football team practiced at Autzen Stadium every afternoon, and the autopsy was scheduled for one o'clock. She might as well check out the girlfriend's address, then go back to Grayson's apartment building and see if his roommate had returned, maybe question his other neighbors. So far, the evidence indicated the football player had died alone in his bathroom, possibly from drugs, or even a hereditary condition no one knew about. It happened to athletes sometimes when they overworked their bodies. But his head injury concerned her, and she had an obligation to discover who might have wanted to harm the player.

As she stood to leave, her phone rang and she looked at the ID: *University of Oregon.* She connected the call. "Detective Evans."

"This is William Davis. I'm with the university's sports center. I'm trying to get some information about Logan Grayson's death."

A PR person? "It's too soon to report anything."

"We heard that he was bleeding from his head. Was he assaulted?" A middle-aged man, trying to sound matter-of-fact.

How did that rumor get started? "He had a nosebleed, but we don't know what caused it or his death."

"Don't jump to any conclusions about the nosebleed. That happens to football players who get tackled and suffer blows to the head."

Trying to quash the idea of cocaine use. "I plan to conduct a thorough investigation and have to get back to work."

"Please call me the minute you know what happened."

Yeah, right. Evans hung up.

The girlfriend lived in an old house close to the UO's music building. Evans had to circle the block three times before finding a place to park. She hated working the campus area but always seemed to end up here. Correction, she hated looking for parking around the campus. Otherwise, the redbrick buildings and majestic trees were attractive, and the students were energetic and often amusing. As Evans neared the house, a young woman with a ponytail and a perky bounce came down the steps. *Cheerleader.* "Are you Danica Mercado?"

"Nope. She's inside. Her boyfriend died, so be nice." Bouncy girl waved and kept moving.

Evans let her go. She had to stay focused. No one answered her knock, so she tried the door, opened it a crack, and called, "Danica?"

"Who are you?" Through the opening she saw the girl sitting lengthwise on the couch, under a blanket, with a bag of Doritos and a laptop.

"Detective Evans, Eugene Police."

"Oh yeah. You called. Sorry, but I don't feel like talking." Pretty face, straight auburn hair, perfect white teeth. She didn't look particularly sad.

"I'm sorry for your loss, but I have to ask some questions." Evans stepped in and pulled up a chair next to the couch. "When was the last time you saw Logan?"

The girl's eyes widened. "Why are you asking me? I know what that means!"

"I'm just trying to establish a timeline. We think Logan died hours before his roommate found him. Did you see him Monday evening?" She clicked on her recorder and pulled out her tablet.

"No. We were mostly over."

"Who ended the relationship?"

"No one, really. He would disappear sometimes, and I know he lied to me about where he went. I think he was seeing someone else."

Disappear was a trigger word. "When did you see him last?"

"Friday, I think. At Taylor's. I was there with my roommate, but I saw Logan and we had a beer. Then he took off."

Holding out the earring she'd picked up in the bathroom, Evans asked, "Is this yours?"

"Where did you find it?" Danica reached for it.

Evans pulled the evidence back. "On the floor where Logan died. Is it yours or not?"

"It's mine."

"If you were there with him when he died, I need to know. Tell me what happened."

Danica put the laptop on the floor and sat up. "I don't even know what happened to our relationship."

When the girl shifted, Evans spotted a bruise on her forearm. "Was Logan abusive?"

She jerked the blanket over it. "No, that happened when I helped my friend move." Tears finally rolled down her face. But her eyes were angry.

Evans didn't believe her. "Did you and Logan fight physically?" Maybe the football player had developed a drug habit. Or took steroids that made him aggressive. Maybe Danica had fought back and struck him on the head. Or was she just being suspicious after a morning at Womenspace?

"No." Danica shook her head. "We argued, but that was it."

"Argued about what?"

"I don't remember."

Really? "His teammates say you cheated on him. Did he confront you?"

She rolled her eyes. "I had dinner with a friend. And yes, it pissed him off, but Logan was the cheat."

"When did that happen?"

"A month ago." Irritation flashed in her eyes. "His death isn't about me!"

Time to get down to it. "Did he take drugs?"

"Not around me." She avoided eye contact.

"But you think he did."

"Maybe cocaine sometimes."

"What about steroids?"

"I don't know."

She was either a liar or they hadn't been much of a couple. "Who else might have been angry with him?"

She shook her head. "Everyone liked Logan."

"But you think he had a new girlfriend?"

"Whatever." She made a dismissive gesture. "We were over. And now he's dead." A strange tone of satisfaction.

The young woman was definitely not grieving. Had she killed him out of jealousy or anger? "Where were you Tuesday night between eight p.m. and early the next morning?"

CHAPTER 9

Jackson woke before his alarm, turned it off, then tried to focus. The sound of nearby breathing startled him. Someone was in his bed! He rolled over and saw the boy. Benjie's eyes opened and a small smile played on his lips.

Jackson grinned back. "Good morning. You must have been pretty quiet when you snuck in here, because I'm a light sleeper."

A bigger smile this time.

"I have to make coffee and get in the shower. Will you stay right here?"

The boy nodded.

Jackson's ex-wife had stayed home with Katie when she was little, so he wasn't sure how much supervision a three-year-old needed. It seemed okay to take a quick shower. His Sig Sauer was in a locked case that opened only with his fingerprint, and the cleaning supplies were on a high shelf in the laundry room. He hurried to the bathroom, took his prednisone, and hopped in the shower.

What the hell had he done bringing the boy here? It was just temporary, he reminded himself. He would find Amanda's family today, no matter what it took. Then Benjie would begin to recover and not need him so much.

Later in the kitchen, he asked the boy what he wanted for breakfast. When he didn't get a response, Jackson opened a cupboard. "I've got cereal, pop-tarts, and toast."

"Junk food."

He spun toward the boy and laughed. "So, you're a healthy eater. My girlfriend will like you. What do you want then?"

"Eggs and fruit."

The boy was not only talking, he was articulate. A good sign. "I have eggs, but I'm not sure about the fruit."

Jackson scrambled eggs for two and found a box of raisins that had been hanging around since before Katie left. They chatted while they ate—a mostly one-way conversation—and Jackson resisted asking questions. Benjie needed time to feel safe. Jackson hoped to catch his mother's assailant without the boy's help at all.

Derrick padded into the kitchen and poured himself some coffee. "Good morning. Who is our company?" His brother was home for a few days between long-haul gigs.

"This is Benjie. I'm trying to find his family."

Derrick arched an eyebrow, but Jackson wouldn't talk about the boy's mother in front of him. He turned to Benjie and finished the introduction. "This is my brother, Derrick."

Benjie smiled and said, "Hi."

It surprised him at first, but then, he and Derrick had similar faces. His brother was taller, blonder, and more attractive, but they both looked like their mother. Jackson took his plate to the sink and spoke softly to Derrick at the counter. "How long are you home this time?"

"Today and tomorrow. I leave early Friday, unless I get a job offer."

"I may need your help with Benjie."

Derrick grinned and punched his arm. "Good luck with that. I'm only up early because I have an interview this morning and another this afternoon. I have to get off the road." He took his coffee back to his room.

Jackson gave the boy a quick bath and some clean clothes, then pulled out the toys from his backpack. A talking computer gadget, some building blocks with letters, and several little trucks. Not much, but it would get him by for a while. He settled Benjie on the couch with his toys and a set of sound-blocking earphones. As an only child, Benjie was probably used to spending time alone, entertaining himself. With an alcoholic mother and no siblings, Jackson's own daughter had become quite self-reliant at an early age. He regretted that independence now and wished he could raise Katie all over. But there were no second chances with kids.

He shook it off. Time to dig up some information.

His first call was to Cricket. He got lucky with a sympathetic manager who agreed to e-mail Amanda's phone records for the past three months without asking for a warrant. Jackson had suggested she call the department to verify his ID and that had tipped the scale in his favor. The files would still take a few hours to arrive, but at least he had a component of the investigation moving forward.

The call to Chase Bank was less rewarding. They wanted him to fax a subpoena. Jackson called Quince and asked him to take care of it, hating his dependency on his team for this case. Schak would also have to interview the homeowners when they came in. But he had to let go of the responsibility. Both detectives were good at their jobs, and he'd get an update at the task force meeting.

That reminded him to send an e-mail with a photo of Amanda to his contact at the *Willamette News*. As much as he hated opening up a line of communication with the media, he owed it to the victim to do everything he could to find her family and solve her death.

After that, he googled nursing homes and started making calls. Forty minutes later, he hadn't found anyone who'd heard of Amanda Carter. He didn't expect her to be on the payroll at either hospital, but he made the calls anyway and hit a dead end. Where else did people wear scrubs? Medical clinics and dental offices. He was skeptical though. With fake ID and a low-rent lifestyle, she was probably a minimum-wage employee. He came back to the nursing home idea and wondered if he'd missed one. He googled *caregiver Eugene*, and Fresh Horizons In-Home Care came up.

That made sense. Amanda could have taken the boy with her to job sites. Jackson called the Eugene office, identified himself, and asked to speak to the director. After a long wait, a man's voice came on. "This is Albert Yamhill. What can I do for you?"

"I'm investigating the death of Amanda Carter and looking for information about her. Did she work for you?"

A funny noise of surprise. "She did. We were just going to call her. She was supposed to work this morning and didn't show up." He made another strange sound in his throat. "I'm sorry to hear she'd dead. What happened?"

"We're not sure yet. Do you know anyone who might have wanted to harm her?"

"I didn't really know Amanda, but she seemed nice. Our clients liked her and she was dependable."

"Did she mention anyone threatening her?"

"Not to me."

"What about family? I need to let them know."

"Let me see who she listed as an emergency contact." The sound of a drawer opening and papers rustling. The director came back. "She put down Lucille Caiden. Do you want the phone number?"

"Please." Finally, someone who knew the victim. "Do you have an address too?"

"No." The director relayed the phone number.

Damn. The 458 area code could be anywhere in Oregon, but not likely Eugene.

"How is her little boy?"

"He's fine, but he needs a family. Do you know anything about his father?"

"No. Our employees work independently and only come in for meetings and training. So they don't really even know each other."

"Can I have a copy of Amanda's schedule and who she was taking care of?"

He hesitated. "I'll send it to you, but our clients are mostly shut-ins. I doubt any of them could be involved."

"I'm sure you're right." But he would check them out anyway. One might have a son who was mentally ill or drug addicted and had become infatuated with Amanda. Jackson gave his e-mail address. "If you think of anything important, please contact me."

He glanced at Benjie, who'd stretched out on the couch and was about to fall asleep. Jackson checked the time. A late morning nap. That was normal, wasn't it?

He poured himself another cup of coffee, then dialed the contact's number, his torso tight with expectation.

As he was about to hang up, an older woman answered. "Hello?" She sounded feeble.

He introduced himself, then jumped right in, asking a loaded question. "How do you know Amanda Carter?"

A sharp intake of breath. "Oh no. What happened?"

Oh damn. He hadn't braced for this. "I'm sorry to tell you she died. We're not sure how. Are you rela—"

The woman cut in, near hysteria. "Where's Benjie? Did he take him?"

Ten questions popped into his brain, and Jackson wanted answers to all of them. He forced himself to proceed slowly. "Benjie is fine. He was hiding under the house where Amanda died." He glanced over. The boy still had on his headphones but his eyes were open. "Tell me how you know Amanda."

"She's my granddaughter."

"What's her real name?"

"I can't tell you."

Oh crap. "Someone murdered her, and I need your help. I need to know everything."

"Murdered? He hurt her? Oh no. I thought he just wanted the boy." The old woman began to cry.

He? A viable suspect. Jackson had to comfort the grandmother first. "We think Amanda died quickly, but we're still trying to figure out what happened."

"He probably found them, but she must have hid Benjie in time."

"Who was stalking her? Benjie's father?"

Silence.

"What's his name?"

"I don't know. Amanda would never tell me. But she was afraid of him."

Frustration made him impatient. This was getting nowhere. "Did he write the threatening note in Amanda's wallet?"

"Yes. He left it in my mailbox and I sent it to her. She wanted it because she thought it might help the police someday if he ever found them."

"What is Amanda's real name?"

"I can't tell you. I promised to keep her secret."

Now he was pissed. "Amanda is dead. You can't help her by keeping things from us."

"Benjie still needs protection. I'm sorry." She hung up.

"Dammit!" Jackson glanced at the boy, who watched with wary eyes. Kids knew when you were talking about them.

Irritated, he jumped up. He hadn't had a chance to ask the woman if she would take care of Benjie. Or if another family member could. Pacing, he redialed the number, but Lucille Caiden didn't answer. If he had to, he would drive down to Drain and talk to her.

But would the boy be safe with Amanda's grandmother if she could take him? Jackson had to shut down his personal emotions and not jump to conclusions. He didn't even know if the father was really a threat. Maybe the father had custody. But if he'd killed Amanda, that paperwork no longer mattered.

He needed a name!

CHAPTER 10

Jackson texted Kera: *Are you at the hospital? What's the update?* While he waited for a response, he took the headphones off Benjie, then talked to the boy as he pushed buttons on the talking toy, which looked like a cross between a cell phone and a mini-computer.

"G is for gorilla," Jackson said.

The boy made a growling gorilla sound.

So cute. Jackson loved this age. "D is for doggie. I don't like dogs. Do you?"

"I like puppies." Benjie shook his head. "Mommy says no."

"Dogs are a lot of work. What is your mom's name?"

"Mommy."

No help. "D is for dad too."

The boy pushed another button and mooed like a cow.

"Do you have a dad?"

"No." Benjie changed the subject. "Do you have puzzles?"

That surprised him. "No, but we'll pick up some at the store."

"Thank you." He made a gesture with his hand on his mouth. "I'm hungry."

"Let's get something."

While he made a PBJ for the boy, he received a text from Kera: *In ICU again this morning. No charge. Could use a break from Micah. But I know you have a case.*

How could he refuse her? He had almost two hours before the task force meeting, and he was babysitting anyway. He could spare an hour. He texted back: *On my way.*

A moment later, he regretted it. He should be working to find Benjie's family and Amanda's killer.

Kera looked so relieved to see him, his anxiety about not working eased. Her expression quickly changed to puzzlement when she saw Benjie. Jackson let go of the boy's hand and Benjie grabbed his pant leg. Jackson hugged Kera tightly, then kissed her—guilt, love, and worry poured into the encounter.

She finally pulled back. "What's going on? Who's the little one?"

"Benjie was hiding at the crime scene yesterday. I haven't found his family yet."

"Why didn't children's service take him?"

"They tried but he was too distressed. He's quite bonded to me—for now."

"I don't blame him." A little smile.

"Anything new on Danette?"

"They've stopped the bleeding in her abdomen, but she's still unconscious and her blood pressure is low.'

"Have you called Maggie?" Danette's mother lived in Corvallis but had little contact with her daughter and grandson.

"She's coming this late afternoon, so I'll be able to go home for a while."

"Go take a break. I'll watch the boys."

Jackson picked up Kera's grandson and said hello.

Benjie made a distressed sound. Jackson put down Micah and patted the other boy's head. "Don't worry. We're still a team." He introduced the kids to each other.

"I like this version of you." Kera grinned and gestured with a circle of inclusion. "Good luck." She headed for the elevator.

He took a deep breath. How had he ended up here, taking care of two little boys? It was odd, yet strangely satisfying. Time to find the playroom on the children's ward.

Later at the department, he ordered pizza for the task force, then updated his case file. He glanced at Benjie, who sat on the floor, playing with an old recorder and laughing at the sound of his own voice. Before that, the boy had been working a puzzle with surprising skill. Would Benjie think the pizza was junk food and not eat it? Jackson felt like a bad influence. It didn't matter. He would drive to Drain this afternoon and not leave the grandmother's house until she agreed to take the boy or gave him the name of a family member who would. Getting attached to Benjie was a bad idea.

Footsteps thundered nearby and Jackson spun in his chair.

"What the hell?" Sergeant Lammers strode up, hands on her ample hips, staring at the boy.

"He was hiding at the crime scene yesterday, and I'm trying to find his family." Jackson stood too, trying to feel more . . . more what? Masculine?

"Mommy my family." The boy grabbed his pant leg. "And Jackson."

"Oh brother." Lammers rolled her eyes. "You need to call Family Services."

"That didn't work out."

She glared for a long moment. "What's the update on your case?"

Jackson started to tell her, then remembered the boy. He grabbed the headphones and put them on Benjie again. The boy grinned. "Warm ears."

He turned back to Lammers. "The victim's ID says Amanda Carter, but we believe it's phony. I located her place of employment and her grandmother, and I'll drive to Drain this afternoon to question her in person."

"Leave the boy with her."

Jackson bristled. What the hell did she care? "That's the plan."

"Any suspects?"

"The teenager next door called in the body, and we're looking closely at him." He wouldn't mention the threatening note and the potential custody issue until he knew more. "We have a task force meeting in a few minutes."

"Keep me posted." The boss moved next door to Evans' office.

He remembered Evans wasn't on his team anymore and wouldn't be at the meeting. That was too bad. She always had a fresh insight. He finished typing up his case notes and printed copies for Schak and Quince. Grabbing Benjie's hand, he headed for the conference room.

Schak arrived early, stood in the doorway, and raised an eyebrow. Jackson didn't know if he was asking about lunch or the little kid who was pushing around one of the chairs. "Yes, I ordered pizza. And Benjie is hanging out with me until I find his family."

"Whatever works for you." Schak lumbered around the table. "I'll take the board since Evans won't be here."

Quince came in, did a double take at Benjie, then smiled. "Your girlfriend's grandson?"

"No." Jackson explained—hopefully for the last time—then asked Benjie to leave the chair alone and try another one of his new puzzles. "I have to put the ear warmers back on for a while."

"Mommy can't hear either."

Poor kid! He ached for the boy but didn't know what to say. "She misses you too." He turned back to the group, feeling awkward. "Let's make this quick." He passed out his case notes. "Amanda Carter, if that's her name, worked for Fresh Horizons In-Home Care. She listed Lucille Caiden as her emergency contact, so I called her this morning. Lucille admitted being Amanda's grandmother but wouldn't tell me anything else."

"That's weird," Quince said.

"She claims she promised to keep Amanda's secret." Jackson slipped the folded paper out of its plastic evidence pouch. "I also found a threatening note in Amanda's wallet. No signature, but her grandmother sounded scared. I think they were hiding from the boy's father. But it's just a guess." He passed the note to Schak, who copied it to the board in handwriting that was nearly unreadable.

"Probably a custody issue," Schak said. "It may explain why she didn't have a birth certificate for the boy."

"I hate custody issues," Quince added.

"Me too." Jackson checked his case file for their assignments, then looked at Quince. "Did you talk to the teenager next door again?"

"I tried, but Dylan wasn't home. When I told his mother about the bloody knife, she looked worried and stopped talking to me."

Jackson had an ugly thought. "Look at reports in the neighborhood and see if there are incidents of animal abuse. Or if Dylan's name comes up in complaints."

A knock at the door, then a desk officer opened it. "Dan and Julie Beckett are here to see Schak."

The homeowners. About time.

A mismatched older couple tentatively stepped in. He was seventy and scowling, and she was fifty, plump, and pleasant.

"Thanks for coming," Jackson said. "Have a seat, please. We won't take much of your time."

The man stayed standing, his wife a step behind him. Dan Beckett demanded, "I want to know who was in the house! It hasn't been rented since February."

That answered the basic question. Still, Jackson tried to clarify. "You don't have a rental contract with anyone right now?"

"No." The man crossed his arms. "Whoever was there was trespassing. Damn squatters."

Well, hell. Jackson handed him a close-up photo of Amanda's dead face. "Do you know this woman?"

"No."

His wife peeked over the man's shoulder, then quickly looked away. "I've never seen her."

"Who has keys to the rental?" Jackson glanced at the boy to see if he was looking at the Becketts or showed any recognition. Benjie was focused on a puzzle and whispering to himself about it.

"No one," Mr. Beckett said. "We don't have a manager for the place. In fact, we've mostly given up on it."

"What does that mean?"

A moment of silence, then Mrs. Beckett blurted out, "We stopped making mortgage payments months ago. Without a renter, we couldn't afford to."

A zombie house. Abandoned by the owners but unclaimed or processed by the bank. They were all over the country. Surprised by the development, Jackson struggled to think of what else to ask.

Schak tapped the board, then looked at the Becketts. "Do you know anyone who owns a blue pickup?"

"Why?" Julie Beckett asked.

"Because someone saw a small light-blue truck in front of the house recently."

"Our son used to do maintenance for us, but he has a big, dark-blue F250."

"He has a key?" Jackson again tried to clarify.

Dan Beckett took over. "Yes, I'd forgotten that. But he had no reason to be there now, and he damn well didn't let anyone stay without signing a rental contract."

"Could Amanda be a friend of his?"

A deeper scowl. "Our son's married, a churchgoing family man." Mr. Beckett shook his head. "They probably broke in. The window in the laundry room doesn't latch well."

"What's your son's name?"

"Charles Beckett, but you leave him alone. This has nothing to do with him."

The desk officer was back with thin, flat boxes. "Your pizza is here."

"Thanks." Jackson started to ask the Becketts another question, but they were already leaving.

He let them go. "We need more information about the little blue truck, but first, let's eat."

CHAPTER 11

Wednesday, September 4, 11:50 a.m.

Evans took the elevator to the basement of the old hospital. Her first autopsy. The thought made her stomach flutter. A lot of newbies passed out or got sick, but she was determined to be stoic.

She pushed into the room and gave it a quick once-over: Smaller than she'd imagined, with lots of stainless steel. Grayson's body lay on a wide, raised table, but she wasn't ready to look at it.

The pathologist glanced up from the back counter, startled. "You're early. What a pleasant surprise. I'm Rudolph Konrad." His round, thick face didn't match his graying hair but he had a nice smile.

"Detective Lara Evans." She looked around for protective gear and saw a shelf with open boxes of gloves and facemasks. "Should I suit up or is it too soon?"

"We're still waiting for Gunderson and an assistant DA. I don't know who this dead young man is, but the district attorney says there's no room for error." The pathologist's smile disappeared. "I don't make mistakes."

"Bullshit." Gunderson strode into the room. "We all do. You're just better at explaining yours." The medical examiner grabbed two paper gowns and handed one to her. "This is your first, isn't it?"

"I'll be fine." Evans tied the gown and pulled on a facemask, feeling like she was about to operate on someone. Watching the pathologist make the big cut in the corpse's chest would be the hardest part. Once he was open, she'd be all right.

Five minutes later, Jim Trang rushed in and apologized for being late. "I didn't know I was supposed to be here until I got the call this morning." His briefcase looked out of place in the room with all the white paper gowns and stainless steel. As he suited up, Trang said, "The DA wants Logan Grayson's toxicology reports prioritized."

Gunderson snorted. "Then he'll have to call the state lab. I sent them out this morning and that's all I can do."

"Let's get started," the pathologist said, moving to one side of the body, and the medical examiner took his place on the other. The two men had probably done a hundred autopsies together. Gunderson, the ME, attended crime scenes, took detailed photos, cleaned the body, and extracted fluid samples. Konrad, the pathologist, conducted the postmortem examination and determined the cause of death. At least that was her understanding.

Following Jackson's advice, she put a piece of mint gum in her mouth and focused her eyes on the dead man's feet. So far the room reeked mostly of powerful antiseptic, but she knew the body smell could get intense when they cut him open.

First, Konrad began an inch-by-inch search of the skin, starting at the toes. He made general comments for the recording, but most were irrelevant to her investigation. Evans found herself staring at the man's incredible physique and muscle structure. He could have passed the damn SWAT test without even trying. A bruise on his chest, about the size of a fist, blended with his mixed-race skin. Had someone struck him? She really wanted to examine his face and head, but the pathologist hadn't reached that point, and she didn't know if she would be allowed to get that close.

After a few minutes, Konrad picked up one of the corpse's hands. "Bruising on his knuckles indicates an altercation, but the yellowish color means it likely happened several days ago."

Evans remembered the outburst by Lamar Owens, Grayson's teammate. Maybe Grayson had struck a wall too. But walls didn't punch back in the chest. Who had he fought with?

"Did you take samples from under the nails?" Konrad asked.

"Always." Gunderson's tone held the same attitude they saw at crime scenes.

For a long moment, the pathologist stared at the man's right knee, then examined it more closely with a magnifier. "I believe he had an arthroscopic knee surgery in the last few years."

"He injured his MCL last year and nearly missed the bowl game," Gunderson said. "Don't you people follow the Ducks?"

Konrad moved on without comment. "A bruise on his chest near the right nipple." The pathologist measured the mark, noted the coloring, then added, "This bruise was likely incurred several days before his death, perhaps in the same altercation where he suffered the bruise to his knuckles."

The fistfight now seemed important. "Could the fight have set off a chain of events in his body that led to his death?"

"Possible, but unlikely. We'll know more when we get inside." Konrad didn't even look up. He shifted his gaze to a new area. "There's a tattoo of the ace of spades on his right shoulder."

Was it supposed to be lucky? Evans started to feel restless and they hadn't even turned him over.

Konrad leaned in and examined the tattoo.

"What is it?"

"I'm not sure. A pin prick maybe."

"Like a needle injection?"

"No. Too small. It may be nothing." He photographed the spot and moved on.

Finally, the pathologist reached Grayson's head. "A significant amount of dried blood, all of it stemming from the nose. But no swelling to indicate a blow there." The pathologist made an unexpected cut into a nostril, drawing a tiny trickle of blood.

"The nasal cartilage shows minor damage, most likely from snorting narcotics." Konrad extracted a tissue sample and placed it on a glass slide to examine later under a microscope.

"Cocaine?" Evans asked.

Gunderson spoke up. "Or meth. Or oxycontin. Drugs users will snort just about anything."

The assistant district attorney cleared his throat. "Speculation is unnecessary, and this information cannot reach the media. The national news teams are in town and pressuring everyone. This is too explosive."

They all turned to stare at him, and Gunderson said, "We don't talk to the press."

"I know," Trang answered. "But you can't tell your wives or coworkers either, or it will leak. The football team is already hurt by Logan Grayson's death."

Evans was surprised the DA's office cared so much. Was this player's drug use just the tip of an iceberg? Or was it simply about keeping the money flowing in?

"I'd like to continue my examination." Konrad's tone was so dry it sucked the moisture out of the room. The pathologist began to search the man's scalp, aided by the shortness of Grayson's curly brown hair. "An abrasion on the left side of the neurocranium, two inches above the temple. Slight swelling and discoloration, but no lacerations and no blood."

A fist to his head too? "What caused it?"

"Either someone shoved his head into a wall, or his head struck something when he fell. The body was found on the floor, correct?" Konrad looked up at her.

"Yes, but none of us saw the body at the scene. I also didn't find any evidence that he hit anything on the way down." Evans remembered the medication in Grayson's bathroom. "He had a prescription for Nardil, an antidepressant."

The pathologist nodded. "It's a monoamine oxidase inhibitor and contra-indicated for food such as hard cheese and cured meat. We'll see what's in his stomach later." He looked at the ME. "Let's roll him over."

The backside examination went quickly, and Evans planned her next steps as Konrad listed moles and scars. Finally, the pathologist said, "Let's look inside."

Evans braced herself, then decided not to watch. She kept her head up, but cast her eyes on the counter as he began the Y-shaped incision on the chest. The room was quiet.

"There. Done."

Just as she looked up, Konrad lifted the chest skin and flapped it over the dead man's face. The smacking sound and rotten smell made a little vomit rise in her throat. She swallowed it back and pinched the skin near her thumb. She would not get light-headed or puke or run out. It was just a dead body. She'd seen a few.

Konrad carefully cut what looked like a liver from the man's cavity. Evans forced her mind to go blank.

Her cell phone rang in her pocket. *Thank god.* She grabbed it and glanced at the screen. An area code she didn't recognize. "I have to take this." She spun and exited the room.

In the narrow white hall, she pulled in long breaths, then laughed at herself. After a moment she answered. "Detective Evans."

"This is Paula Grayson. The police department said to call you to find out what happened to my son Logan." A current of panic under her careful words.

The desk officers normally didn't give out her cell number, but today everyone seemed to have it. "I've just started my investigation, and the autopsy is happening now, so we don't know the cause of death yet."

"Was he using steroids? I want to know. I think the coach pushed him to bulk up."

Whoa! A whole new line of inquiry. "We won't know until the blood toxicology reports come back from the state lab. That can take weeks, but this case has been prioritized." Evans reached for a notepad, unable to get her tablet computer going quickly enough. "What makes you think the Ducks' coach was pushing Logan to use steroids?"

"He hasn't been himself lately." The mother's voice broke. "He's been avoiding us, except when he needs money. And he seemed easily irritated."

That could describe any college student under pressure. "What makes you think his coach was involved?"

"Coach Harper was always pressuring him to work harder and push his limits."

Evans jotted notes as quickly as she could. "Did Logan ever specifically mention steroids?"

"No, but this all started after his injury last year."

A man's voice yelled in the background. "Who are you talking to?"

Mrs. Grayson kept her voice muted. "The detective."

From the background again, "I told you not to call him!"

"We need to know," the mother argued.

The connection terminated. Evans would call Mrs. Grayson again later in the day. For now, she had to man up and get back in there. She pushed through the door.

Konrad held a reddish-purple organ in one hand and a magnifying lens in the other. Grayson's heart. Evans' heart contracted in sympathy.

"Well?" the ME prodded.

"I think this young man had a heart attack."

CHAPTER 12

Wednesday, September 4, 1:35 p.m.

As Jackson got ready to head out, his cell phone rang. *Sophie Speranza.* A little redheaded reporter at the *Willamette News.* He usually ignored her until he couldn't anymore, but he had reached out to her this time, so he picked up. "Hey, Sophie. We have to make this quick. I'm in the middle of something."

"Jackson! Thanks for taking my call. But you sent me a photo of a dead woman. Don't you have any other image of her?"

"A driver's license, but it's too small to use, and she's changed her hair color."

A sigh. "Okay, I'll run it, but my boss won't be happy."

"Thanks, but I found the victim's grandmother and may not need the public's help."

"I guess that's good news." She sounded a little disappointed.

"I still don't know much about her, so go ahead and run the photo."

"Should I use your desk phone or the department hotline?"

"My desk phone. I've gotta go."

"Wait! You have to give me something to fill out the story."

He hated sharing with the media, but he owed Sophie. She'd given him useful information more than once. She also seemed to know everyone and was a good resource. "The dead woman has ID that says Amanda Carter, but we think the name might be fake."

"How did she die?"

"Let's just call her death suspicious. That's all I can tell you for now."

"Do you have a suspect?"

"We're looking at a couple of them."

"Come on, Jackson. Give me one specific detail. Something that won't affect your investigation."

Sophie's eagerness sucked him in. She loved a good case and stuck with it as obsessively as he did. "Her body was found in a nearly empty rental house."

"Interesting. We've heard reports of homeless people breaking into zombie homes and squatting."

"That's not the case here. She had a job and a car. Call me if you get any tips from the photo." He hung up as she thanked him. He'd come to respect Sophie, but he knew better than to give her another opening.

Jackson stopped to buy juice and snacks for Benjie, then hit the freeway heading south. He'd found Lucille Caiden's address in the white pages, and it matched the address on the victim's license. Even if Lucille had moved, Drain was small enough that someone would know where she lived and would tell him if he flashed his badge. He tried chatting with Benjie, glancing over his shoulder at the car seat, but after saying "road trip" with a sad smile, the boy went silent. The next time Jackson checked, Benjie had nodded off. Car rides did that to kids.

When he reached the small town an hour later, he stopped at a gas station and keyed Caiden's address into the GPS locator on his phone. He hadn't mastered voice commands yet, but he would. Benjie woke up and started whimpering.

"Hey, big guy. What's wrong?"

"I want Mommy."

Poor kid. What should he say? "I know you do. I'm sorry. She's not here anymore." Did three-year-olds understand death? They understood lonely, that was for sure. "We're going to see your grandma. Do you know Grandma?"

Benjie didn't answer.

Jackson checked the directions, relieved he was only a half mile away.

Lucille Caiden's red-shingled house sat back from the road, enveloped in oak trees. Moss grew on the roof and chickens wandered in the yard. An old diesel Mercedes in the driveway gave him hope that Lucille was home. Jackson parked and helped Benjie from his car seat.

"We're here?" The boy rubbed his eyes. "I have to pee."

"We'll go inside and find a bathroom."

They cut across the dried grass, holding hands. Benjie stopped near the front steps. "I don't like this house."

"Have you been here before?"

"No." A pause. "Yes."

"I think your grandmother lives here. Let's go see." Jackson had the headphones in his pocket. He needed to question the grandmother whether she liked it or not.

Benjie inched closer to him. Jackson knocked on the door and waited. He pounded louder, then called out, "It's Detective Jackson. We need to talk."

"Jackson?" The little voice beside him was quiet and worried.

"What is it?"

"Let's go."

"Why don't you play with your little computer? I need to make a call." Jackson steered Benjie to a well-worn porch swing and lifted him up. "Do you like to swing?"

"Not here."

The boy was obviously uncomfortable. Had something bad happened to him here? Jackson couldn't leave without information. He checked the front door. Locked. He looked around. The nearest neighbor was seventy yards away with no cars in the yard. No traffic on the road either. He heard a lumber mill nearby. Was it safe to leave Benjie sitting here while he went around back? Even if it was, the boy would probably grab him and tag along.

"How about a piggyback ride?"

"Can I chase chickens?"

Jackson laughed. A boy after his own heart. "We'd better not." He squatted, his knees complaining, and Benjie climbed on his back. Once again, the little arms went around his neck and he liked it. He had second thoughts about leaving the boy with his grandmother. Lucille had sounded old and frail, not an ideal person to raise a young boy. And Benjie didn't like the house, whatever that meant.

Around back, a kitten slept in the sun on the cement step.

"Kitty!" Benjie scampered down and ran for the cat.

"Gentle, please."

At least it wasn't a dog. While Benjie played with the cat, Jackson knocked on the back door, then began to look in windows. From the dining room glass, he could see into the living area. A gray-haired woman sat on the couch, her head leaning forward. A TV played in the background. As the situation became clear, his chest heaved in a huge sigh.

Lucille Caiden was dead.

CHAPTER 13

From the outside, Jackson saw no blood or damage, but the grandmother could have taken a bullet to the other side of her head. Damn. Had he set this in motion by calling her? He'd just been doing his job. What the hell was going on here? He slipped the headphones back on Benjie. Enthralled by the kitten, the boy paid no attention.

Reluctantly, Jackson called the front desk of his own department and reported his location. "I came to question Lucille Caiden in a case I'm working, but I think she's dead. I'm going into the house. Let the local sheriff's office know."

"Copy that. Should I send backup?"

"No. It could be natural causes and we'll trust the sheriff's office to work with us." He hung up, wishing he'd allowed himself more time to search, but calling had been the right thing. Sometimes he wished he could be a rule-breaker, but he also liked to keep things simple. Watching his older brother get into trouble over and over had turned him into a straight shooter at a young age. At the time, Jackson had thought he was trying to make his mother happy by being the good son. Now he wondered if he was just a coward.

The memory of a disturbed young woman pointing a gun at his head reminded him that cowards didn't become police officers—unless they were trying to face their fears. Jackson shook off his doubts. He had to get busy and learn what he could before the local law enforcement showed up. Jackson jogged back to his car to grab his carryall, and pulled on latex gloves.

How to get in the house? He tried the back door and it was unlocked, but it didn't look jimmied or busted. Lucille couldn't have been too afraid if she'd left her back door accessible. Or maybe she'd let someone in. Jackson glanced at Benjie, who was chasing after the cat. He had to take the boy inside where he could keep an eye on him, yet not let him see the body. *Oh hell.* Nothing like trying to do his job with one arm tied behind his back.

Jackson called to Benjie, then rounded up the kitten, glad none of his task force could see him now. After pulling the headphones off the kid again, he went into the house, a boy in one arm and a kitten in the other. The back door opened into the kitchen, where he left Benjie. On the other side of the narrow galley was the dining area. He grabbed two chairs and created a barricade. It wouldn't keep the cat in the kitchen or deter the boy if he became aggressive, but it would buy time.

"Please stay here in the kitchen while I work."

"I'm thirsty."

Jackson found a glass and poured the boy some water, feeling a pang of guilt about messing with the crime scene. What if there was trace evidence on the floor? Or fingerprints on the back doorknob?

"Don't touch anything but the cat, okay?" A waste of breath. The kid was three.

He stepped out of the kitchen, pushed the chair back in place, and rushed to the dead woman on the couch. A quick appraisal revealed no obvious wounds. A yellow nightgown covered much of her body, and she could have been beaten where it didn't show. Some men were good at that. Caiden's short gray hair, deeply-lined face, and white compression stockings signaled that she was elderly. Her death could have simply been from natural causes. Brought on by his phone call and news of her granddaughter's death?

He snapped four quick photos and checked her hands for defense wounds. None that he could see. With only a few minutes before a deputy arrived, he had to focus on finding information about Amanda. After a quick check on the boy, Jackson began to search for paperwork. Under the newspaper on the kitchen table, he found a pile of mail. Most of it was local bills, but one envelope caught his eye. A personal letter from Salt Lake City. Jackson wanted to pocket it to read later, but he didn't. This wasn't his scene or jurisdiction. And he would never impede another officer's investigation.

He charged down the hall and turned into the first bedroom, which was filled with boxes, blankets, and rarely used household items. He moved on to the next. An old-lady bedroom with a floral bedspread and a collection of colored-glass bottles. He riffled through dresser drawers, looking for more letters. In the nightstand, he found an address book, but Amanda Carter wasn't among the names. No computer in the room, only an old-style phone on the nightstand. The grandmother probably didn't have a cell either.

Back to the first bedroom. Jackson scanned cardboard boxes to see if the old woman was storing some of her transient granddaughter's possessions. Bingo! A box labeled *Andra Caiden*. Much like the Amanda Carter she called herself now. Jackson pulled out his utility knife and cut through the packaging tape.

The sound of an engine slowing down. *Crap.* His time was up. He pulled the flaps open anyway. Filled with sweaters, books, and childhood art projects. *No help.* He rummaged to the bottom and found a high school yearbook. *Yes!* He scanned the messages on the inside flap. One was signed, *Your BFF! Christy Blesser Chadwell.* He made a mental note and closed the book, keeping it under his arm. He shoved the box back into the stack and ran to the kitchen. Sliding the chairs back into place, he grabbed Benjie and the cat and headed out.

Once he rounded the side of the house, he realized the car he'd heard had arrived next door. Relieved that he had another minute, Jackson hustled to the front yard. His own arrival in the parking area had likely destroyed any tire track evidence, but he sat the boy down under an apple tree, tossed the yearbook on the hood of his car, and looked for viable footprints in the dirt next to the Mercedes. The dry summer had left the ground packed hard and nothing showed. But near the start of the walkway, a hose bib dripped, creating a three-foot wet spot. In the middle was a clear print. A man's dress shoe, he guessed. About a size ten. He squatted and took close-up photos. The sheriff's department would make a mold if he pointed it out to them, but the state lab might not process it for weeks.

An engine slowed nearby, then tires crunched on fir cones. He took one last glance around for potential evidence. Sometimes he got lucky and found a dropped cigarette butt or a gum wrapper. Not today. A dark-green sedan rushed down the driveway.

Jackson stood and turned to Benjie. The boy scampered toward him, a panicked look on his round-cheeked face and his little legs nearly tangling. Jackson scooped him up. "It's okay. He's another police officer."

An older man in a tan uniform climbed from the car and strode over.

Jackson introduced himself, but still holding Benjie, he didn't offer a hand.

"Deputy Walt Harwood. What are you doing here?"

"Investigating a suspicious death in Eugene. Lucille Caiden was my victim's grandmother."

"And now Lucille's dead?" The man raised a bushy eyebrow. "Where is she?"

"On the couch." Jackson set down the boy and slipped the headphones back on. "She may have died of natural causes. How old was she?"

"I didn't know her that well." The deputy squinted and frowned. "Were you in the house?"

"Yes. I wanted to check on her. She might have needed an ambulance."

"Bullshit. You busted into my death scene trying to help your own case."

Jackson couldn't argue. He held up his gloved hands. "I just took some pictures and looked at the mail on the kitchen table."

"You shouldn't have done that."

"I have a homicide to solve, and Lucille Caiden is the only contact I could find. I hope you'll let me help search the house."

"Not a chance." The deputy stared at Benjie. "Who's the boy?"

"Lucille's grandson. Did she have any relatives around here?"

"A brother, I think, who died a few years back." Harwood took a step toward the door and noticed the yearbook on Jackson's car. "Is that from inside?"

"Yes. It's the granddaughter's. I'd like to take it and track down *my victim's* friends or family."

"You're not taking anything from this scene until I've had a chance to look it over."

Jackson willed himself to be civil. "We should work together."
He wanted to share the threatening note and his suspicion that the
stalker might have come here looking for Andra Caiden and her
son. But he wanted something in return. "Let me look through
the yearbook and I'll tell you what else I know."

"I don't think you have anything to trade. And no one trusts
the Brady Bunch at the EPD."

Ouch. He tried not to visibly cringe. The evidence locker scandal—on the heels of sexual-assault convictions for two officers—
had sealed the department's reputation as a bunch of crooked
cops. But they weren't all that way and he wanted to change this
man's mind. "There's a fresh footprint in the wet dirt by the sidewalk." Jackson pointed. "I would get some tape around it and have
a crime scene tech make a mold."

"Are you sure it's not yours?" Derision saturated his tone.

"It's not. I walked across the grass."

"Did you touch the door handle in front?"

"Sorry. I didn't know she was dead until I went around back."

"You're a pain in the ass, and I want you out of here."

He had no legal right to stay. "The front door was locked, but
the back door was open. Just information."

"Write up a full statement and e-mail it to me as soon as you
get back to your office."

He had his own case to solve. "I'll do what I can."

A white sheriff's truck pulled into the driveway. The deputy
made a dismissive gesture. "Give me that yearbook, then get out
of here, so we can do our job."

CHAPTER 14

Wednesday, September 4, 3:05 p.m.

Evans left the medical center and drove toward Autzen Stadium on the other side of the river. The football team would be practicing, and the head coach might even be on the field. She hoped Grayson's roommate would be around too. Both messages to him had been ignored, and she was feeling testy. People who avoided the police tended to have something to hide. And if they wouldn't come to her, she would find them. She'd considered the possibility that the squad might take a day off to grieve Grayson's death, but rejected it. Football was a moneymaking machine that didn't stop for anything.

Outside, the temperature had hit ninety-plus again—one of about ten hot days they had each summer in late August or early September. Her car was even hotter inside, so she pulled off her blazer and cranked up the AC. How did the players practice in this heat with all that gear on? That was one of the things that had bothered her most as a patrol cop—long sleeves, flak jacket, and a belt full of gear on summer days. She loved the freedom of dressing in nice clothes and not having to wear a flashlight and a pager. No one looked good with thirty pounds of gear on their waist.

The stadium came into sight as soon as she pulled off Ferry Street Bridge. New skyboxes had been added a few years back, and it was now the most imposing structure in the valley. But that had been just the beginning. Nike money had built a new football "performance center," which was the envy of colleges across the country. The sleek building sat next to the boulevard and connected to the existing retail shop and coaches' office. She'd read a news article about the plush amenities in the new performance center and was curious to see the inside.

The first driveway took her under the building, where she parked, grabbed her phone, and left Coach Harper another message: "I'm here at the stadium and need to talk to you about Logan Grayson's death. Call me ASAP." Evans texted a similar plea to Jake Keener, the roommate. After hearing at the autopsy that the quarterback had suffered a heart attack, she doubted that he'd been murdered, but he could have been a victim of someone's greed, stupidity, or earlier violence.

She rode the elevator up to the main floor and stepped out into an expansive, high-ceilinged lobby, appointed in various shades of charcoal. A wall of video screens wrapped to the left, a fifteen-foot glass trophy case stood directly in front, and to the right was a sitting area surrounded by floor-to-ceiling windows. A receptionist sat behind a small counter reading. She would give the guys five minutes to call or show up, then she would go out to the field looking for them. While she waited, she would explore the rest of the building and see what all the fuss was about. As she started to get back on the elevator, a young woman in a Ducks T-shirt trotted up.

"Excuse me, but you can't get on the elevator. The rest of the building is for football players. The public is only allowed in the lobby."

No kidding? "I'm Detective Evans with the Eugene Police. I'm here to talk to Coach Harper and Jake Keener."

The receptionist, who looked sixteen, seemed uncomfortable with her security duties. "I'm sure they're practicing now."

"Tell me how to get to the field from here." Evans had never attended a Ducks game in person, and the complex appeared to be a mass of buildings, stone walls, and locked entries.

"Which field?" the girl asked. "There are five."

Five football fields? Evans tried to hide her incredulity. "Please tell me where Jake Keener is practicing."

"I think the offensive team is up front today. Go out those doors and turn right. You'll see it." She pointed at the glass wall.

Voices near the front made Evans turn. A group of men carrying video equipment and microphones crossed the lobby. Sports reporters. The first wave of national media had arrived to speculate about the effect of Grayson's death. The receptionist hurried back to the counter. Evans watched to see if the girl would turn the reporters away.

"Coach Harper is running a little late," she said, her voice almost too timid to hear. "When all the newspeople are here, I'll escort you to our media room."

Harper had scheduled a press conference. His phone had probably been ringing nonstop. She would try to catch him before the reporters used up his time.

Evans strode past the sitting area, remembering that the news article had said the chairs were upholstered with the same material they used in Ferrari seats and that the couches were imported from Italy. Two other details came to mind. The walls in the locker room were covered in football leather, and the floor in the weight room was constructed of Brazilian hardwood so dense it wouldn't burn. That, she wanted to see, but wouldn't likely get the chance.

Outside, she trotted down wide stone steps and came to a football field enclosed by a wall of massive dark stones in the front to block out the traffic and rows of tall evergreen hedges in the back. How much money had been spent on the complex—for a team of seventy or so players?

She remembered the article had estimated the cost at $68 million. The new police department building, plus renovations for the old one, had cost $27 million—for two hundred and fifty officers. Another reminder that law enforcement was not a priority in this town.

Wearing white practice jerseys, the players sprinted up and down astroturf-covered ramps. A middle-aged man in slacks and a T-shirt trotted over and politely asked what she wanted. Evans returned his smile and told him.

"I'll get Jake now, then call the coach. He's in his office." The assistant coach headed back to the players, who were sweating and grunting in the sun.

Moments later, a player trotted over and pulled off his helmet. Except for the dyed canary-yellow hair, he was handsome, but unsmiling. "I'm Jake Keener. You must be the detective."

"Lara Evans."

He surprised her by shaking her hand—and not crushing it with his powerful grip.

"Let's go inside out of the heat. That way I can take notes."

"Let's stay here. I don't have much to say or much time. I need to get back to practice."

As if the damn game were more important than his friend's death. "I have a job to do as well. If you'll be as honest and detailed as you can, this won't take long." Evans headed for the nearby steps and he followed. If they were going to stay in the heat, she wanted to take off her jacket—but couldn't because her weapon would show.

It was too bright to use her tablet computer, so she took out her recorder and a notepad. "When did you last see Logan Grayson?"

"Monday at practice. Then I found him on the floor in the bathroom at home Tuesday after practice."

"Where were you in between?"

"With my girlfriend overnight on Monday and here at practice the next afternoon. Her name is Alicia Zepher, and I'll give you her number if you want to check out my alibi."

He'd had plenty of time to come up with that tidy response. "I'll see what she says." Might as well jump right into the ugly stuff. "Logan had a heart attack, and his mother says Coach Harper pushed him to use steroids. Tell me about it."

"No way!" Keener slammed a fist into his thigh. "I don't believe it." He shook his head. "A heart attack?"

"It's unusual for someone his age, unless he took steroids."

"I think Logan did coke sometimes but not steroids."

"You think he did coke or you know because you saw him snort it?"

"I'm not talkin' about it." He wouldn't look at her.

So he used coke sometimes too. She remembered the dried blood and Keener's 911 call. "When you found Logan, what made you call for an ambulance?"

He grimaced. "I'm not stupid. I was just scared. And I didn't want to believe he was dead."

Time to move on. "Who did Logan fight with over the weekend?"

"He said it was some dude who'd been hitting on Danica. But he wasn't with her. I know because I talked to Danica."

"What do you think happened? Why would he lie?"

"I think he owed someone money. I heard him arguing about it on the phone last week."

"Did you hear a name?"

"No." He fidgeted, one leg vibrating. "In the last few months. . ." Keener stopped and glanced over at his teammates on the field.

"Tell me. I want to find out what happened to Logan."

"He changed recently. He was, like, stressed and secretive. He would be gone all weekend and not tell me where. I think he had another girlfriend. One he didn't want anyone to know about."

Interesting. "Why would he keep her a secret?"

The roommate shrugged. "I don't know."

"Any idea where I can find her?" Evans wasn't sure how a secret girlfriend connected to a fistfight or heart attack, but she wanted to find out.

"I think I saw his red Miata at some apartments off Willamette, near Twenty-ninth."

"Tell me exactly which apartments and where it was parked."

When she had the information, Evans let him get back to practice. Except for the cocaine issue, Jake Keener had seemed straight with her. If he and Lamar Owens were hiding something, they were practiced liars. She hurried back to the performance center. Time to track down the coach in his office.

Before she reached the building, a heavyset man rushed across the plaza, brow creased and jaw set. Harper's head seemed too small for his body, giving him a cartoonish look for a man who made $1.8 million a year.

Evans moved to intercept him. "Coach Harper?"

"Not now." He waved her off.

She kept pace at his side. "I'm Detective Evans. We can do this now and easy or at the department."

"I only have a few minutes." Stress filled his voice. "Logan's death, plus Trey being in the hospital, has been a huge blow.

We've been scrambling to rethink our lineup, and now I have to convince the media that we can still win games."

"Can we talk in your office?"

"No. I'm late for a press conference. Let's step into the lobby." He reached for the glass door.

Evans hoped the reporters had been taken to the media room. "Who's Trey and why is he in the hospital?"

"Trey Sandoval, a linebacker." Harper scanned the lobby, like a man braced for an assault. "He was in a car accident Monday, but at least we didn't lose two from the same squad."

She pivoted to face him. "Two players in one day. That's rather unusual."

"Only because they weren't involved in the same incident. Trey and Logan were good friends."

"But not roommates?"

"Trey lives with his sister. His parents insist on it."

They sat facing each other on a low black sectional couch. Evans pulled out her recorder and tablet, the scenario making her feel more like a reporter than a detective. "Did you know Logan Grayson used cocaine?"

Harper tensed. "I don't believe it."

"I just came from his autopsy. His nasal tissue was damaged, and he'd had a heart attack." She gave him a moment to process the information. "Logan's mother thinks you pushed him to use steroids."

The coach shot forward, eyes blazing, and grabbed her recorder. "That's a load of crap!"

Evans willed herself not to overreact. "Settle down or I'll take you into the department for a real interrogation." She reached out for the device. "I'll stop recording." *Like it mattered. Every word would go into a report.*

He held onto the recorder. "Mrs. Grayson is upset about Logan's death and wants to blame someone. But I have *never* encouraged my players to use steroids. Just the opposite."

She couldn't read him. His anger could have been masking deception. "So why do you think a twenty-year-old would have a heart attack?"

"I don't know."

"Did he seem different to you lately?" She keyed into her tablet as they talked.

"Maybe a little distracted."

"In what way?"

"Late to practice sometimes. And his mind was elsewhere during strategy sessions."

Some kind of external pressure. She made a note. "His mother said it started with his injury last year. What happened?"

He took a deep breath, barely able to contain his impatience. "Logan tore his medial collateral ligament and had to have surgery. He missed a month of the season and it probably cost him the Heisman Trophy."

"Did the setback cause a change in behavior?"

"I don't think so."

"Did you know Logan took antidepressants?"

Another scowl. "No. I'm his coach, not his mother or his therapist."

"Who did he exchange blows with over the weekend?"

"I have no idea. But Logan could be a hothead."

"Do you know anyone who might want to harm him?"

He pulled back, seeming confused. "Why would you ask?"

"I work Violent Crimes. His body had a head injury and a nosebleed, so the officer who responded to the call reported it to our department."

"He could have been hurt in practice." A pause. "Although the players always wear helmets. Maybe Logan fell while he was goofing around at home or with friends."

Or maybe he got into a fistfight. She asked a few more questions, but learned nothing. Harper stood and terminated the conversation. "Please don't report the steroid bullshit to the media. Or the cocaine use. We've had enough bad press with the DUIs last year."

"We won't report anything until we have lab results back." Evans stood too. "Thanks for your time."

He was already headed toward the cafeteria.

She walked to the elevator, but the receptionist intercepted her again. "Will you please go out the front door?"

"Seriously? I parked under the building. I came up on the elevator."

The girl looked sheepish. "You weren't supposed to."

Evans wanted to defy her, but the elevator pad didn't have normal buttons and looked like it required a code. She shook her head and headed toward the front, hoping she could find her car again.

As she walked down the ramp, her phone rang. A male name she didn't recognize. What if it was one of Grayson's friends, calling with information? She connected the call. "This is Detective Evans."

"Marcus Sanyo, a sports reporter with the *Willamette News*. Are you investigating Logan Grayson's death?"

A local reporter. Was he calling her from the media room or had he been left out of the national press conference? "Yes, but it's too early to report anything."

"A witness says Grayson was bleeding from a head wound. Was he murdered?" The reporter sounded young, with an underlying eagerness.

What witness? Jake Keener? "Grayson had a nosebleed prior to his death, but it wasn't from an assault."

"A nosebleed is consistent with cocaine use. Did he die from drug abuse?"

"He had a heart attack, but we're waiting for a toxicology report. I have to go." She hung up before he could respond. At least someone wanted to dig for the truth rather than worry about whether the Ducks could still win.

CHAPTER 15

On the drive home from Drain, Jackson notified his team of the victim's real name, then pondered his next move. It seemed critical to identify Benjie's father and the person who'd threatened his mother. He knew better than to assume they were the same person, but custody issues often turned into kidnap cases and violent interactions. Salt Lake City kept coming to mind. If the grandmother had contacts there, then Andra Caiden probably did too. Maybe he should run a photo of Andra in the Utah newspaper to see if anyone recognized her. He had a friend's name from high school, but she could be anywhere by now and married with a different ID. He wasn't optimistic about locating Christy Chadwell or gaining any useful information from her.

"I miss kitty."

Jackson glanced at the boy in the backseat. "Sorry, pal, but it ran away." Benjie had wanted to bring the cat, but it had fought to get free and run away. Jackson's relief had been short-lived as Benjie had cried and called for "Mommy" to come back. Having the kid name the cat after his mother had been heart-wrenching. What could he do to help the boy recover?

"I have to pee," Benjie said.

"Hang in there. We'll stop in a minute." Jackson hoped it wouldn't be too late.

"Can we get more puzzles?"

"Sorry, they're at home." He wished he'd brought some, but they hadn't seemed appropriate for a car ride.

A few minutes later, Jackson pulled off at a rest stop. Benjie opened the door and climbed out before Jackson had unbuckled.

"Hey, wait!" He scrambled to get out as the boy darted up the path to the white brick building. Only a few cars were at the rest area, but all it took was one pervert presented with an opportunity for a tragedy to happen.

He caught up with Benjie just inside the dark cement-block restroom. Relief made Jackson laugh. He'd forgotten how precarious a parent's job was at this age.

When Benjie came out of the stall, he asked, "Where's Mommy?"

Oh no. Did he mean his mother or the kitten? He hugged the boy. "She's not here anymore. We'll find you a new mommy." Could he keep that promise?

Back on the road, he decided that running Andra's photo in the Utah paper might not be a good idea. What if it alerted the father/stalker to Benjie's new location? What if he was a criminal or pedophile? Jackson knew he had to be careful. He would try to find Andra's friend, then call the Salt Lake police department and see what he could find out. The contact would probably be a waste of time. Someone would take his name and number and forget about it. Or wait a few days, hoping the urgency would go away. Law enforcement everywhere was overworked, and no one took on someone else's problems unless they were forced to.

As he took the Eugene exit, his cell phone beeped. A text. Jackson stopped at the intersection on Franklin and glanced at the message. Katie. She'd finally responded: *What boy? Why my help?*

He didn't have the time or patience to explain with keyed-in messages. Jackson put in his earpiece and called her, hoping she would talk to him.

"What's up?"

The sound of his daughter's voice filled him with a sense of peace. "Same old. I'm working too hard and still missing you."

"I text you all the time." A TV played in the background, so at least she wasn't on the street somewhere.

"I want to see you."

"What's the deal with the little boy you mentioned?"

Jackson closed the glass between the front and back seat, so Benjie wouldn't hear. The traffic light changed and he looked for a place to pull over and talk. "His mother was killed, and he may have witnessed her assault. He's pretty sad, and I'd like you to come over for a few days and keep him company." Jackson counted on Katie's big heart wanting to help. School would start soon, and he hoped she would decide to stay with him.

"Why isn't the kid in foster care?"

He was tired of explaining. "Benjie cried the whole time he was with Mrs. Martin, so I took him home with me."

"You always wanted a boy." Her tone was only half joking.

It ripped Jackson's heart. "I loved you from the moment I laid eyes on you. You're everything to me."

"I was teasing. And I know you're not keeping him."

Unless no one else turned up. "What do you say? Help me out for a few days? I can pick you up right now."

"Give me a couple hours to pack some things and talk to Trevor. I'll call you back." She clicked off.

Who was Trevor? Another boyfriend, of course. Jackson was slowly coming to terms with the fact that Katie considered herself an adult . . . and had adult relationships. It was best not to dwell on it. Everything had changed between them and he had to accept whatever she offered.

They were parked near the Market of Choice, so he took Benjie inside and picked up a couple of sandwiches, then went next door to Hirons and bought a pack of more-complex puzzles. The boy had mastered the others too quickly. Jackson felt self-conscious about walking around with Benjie, as if one of the victim's friends or family members would see them and accuse him of kidnapping. Instead, everybody smiled at them. The kid was a cutie.

Later at the department, he settled the boy and his playthings in an open area in front of the windows. He felt grateful for the new workspace. The Violent Crimes Unit had one whole end of the second floor, and no one was around to be bothered by the sound of a little boy playing.

He made a call to the Salt Lake City PD, explained his case to a desk clerk, and was promised a return call. *Yeah, that would happen.* Concerned that he hadn't heard from his team, he texted Schak and Quince to set up a task force meeting right after the autopsy the next morning. Now he had to find Christy Blesser Chadwell, who'd been Andra Caiden's best friend at Skyline High School. The online white pages weren't helpful, so he keyed her name into Facebook, trying both last names, relieved to find only three Blessers and eight hits for Chadwell. One pretty blonde, aged twenty-four, listed her hometown as Salt Lake. Finally! Something had broken his way on this case. He hoped. Christy might not have talked to Andra since graduation.

He clicked her About section and found a phone number. Nice for him, but what the hell was she thinking? Maybe she didn't realize she'd made the information public. He called the number, and when she answered, he was so surprised he fumbled a little at first. "Wade Jackson here. I'm a detective, and I'm trying to locate a friend or family member of Andra Caiden. Do you know her?"

A gasp, then she blurted, "I'm not helping you find her," and hung up.

Jackson mentally kicked himself and tried again. She ignored his call, so he left a clarifying message "I'm with the Eugene Police Department, and I'm investigating Andra's death. I need your help. Please call back."

He put down the phone and rubbed his pounding temples. It didn't help, so he reached for the aspirin he kept in his desk. He needed more caffeine.

Lammers' voice boomed outside his cubicle. Who was she talking to? Jackson jumped up and rushed out. His boss was squatted next to Benjie and chatting with him about the puzzle he was putting together. The boy was silent, watching her with big eyes.

Jackson hurried over, feeling protective. "I hope it's okay to have him here."

"Not really." She stood and motioned for him to follow her into her office.

He reassured Benjie he'd be right back, then left Lammers' door open so he could see and hear the boy.

"Have you made any progress on this case?" His boss drummed the desk with a pen. One of her many annoying quirks.

"Yes and no." Jackson summed up his trip to Drain, highlighting that he now knew the victim's real name and possibly where she was from.

"What about suspects?"

"The victim had a threatening note in her wallet, and I'm trying to find the boy's father. He may be the assailant."

"You should take the kid to Family Services and get focused. You usually have someone in for questioning by now." Deadpan voice, unblinking stare.

He tried not to hate her. She just didn't understand this case. "Katie will watch Benjie for me tomorrow. After the autopsy, I want to fly to Salt Lake City."

Lammers made an odd laughing noise, then crossed her arms. "This had better be good. Our travel budget is gone."

"The victim was hiding from someone. Her grandmother was afraid for her. They're both from Salt Lake City. I'm betting the father is there."

"So, run a photo of the mother and child in their paper." She shook her head, as if dealing with an idiot.

Jackson paused to calm himself. "What if Andra Caiden was running from an abuser or a pedophile? Announcing publicly that his son is in Eugene could be dangerous. I'm not willing to jeopardize the boy."

After a long moment, Lammers said, "I'll give you two days. But I think you're wasting your time and our money."

"I'll submit a travel form." He stood and walked out.

Benjie stood near the door, looking worried.

"We're fine." He picked up the boy and his puzzles and took him into his cubicle. A few more tasks and he'd head home.

Jackson checked his e-mail. One from Jasmine Parker, the evidence technician, caught his eye:

The prints on the bloody knife found at the Pershing house don't match anyone in the system. But they are smaller than average. A woman perhaps? Also, the blood type on the knife doesn't match what the ME sent us from the victim. I sent a sample to the state lab for testing. A strand of hair found on the victim's chest is definitely from another person. It's shorter, darker, and thicker. All we need now is a suspect and a DNA swab to compare it to.

He didn't have either of those yet, so he focused on the knife prints. Smaller than average. A woman, or perhaps a fourteen-year-old boy. He called Quince. "Hey, have you found Dylan Gilmore?"

"Not yet, but I'm downtown showing his photo around."

"If you find him, bring him into the department for questioning and let me know. The prints on the bloody knife are small, like a woman or a teenager." Jackson grabbed his jacket and carryall. "After we question him, let's book Gilmore into the juvie system so we can get his prints. If they match, we'll get a subpoena for a DNA swab."

"Should I put out a bulletin?"

"Why not? Call me if you find him. Otherwise, I'll see you in the conference room at ten tomorrow."

As he hung up, his cell phone beeped. A text from Katie: *Pick me up at the fairgrounds. But don't get excited. It's only short term.*

Yes! His daughter was coming home, at least for a day or so.

His joy was short-lived as he remembered Danette was in the hospital. Kera needed to hear from him. As he headed downstairs with Benjie in tow, he called. She picked up, sounding resigned. "Hello, Wade."

No one else called him that. "How's Danette?"

"Getting worse. Her brain is swelling."

"I'm sorry to hear that."

"Even if she lives, she'll probably never be the same."

"Oh no." Jackson knew he should ask about her plans for her grandson, but he wasn't ready for that conversation. Little Micah needed a father too, and the thought overwhelmed him. "I'm sorry I can't be there. I've got a case and a lost little boy too. But you sound pretty calm."

"Daniel is here, helping me look after his grandson."

Not good. Jackson's stomach tightened. Kera hadn't talked to her ex-husband in months. "You called him?"

"Yes. Micah is his grandson too. And we have to do something about his future."

Jackson burned with inexplicable jealousy. "Please don't make any decisions while you're distressed. I want to be part of the discussion."

"Then get involved. I have to go." She hung up.

CHAPTER 16

Evans pulled into the parking lot at the department and saw Jackson walking to his car with the little boy. What a good man. He obviously hadn't found a family member yet and didn't want to abandon Benjie to the foster system. Old feelings bubbled to the surface again. Would it always be this way if she kept working with him? Maybe it was time to get out of his department. Ben might be able pull strings and get her a position with Special Investigations.

Parking next to his car, Evans climbed out. "Hey. No luck finding his family?"

"Yes and no. I'll update you later." He gestured with a head nod at the boy.

"How's the case in general?"

"We're struggling. Schak is searching for anyone who might have seen another vehicle at the house, and Quince is looking for the teenager next door." Jackson buckled the boy into a car seat.

"I have the name of the victim's best friend, and I'm hoping she'll tell me something about Benjie's father."

"My case might wrap up today, so I should be able to help soon."

"Thanks, Evans."

Had he ever called her Lara? She wanted to hear it from him, just once. "Let me know if you need anything."

"I'm fine." Jackson looked as distressed as she'd ever seen him—and he'd been through hell and back a few times during the few short years she'd known him.

On impulse, she put her arm around his shoulder and squeezed. "You're a sharp investigator. You'll work through it." What else could she say?

Jackson surprised her with a return hug. For a brief moment, everything was right in her world. Then he let go, climbed in his car, and drove away.

Upstairs in her new cubicle, Evans typed up case notes, unsure of what to do next. Grayson's death was not likely a homicide, and without a toxicology report, she couldn't make a case for anything else. Reluctantly, she headed for Lammers' office. Her boss was just heading out.

"Make it quick, Evans. It's been a long day."

"Logan Grayson's autopsy revealed he'd had a heart attack, but he was also in a fight sometime before he died. Plus, he used cocaine. I'd like to keep investigating."

"What did the pathologist rule?"

"He's waiting for toxicology, but his report says"—Evans glanced at her notes—"hypertensive crisis followed by cardiac arrhythmia." She looked up. "Or, extremely high blood pressure that brought on a heart attack. Which could have resulted from cocaine or a bad mix of prescription drugs."

"Then wrap it up. Call the DA first, then have our spokesper-son issue a statement. She's tired of media calls." Lammers locked her office and started toward the stairs.

Evans knew better but said it anyway. "There's more to this case. Grayson's mother thinks his coach pushed him to use ste-roids, he had a secret girlfriend and would disappear for days, and he owed someone money."

Lammers shook her head. "A jock with bad drug habits. His death doesn't concern our department. Make the calls, then get back on Jackson's case. He needs help." The boss rolled her eyes. "He'll end up adopting that kid if you don't find a family member soon."

With mixed feelings, Evans returned to her desk and called the district attorney's office, leaving a message for Trang. She noti-fied the department's spokesperson and told her to make a state-ment about Grayson's heart attack to the eager press. More upbeat about her next task, Evans texted Jackson, letting him know she was back on his task force.

But even after opening her notes on Carter/Caiden, she couldn't focus on the case. The dead football player's secret girl-friend was a loose end that bugged her. What would she have to say? If Grayson had been with her before his death, she might provide some insight into what had been going on in his life. His parents deserved more than just a medical statement about how his body had shut down. She could drive over to the apartment complex and . . . and what? Knock on every door?

She clicked off her computer and stood to leave. Grayson's computer! She'd dropped it off with Detective Dragoo, a tech expert, hoping he would be able to get around the password. She hustled down the spacious walkway to the front of the building. The Vice unit had a view of the golf course across the road, but the building was quiet and she suspected everyone had gone home.

Dragoo was still in his cubicle. *Yes!* "Hey, buddy."

"Oh no, you must want something."

She smiled. "Sorry. Just checking to see if you made any progress on the laptop I brought you this morning."

"I got into it, looked around, and got bored. No criminal activity, unless you consider porn a crime." He grinned, rolled his chair back, and reached for a laptop in a plastic bag. "Here you go. I turned off the security, so you'll have free access."

"Thanks. I appreciate your help."

He held on to the computer. "Enough to go out with me sometime?"

Dragoo was married and the joke was old. "Your wife keeps telling me you're a cheap date." She winked, smiled, and pulled the laptop free of his grip. "See ya."

Evans hurried back to her own workspace. Stomach growling at the late hour, she accessed Grayson's laptop and opened a browser. His Gmail account loaded automatically. He must have figured the laptop password was privacy enough.

She scrolled through his messages, ignoring anything from a guy or a business for now. The e-mails from Danica Mercado, the cheerleader girlfriend, were mostly annoying. She wanted to know where he was and why he wasn't talking to her. Grayson had only responded to one and said: *I'm going thru some stressful stuff right now. Please give me space. I care about you.*

What stress? Evans tried to understand his world. Had he felt pressured to win the Heisman Trophy? As well as the championship? Money had obviously been a concern too. But Grayson had been taking a powerful antidepressant and may have had personal problems or a mental health issue.

Five minutes later, she hit the end of the in-box's first page and hadn't found the other girlfriend. She opened several folders and found e-mails from Grayson's mother, his bank, and a social networking site. Why had he saved those? Not until she spent ten minutes scanning through deleted e-mails did she find a possibility. From a sender labeled Cat7790@gmail.com: *I know I'm not supposed to e-mail you, but I miss you. It's been 10 days! And the rent is due. Please call me. —C*

Evans' first thought was, *How could he afford to pay his secret girlfriend's rent?* Grayson didn't have a job as far as she knew. She suspected none of the players did. Once classes started, they wouldn't have the time, and they were expected to focus on football. Evans also wanted to know what Cat stood for. Cathleen? Catlin? Catrina? It wasn't much help without a last name. But the numbers could be a birthday: July 7th, 1990.

If the girlfriend wasn't supposed to e-mail Grayson, then she probably called or texted. Frustrated that the paramedics or the hospital had lost his phone, she called North McKenzie and asked about it again. The hospital's receptionist put her on hold, so Evans did push-ups while she waited. She stopped at sixty and was still breathing hard when the woman came back on. "They found the cell phone in the ambulance. The ER will send it to the front desk, and I'll hold it until you come in."

"Thanks." If this had been a homicide, the delay could have been costly. But it was no longer an active investigation, she reminded herself.

On her way to pick up Grayson's phone, she called Ben.

"Hey, Lara. Everything okay?"

They typically only saw each other on weekends, with texts and e-mails in between, so her call must have surprised him.

"I was just going to get some dinner and wondered if you wanted to join me."

A pause. "It's a lovely thought, but Kurt and I already had dinner. Now we're looking at classes and trying to figure out his school schedule."

Brushed off for a class schedule? "It's that time of year." She wanted to shake things up. "What about later? Would you meet me for a drink?"

"What's going on? Is it important?"

"Not particularly. I just wanted to see you. Maybe discuss a case I'm working, or sneak in some midweek sex."

He chuckled. "I love the idea, but my son is grounded and I can't leave him home unsupervised. I'll call you after a while and we can talk."

"Okay. Bye." What had she learned? Their relationship was going nowhere until his teenage son was out on his own, and with some male offspring that took until age twenty-five. As much as she liked Ben, she was too impatient for that. More important, after all this time, neither of them had ever said *love*.

Impulsively, she called Jackson and he picked up right away. "Evans, what have you got?"

"I need to talk about the Grayson case. Can you meet me for a drink?"

"I've got Benjie here. And Katie. So it's not a good time to leave." A pause.

She started to say *Never mind*, but he continued. "You can stop by for a while. Katie and Benjie are getting along well, and we can step out on the deck, drink a beer, and talk."

That he would make time for her meant everything. Especially after Ben had blown her off. "Thanks. It'll be a quick stop. Do I need to bring the beer?"

He laughed. "You know me too well."

CHAPTER 17

Evans' call had surprised him. Having her stop at his house was even more unusual, but turning her away seemed wrong. If Schak or Quince had wanted to talk in person, he would have made time for them. Evans was as much a friend as any of the guys on his team. Also, she had never asked him for special favors or attention, so something must be weighing on her mind. He wondered how Kera would feel about Evans stopping by—especially since he was avoiding his girlfriend rather than be at the hospital with her, waiting for Danette to die. Jackson couldn't face more grief right now. Instead, he had guilt and worry rolling around in his gut. He was surprised Kera had called her ex to the hospital. Daniel had been mostly absent from his grandson's life.

Jackson returned to the living room, and the joyous sight of Katie and Benjie playing hide-and-seek pushed his guilt and confusion aside. For a delirious moment, a fantasy played out in his head. He would adopt Benjie, and Katie would move home to help raise him. They would all bond, and Benjie would fill the hole in their lives left by the death of Katie's mother. They would be a family. Kera and Micah too. Benjie could grow up with Kera's grandson as his stepbrother. Maybe they'd all move in together. They could make it work.

Derrick strode up the hall and interrupted his happy thoughts. "I'm going out for a while. The noise is a bit much for me." His brother slapped his arm with a rolled-up magazine.

"I'm sorry."

"Don't be. I'm happy to see Katie. She looks good."

His daughter turned, stuck out her tongue at them, then chased Benjie down the hall, laughing. She was still gaunt, still dressed in black, and had straightened her curly hair, but she seemed sober. Jackson had asked her to show him that she didn't have alcohol in her backpack and had made her promise not to drink while she was home. "I'm not like Mom," was all she'd said.

Jackson walked outside as Derrick drove off. The sun was sinking in a pink-and-charcoal sky, and the air had started to cool. He loved this time of day. Evans pulled in moments later. Neither she, nor anyone on his task force, had ever been to this house, which he'd only lived in for the last year. He'd grown up in the house as a kid, then gotten married and moved a mile away with his wife and daughter. After he and Renee divorced, he'd finally sold their house to get out of the joint mortgage and had moved back in here with his brother, who was typically not at home.

Evans walked up the driveway, moving a little slower than usual. Did she look sad? He was glad he'd hugged her earlier in the parking lot. Something was going on.

"Hey. It's a nice evening for a brew on the porch with a friend."

"Sure is." She pulled two beers from a sack, opened them, and passed him one. "Is that Katie I hear inside?"

"Yep. She's home for a few days to help with Benjie. They seem to like each other."

"Good news."

They sat side by side on the front porch, enjoying the dusk, and didn't speak for a while. Evans drank like a thirsty person while Jackson sipped his beer. He hadn't eaten dinner and rarely drank, so he could feel his tension slide quickly away.

Finally, she said, "I know you're busy with your family and I don't mean to stay long. But there's more to the Grayson case than a jock having a heart attack from snorting cocaine. He had a girlfriend on the side, one that he paid rent for."

"He sounds like a man under pressure."

"I think so too." She turned to face him. "Lammers wants me to drop the investigation, but I plan to find the other girlfriend and see what she has to say."

"That's probably what I would do too." He patted her leg. "Let me know what you find out."

Evans put her hand on his leg and left it. "I knew you would say that."

Jackson didn't know what was happening, but he liked it. Too uncertain to move, he sat quietly, enjoying the feel of her body so close to his.

Her voice was soft. "Do you think it's possible to be in love with two people at the same time?"

Who was she really asking about? "It happens." He tried to sound casual.

"But eventually something has to give, doesn't it?"

"Yes."

"I think that's what happened to Logan Grayson." She kissed his cheek and slipped away.

Later, he was reading through his case notes and nodding off in his chair when his phone rang. He recognized the number as the department's front desk. What could it be? He hadn't asked for any bulletins yet. "Jackson here."

"You're running the homicide case out of 2395 Pershing?"

"Yes. What have you got?"

"That house is on fire. The dispatcher who took the call recognized the address and notified us."

The evidence! "What happened?"

"It was just called in. I'm sure the fire department is still out there."

"Thanks for the heads-up." He clicked off.

It had to be arson. And the person who came to mind was Dylan Gilmore, the budding young sociopath who lived next door. What was he trying to cover up?

CHAPTER 18

A year earlier

Logan Grayson clenched his teeth. A hot knife of pain twisted into his left knee as they lifted him onto the gurney. "Motherfucker!" Four games left before the BCS Championship game and now he was injured. If he had to have surgery and sit out the rest of the season, his shot at the pros could be ruined.

Coach Harper ran alongside the gurney as the paramedics carried him off the field. "Don't worry, son. We'll get you the best orthopedic in the business. You'll be back in no time." The coach called every player *son*, so his message wasn't personal. Still, the words gave him some comfort. Logan prayed it wasn't his ACL. Many athletes never played sports again after a serious outer ligament tear.

In the hospital, he learned that he'd torn his medial collateral ligament. "That's the good news," his doctor said. "It could be much worse. The bad news is that you need surgery and a month of rest. But you will play again."

Logan looked to his mother, who'd flown to Portland to stay with him. "I'll miss the bowl game and my shot at the Heisman."

"You still have next year. And you'll be a senior."

Would he? Some players were never the same after major surgery. They did all right and finished out their college careers, but then it was over. They no longer excelled and caught the pro scouts' attention. He couldn't let that happen to him. Football was all he had. He wasn't smart enough to have a real career. And after a taste of the limelight, how could he spend his life working in one of his father's auto shops? His depression would overtake him.

By the second week of recovery, he was too restless to sleep at night. He couldn't run or work out or do anything physical, and his frustration was building to a breaking point. He gave up trying to sleep, grabbed his laptop from the nightstand, and clicked open his Chrome browser. When his bookmarked tabs loaded, he opened his Gmail. Nothing new but promotional crap. He thought about starting a chat with his girlfriend, but she would be asleep and not appreciate hearing from him. Danica had been avoiding him since his injury, and he suspected she was cheating on him. Going without sex wasn't easy for him either. She could have at least given him a few blow jobs. Some girls just didn't understand how important that was.

A quick glance at Facebook, then he clicked over to the next tab. He signed in with a password, checked a box that said he was over eighteen, and his favorite poker site loaded. He'd discovered online gambling after getting bored with late-night porn. Logan wasn't a sidelines kind of guy, and with gambling, he could participate. The real-money aspect of internet gambling gave it even more of an edge. He'd already maxed out one credit card, but his skills were improving all the time. He was due for a big win.

After a few hours, his leg started to ache and he reached for another Percocet. The pain pills worried him more than the gambling debt. He'd battled and beaten a cocaine addiction in high school, and he never wanted to go back into that world. Opioids were wonderful. And evil. Sometimes he felt the old cravings. Logan shook it off. It was one pain pill, and he was healing. In a few weeks, everything would be back to normal.

Except it wasn't. Without exercise and purpose, his energy leaked away and his depression came back. His mother talked him into trying a new kind of antidepressant. SSRIs had never worked for him. *That's because you're bipolar,* a little voice in his head chirped. Logan shut it down. He wasn't mentally ill. He just got depressed sometimes in the off-season—or when he was sidelined. Logan called his old doctor from high school, and without even seeing him in person, the doc called in a new prescription.

The new meds kicked in quickly, his knee healed, and he started to practice lightly with the team. But he still had a constant mild pain and his energy hadn't rebounded. At six weeks, his surgeon cut off his Percocet. Logan woke the next day sweating, shaking, and nauseated. At first, he thought he had the flu, but he scored a Vicodin from a teammate at practice, and as soon as it hit his system, the nausea passed. He needed a new doctor and a new pain prescription. He couldn't afford to be sick or look weak. He had a reputation to maintain. His teammates needed him to be strong and throw touchdown passes. His girlfriend, fellow students, young football players, and Duck fans everywhere counted on him to be a shining example of athletic prowess, public charm, and decent academic performance. More important, he had to maintain his scholarship. If he didn't perform for the team, the coach would boot him and the school would cut him loose. He would have to give up his sweet apartment, drop out, and go home. Failure was not an option.

Sometimes he felt like a slave—paid just enough to live, eat, train, and nothing more. He went out on the field every day, where he was broken down physically and mentally, with time off only to attend classes he hated. During games, he and his teammates put on a show for spectators, who placed bets and objectified them. The fans loved him, but only when he performed well and won games. If he made mistakes, they screamed obscenities and posted hateful things online. Some days, he didn't even feel human.

Then, one night at a party, he was introduced to an incredible woman. Tiny, with long platinum hair and full breasts. But her face was what drew him in. Dark-green eyes that hinted at sexual secrets and plump lips the color of cinnamon. When she touched his shoulder, an electric spark shot through his body. Later, when she offered him a line of coke, he fell in love. His energy was back in minutes, and he knew what he'd been missing. Later, she blew his mind—and other parts—with the most amazing sex he'd ever had. He needed her in ways he'd never needed anyone. But Catalina didn't fit into his world. She wasn't a student, she didn't have money, and she wasn't pretty the way Danica and her friends were. Catalina wasn't someone he could ever introduce to his mother.

Yet, he couldn't live without her.

CHAPTER 19

Thursday, September 5, 5:26 a.m.

Evans' first waking thought was that she was back on Jackson's task force and would see him at noon. She shut it down. She was an investigator with important things to accomplish. But first, a workout.

She shortened her normal forty-minute kickboxing routine to practice for the SWAT physical. Out in the backyard, the sun was just coming up. Evans assessed the object of torture for the morning: a piece of carpet rolled up around three pressure-treated fence posts. The effect was about the same as the one-hundred-eighty-pound dummy she would have to carry from a building as part of the test. She squatted next to the roll, swung it up into a fireman's carry, and started across the small grassy yard. The weight was overwhelming—at least forty-five pounds heavier than her own body. After ten feet, a sharp pain in her lower back made her drop the heavy load.

Fuck! She'd made it all the way across the yard the day before. Evans stretched her back muscles, jogged around, and tried again. She hit the halfway point this time, then lost control of the load. Clearly, she needed more work on her core. But not now, when she was hurting. She went out for a three-mile run to cheer herself up, then showered and headed to work.

Her first stop would be North McKenzie Hospital. She'd picked up Logan Grayson's phone at the reception desk the night before and spent an hour reading his recent texts and noting who he'd contacted. Two numbers popped up repeatedly. One didn't have a name label, but it matched a single text from the same number, a text with the same tone as the e-mail from *Cat*. They obviously limited their communication to phone calls as much as possible. Because calls left no incriminating details for his other girlfriend to find? Through the citizen database, Evans had tracked that number to Catalina Morales, complete with an address. As eager as she was to question the secret girlfriend, the early hour wasn't best for most people.

But in a hospital, it didn't matter; the patient was either able to communicate or not. And the second, more-frequently-called number belonged to Trey Sandoval, the player who'd been in a car accident Tuesday. She was on her way to see him now and hoped he was able to answer questions.

As she walked across the hospital parking lot, enjoying the early morning coolness, she couldn't stop thinking about how the best friends had experienced traumatic incidents within twelve hours of each other. The image of Grayson's bloody nose popped into her head. What if Grayson and Sandoval had both ingested tainted cocaine? Giving one a heart attack and the other a seizure or something that had caused him to lose control of his car? Evans warmed to the idea but worried it would be hard to prove unless she could find a sample of the drug. Was Catalina the supplier?

After she showed her badge, the receptionist directed her to a room on the seventh floor. Evans rode the elevator with a sad older couple, then strode through quiet hallways. The new hospital was massive, ornate, and half empty—the corporate owners had overestimated the local need.

The door to Sandoval's room was open, so she tentatively stepped in and said her name. A young woman in shorts and a tank top sat in the chair next to the bed, typing on a laptop. She looked much like the young man in the hospital bed—dark eyes, silky straight dark hair, and muscles popping out of her smooth skin. The patient had a bandage around his head and a cast on his right arm. And possibly more injuries concealed by the white blanket.

"Did you say detective?" Sandoval sat up and clicked off the TV.

The young woman, probably a sister, eyed her warily. "The state investigator was already here."

"I'm with the Eugene Police." She turned to the injured young man. "I need to ask you about Logan Grayson."

His face crumpled. "I can't believe he's dead."

Thank goodness he already knew. Evans asked the sister to give them a moment alone.

"It was an accident," she said on her way out.

Logan or Trey? Evans started to call her back, then changed her mind. Just a family member being protective. She moved closer to the bed. "Let's get right down to business. I want a sample of the cocaine you and Logan were snorting."

He started to deny the accusation, but she held up a hand. "Don't bother. It'll be in your blood work. And Logan snorted some before he died." She didn't know that for sure yet, but the nosebleed made her think so. "I want to know what it was cut with and who sold it to you."

"You think the coke killed him?" His doubt was obvious.

"Logan had a heart attack. Can you think of another reason why he would?"

For a long moment, he stared at the wall behind her. "My lawyer told me not to talk to anybody. Not the media or the police. I still have a football career, and I'm not blowing it."

"Your best friend is dead."

His jaw trembled. "It's not my fault."

Why would he have guilt? Had he given the drug to Logan or was his guilt about the car accident? "Was someone in the car with you?"

He nodded, his eyes watery. "She might not make it. But it was an accident! The truck was in our lane when we came around the corner."

Her empathy was limited. "If your passenger dies and you were intoxicated, you'll be charged with manslaughter." She flipped open her notepad. "Why don't you do yourself a favor and tell me who sold you the coke."

Silence.

"Was it Catalina Morales?"

He blinked in recognition but said, "I don't know who that is."

Liar. "I think you do."

"No."

"Who was your passenger?"

More silence.

She was done wasting her time. She would go to the source— the mystery girlfriend—and call the state police to ask if any cocaine was found in the wrecked car. Leaving a business card on Sandoval's bed tray, she said, "Call me if you decide to help yourself and tell the truth."

Out in the hallway, Evans stopped short. Was that Kera Kollmorgan at the nurses' station? She remembered Jackson mentioning a family accident, then leaving for the hospital—the day they'd been called out to the homicide.

Evans had to approach her. If Kera knew the passenger in Trey Sandoval's car, maybe she could get somewhere. She'd seen Jackson's girlfriend before but had never met her. Evans' stomach fluttered. "Kera?"

The woman turned.

Damn, she was gorgeous. And tall. "I'm Lara Evans. I'm in the Violent Crimes Unit with Jackson."

Kera smiled, but her eyes were sad. "It's good to meet you." She held out a hand. "Jackson speaks highly of your work."

"Good to know." The scenario felt awkward on so many levels. "Can I ask who you're here to see? I just talked to Trey Sandoval and he won't give me any information about his passenger."

Kera bit her lip. "My daughter-in-law, Danette Blake, was riding with Trey. She's in the ICU. I just came up here to check on Trey. I wanted to ask him some questions."

"Good luck. His lawyer advised him not to talk to anyone. He's worried about his football career."

Kera twisted her hands together. "Danette might die, so I don't really give a shit about his career." The tall woman stepped away from the counter. "Are you investigating the accident? I thought the state police were."

"I'm looking into another incident with a football player." Evans paused, not sure how far to push. But she had to ask. "Did Danette use drugs? Cocaine in particular?"

Kera didn't seem upset by the question. "I don't think so. I know she drank at parties on the weekends, but she seemed to be doing fine in school."

"Have the investigators searched her belongings?"

"I don't know."

She had pushed the distressed woman far enough. "I'm sorry you're having to deal with this. I hope Danette recovers."

"Me too. She has a little boy."

A child that lived with Kera. That Jackson and Kera might end up raising if Danette died. Evans couldn't help herself. "Have you met Benjie? The boy from the homicide case Jackson and I are working?"

"Briefly. Have you found his family?"

So Jackson hadn't updated her. "Not yet. But Katie's back home, and she and Benjie are bonding."

Kera's eyes widened and her mouth tightened. After a startled moment, she said, "That's good news about Katie. I suspect you're seeing more of Jackson right now than I am."

"I just stopped by there last night to discuss the case. This one is a real stumper."

Kera looked crushed, and Evans felt guilty. But she had a job to do. She pulled out another business card. "If you find any drugs in Danette's possessions, please call me, so I can get them analyzed. More lives could be at stake."

CHAPTER 20

Thursday, September 5, 5:45 a.m.

Jackson dreamed about Lara Evans. They were at the new police department, only it was different, smaller, and they had to share a cubicle. At one point while he was on the phone, Evans rolled her chair over to his desk and kissed him on the mouth. Electrifying!

He woke up, startled and sweating. Reaching to shut off the alarm, he climbed out of bed. What the hell was that about? He let himself mull it over for a minute and decided it didn't mean anything. Evans was attractive, and they'd had a little moment the night before, so she'd been on his mind. That was all.

On the way to the kitchen to make coffee, he stopped outside Katie's room and quietly opened her door. Yes, she was still here, and Benjie slept next to her. The sight filled him with joy. At Benjie's insistence, he'd set up a small mattress on the floor next to Katie's bed, and the boy had started his night there. Jackson wasn't surprised to see him end up in her bed. Benjie still had a long way to go before he felt secure again. Jackson wanted to talk to Katie before he left for work—an old habit—but the autopsy started at eight, and there was no point in waking her. Communication was so much easier now, and he could talk with her later.

Feeling energetic, he went for his first run in weeks. Only a couple of miles, but it felt great to be in touch with his muscles and cardiovascular system again. He vowed to do it more often. Back home, he showered and packed an overnight bag for his flight to Utah that afternoon.

Surgery Ten's glaring bright lights and small windowless space reminded him of an interrogation room. Which it was, sort of. The pathologist would pry open the victim's secrets in the only way he could.

"Jackson." Konrad greeted him, then looked up at the clock and grunted. The pathologist stood on the right side of the raised table.

"Yes, I'm five minutes early."

Gunderson, the ME, was on the other side, staring at the corpse's midsection. Together, they removed the sheet, exposing Andra Caiden's pale body. Jackson braced himself. Dead young women made him think of dead young daughters, and he couldn't afford those emotions right now. His heart felt pulled in so many directions, it actually hurt. Or maybe the run had been too much.

"Do all young people have tattoos now?" Gunderson muttered. "On women, they're just not right." He was staring at the purple butterfly on her hip.

"It's definitely a trend." Katie had recently tattooed her dead mother's name over her heart. Jackson was still pissed that some idiot would stamp permanent ink into someone so young, but all he could do was hope it would be her only one.

"This tattoo is odd," the pathologist noted. Konrad grabbed his magnifier and leaned in. "It has raised ridges." A long pause. "No, those lines are independent of the ink patterns." He handed the magnifier to Gunderson. "Take a look and tell me what you think."

After a moment, the ME said, "I'll be damned. I think it's scar tissue. She tried to hide the scar with a tattoo."

Konrad nodded. "I think it's a brand."

A what? "You mean someone marked her?"

The pathologist took the lens back and studied the tattoo again. "She was burned with something circular. It could have been an accident, but it looks deliberate. I've heard of pimps branding their girls."

Jackson's stomach rolled. "What exactly is the mark?"

"I'm not sure. But it's circular with something smaller in the middle."

Jackson thought about local gangs and their markings and couldn't make a connection.

"We'll come back to it," Konrad said. "For now, we'll start at the feet, like always."

As the pathologist conducted his examination and gave a running verbal report, Jackson tuned in and out, and planned his order of business once he arrived in Salt Lake City. The important details he filed away in his head for later: Blood had pooled in her backside, so she'd died right where they'd found her, and the time of death hadn't changed from the window of eight-to-ten Monday evening.

When the pathologist cut into the victim's neck, Jackson snapped to attention.

"Her trachea and hyoid bones have been crushed." Konrad's tone expressed a rare element of surprise. "The lack of bruising isn't typical in strangulation cases." A moment of quiet while he prodded the opening he'd made. "Perhaps the assailant pressed something against her throat. Like a forearm. The subconjunctival hemorrhage indicates asphyxiation as well."

As Jackson visualized the scenario, the ME spelled it out. "He had one arm over her throat and his other hand over her nose and mouth. Perhaps to keep her quiet while he raped her."

"That fits with the physical evidence." Konrad's voice had a little catch. "Or maybe he burked her." The term referred to a killer who had kneeled or sat on his victims, so their lungs couldn't expand, while he also held his hand over their mouth and nose. The murder left no trace. "But in this case," Konrad continued, "he would have kneeled on her throat."

Jackson felt queasy. Had Andra been branded by a pimp, then escaped with his child—only to be brutally murdered when he found her again?

After leaving the medical center, he drove by the Pershing house, surprised and pleased to see it still standing. The fire marshal's truck was out front, so he stopped to find out what he could. Inside, the house reeked of smoke, but little of it seemed burned. He heard movement in the kitchen, which faced the back, and crossed the wet carpet. A fire investigator was scraping up samples of the blackened floor. The cabinets and ceiling were also charred, and it looked as if the blaze had been contained to this part of the house.

The investigator turned and Jackson introduced himself.

"Brent Ottovich." The stocky man wore gloves and didn't offer a hand. "This is an unusual case, but I'm pretty sure it's arson."

"Tell me what you know."

"The fire originated in the laundry room, most likely around the dryer." He pointed through a blackened doorway. "If someone were living here, that would seem typical. Overheated lint has started thousands of fires." He held up an evidence bag filled with blackened clumps. "This was in the barrel of the dryer, and more like it was on the floor nearby. I think testing will confirm that it was soaked in kerosene. We had a canine out here earlier who alerted us to its presence."

"You must have gotten here quickly."

"The woman next door spotted the fire and kept it under control with a hose."

"Tess Gilmore?"

"Yes."

"Will you send me your report? I've got a suspect in mind that we'll bring in for questioning. We'll add arson to our list of possible charges."

"You think he was trying to destroy evidence in another crime?" Ottovich asked.

"Seems likely. Which makes me wonder what we didn't find here."

"Let me know when he's in custody. I'd like to question him."

"I'll be in touch."

Jackson headed out. He didn't have time to search the house again before the meeting, but his team could do it while he was in Utah. Had Gilmore tried to burn any fingerprints he might have left in the house? Or did he think that if he destroyed the crime scene, they wouldn't be able to convict him?

On his way to the department, he checked in with Katie, who reported that she and Benjie were going to the park to play. Jackson called Kera too, but she didn't answer. Troubled, he drove to the hospital but couldn't find her. The desk nurse in ICU told him Danette was in surgery to reduce the swelling in her brain. Jackson called Kera again and left a message: "I'm at the hospital, checking on Danette, and hoping to see you. I have to make a trip out of town for a couple days. Please call me. I love you."

He could feel Kera pulling away again, and he didn't blame her. He tended to put work and his own family first. Plus, for the last few months, he'd been grieving his ex-wife's death and his daughter's absence from his life. Crappy company at best. Jackson vowed to change all that. He loved Kera and couldn't bear to lose her. She was the most rewarding part of his life and put up with his crazy schedule the way few women would. He needed to make another grand gesture. No, he corrected himself. He simply needed to invite her, and all her baggage, to be part of his family. Katie and Derrick—and maybe Benjie—would just have to deal with it.

At his desk, he typed the new case notes into his Word file and filled out travel forms. He wished he had subpoenas to write, but without a suspect, this case was at a standstill. Quince called as he prepared to order lunch for the meeting.

"I've got Dylan Gilmore in custody. A patrol cop spotted him near the university."

"Great. Bring him in. I'll call his mother and let her know we have him for questioning."

"Soft or hard interrogation room?"

"Hard. I want to scare him. I think he set fire to the crime scene last night, making him look pretty damn guilty."

"No shit?"

"Good thing we caught him young. Maybe the juvie system can save him."

Jackson ordered sandwiches, poured himself more coffee, and read through his notes about Dylan. Evans had done the initial interview with the kid, so he called her and asked her to come in for the interrogation. Quince could watch from the conference room and monitor the kid's reactions that they might not see.

He wasn't sold on the idea that the skinny fourteen-year-old had strangled Andra, but the little shit's fingerprints were probably on the bloody knife—and he may have tried to burn the crime scene—so Dylan had something to confess.

CHAPTER 21

Thursday, September 5, 10:35 a.m.

Catalina Morales lived in a small complex made of ugly concrete, not far from a busy South Eugene shopping center. The location was desirable and surrounded by owner-occupied homes, so the rent was likely higher than average. Had Grayson been paying for this apartment in addition to his own plush penthouse near campus? Evans had to wonder about the extent of his scholarship and financial support. And if financial pressures had contributed to his death.

She knocked on unit six, not expecting a response. But a young woman jerked open the door, looking disappointed when she saw who it was. Evans introduced herself, giving Catalina a once-over as she did. Striking, with sharp features and green eyes, but not exactly pretty. Platinum hair down to her waist and bronze-toned skin. Pregnant too. Maybe four or five months. She was so small-framed, it was hard to tell.

Grayson's secret was a little more complex than she'd thought.

"Why are you here? Is this about Logan?" The woman blinked back tears.

"Yes. Are you Catalina Morales?"

"How did you find me?"

Evans showed her badge. "I'd like to come in."

The tiny woman didn't move. "I can't help you." She started to close the door.

Evans stuck her foot into the gap. "This isn't optional. And you won't be the first pregnant woman I've cuffed and arrested for not cooperating." The first had come at her with an umbrella when Evans arrested her boyfriend.

Catalina glared but finally moved aside. Evans stepped in, startled by all the color and tiger figurines everywhere. The tiny woman curled up on the couch, pulling a blanket over herself. The cover made Evans nervous. Suspects hid knives and guns and did unexpected things. "Keep your hands where I can see them."

"Oh, please. Do I look like a criminal?"

Evans shifted gears and softened up. "No, you look like a woman who's grieving, and I'm sorry for your loss. How long had you known Logan?"

"We met last winter at a party. I wasn't invited, but my cousin has a thing for football players and dragged me along." A wistful expression. "I never thought I'd end up dating one."

Evans wanted to ask about the secrecy but thought it would be better to wait. The subject was probably painful for her. "When did you last see Logan?"

"He was here Monday night."

"When did he leave?"

She shrugged. "About two in the morning, as usual. He sometimes stayed over on the weekends but never during the week."

Evans jotted down the time. "Did you snort coke with him?"

Catalina made a clucking sound. "As you can see, I'm pregnant. No, I didn't do any lines."

Evans didn't believe her. "Did Logan?"

"No." She glanced away.

"Tell me the truth. He had a heart attack, and it wasn't from heart disease."

"Okay, he did a line when he first got here, but he was fine when he left. Why would he have a heart attack later at home?" She started to cry.

"When did he arrive?"

"Around six thirty." She spoke through tears.

The autopsy had revealed that his stomach was empty. "He showed up, snorted some coke, then hung out until two in the morning and left? Is that correct? What am I missing?"

Catalina let out a bitter laugh. "A few beers, some mind-blowing sex, and an hour of sleep."

Just an average night for a college football player. "Did Logan leave any of the cocaine here? I'd like to have it tested for impurities."

"No." She sat up a little and dried her eyes.

"Where did he get the coke? Give me a name."

"I'm not getting anyone into trouble."

"What if someone else dies? Two other people are in the hospital. Why are you protecting a dealer who's putting bad product on the market?"

She was quiet for a moment. "I think his name is Marcos."

"Where can I find him?"

"I don't know."

"Try harder. I'd hate to have to arrest you."

She glared at Evans. "There's a party on campus tomorrow night, and I'm sure he'll be there. Do you know the big brown house on the corner of Fifteenth Alley and Hilyard Street? It'll be rockin' around ten, and Marcos will be laying lines and makin' money."

"Thanks." Evans keyed the location into her tablet. "I'm just trying to keep people safe."

"Do you know when Logan's funeral is? I don't know any of his friends to ask."

"I'll find out for you if I can. Why don't you know his friends?"

"He was ashamed of me. He never said that, of course, but he was." She choked back a sob. "He said he could lose his scholarship if they found out he paid my rent, but he never had enough . . ." She trailed off.

"Enough what?"

She shook her head. "Logan was sweet, but he spent money like a rap star."

"Even football scholarships aren't meant to cover two rent payments. Did he have a job or another source of funds?"

"No, but he could have let me move in with him."

"Is it his baby?" It would have been foolish not to ask.

"Of course."

"Did Logan plan to acknowledge the child or help you raise it?"

She sighed. "Yes, but not until he graduated. After that, he said he would be free."

"Free from what?"

"From his scholarship, his parents' expectations, and stupid social pressure. Logan would have been drafted by the pros, and we planned to move somewhere together. We didn't even care where."

Every athlete's dream. Evans felt sorry for the woman. But at least now Catalina would never face the harsh reality of Grayson's final betrayal—when he would have signed the pro contract and left her behind.

Catalina stood, still clinging to her blanket. "I'm tired and I have to lay down. Please let me know when the funeral is." She padded toward a bedroom, not looking back. Evans let herself out, thinking it was time to let go of this case, as she'd been ordered to do.

CHAPTER 22

The new interrogation room was twice the size of the old one but still claustrophobic. Jackson took a seat and Evans sat next to him, their silence an opening strategy. Dylan Gilmore sat behind the table, facing the door, the physical/psychological equivalent of being trapped. Sporting an unknown band T-shirt and long skater shorts, Gilmore was the youngest suspect Jackson had ever sat across from. A few months earlier, he'd had to take a statement from a teenage girl who'd faced murder charges, but she had been a little older. Homicide rates for teenagers were on the rise, even though violent crimes overall were declining.

"Everything you say and do here is being recorded and will be used against you in court, if necessary." Jackson set his own recorder on the table, so he'd have a personal file to refer to. Quince had activated the video camera from the conference room. Not all interrogations were filmed, but since Gilmore was fourteen, it was best to protect themselves with documentation. The kid's mother hadn't shown up yet.

"I didn't hurt that woman, I swear." Dylan was already in panic mode.

Jackson put the bloody knife on the table. The murder investigation had to come first. "Your fingerprints are on this weapon. We know it's yours. Who did you stab?"

"No one. I cut myself accidentally." He scratched his neck as he talked.

"You're lying," Evans cut in. "We found the knife in your dead neighbor's backyard, and your prints are on it. You're going away for a long time no matter what you say here."

Jackson added, "You might as well help yourself and tell the truth." If the kid had killed Andra/Amanda, then he knew she hadn't been stabbed and the blood wasn't critical evidence. But he had stabbed somebody or something—and possibly set the house on fire—and that kind of violence made him a likely suspect for murder as well. They just had to wear him down.

Dylan slumped in his chair, both hands on his head, eyes closed. In the silence, his rapid breathing filled the room.

He looked up. "I killed a cat. Okay? That's animal blood on the knife, and the CSI people should know that."

A budding psychopath and a fan of crime shows—they had to get him out of circulation. "Let's start at the beginning. Whose cat? And what day did it happen?"

The kid spent five minutes talking about how the cat kept pooping in his mother's flowers and around his skate ramp in the backyard. He didn't know who it belonged to, just that the cat was a nuisance. "I caught it in the act that morning and I kinda snapped. You know?" He paused for empathy.

Jackson had none but faked it. "It happens to people. So what did you do?"

"The cat ran, so I hopped the fence and caught it in the yard next door." He picked at something on his hand and didn't make eye contact. "Then I killed it."

His story didn't quite add up.

Evans made a scoffing sound. "You caught a cat that was running from you? Bullshit. You lured it in, more likely."

Jackson wanted to focus on their victim. "What day did this happen?"

"Monday. The same day I saw the dead lady."

"Was that before or after you killed the cat?"

"After. That's why I forgot to pick up the knife. I saw her in the window and got worried."

Time to push for the truth—by telling some lies. "Amanda's wounds match your knife. How do you explain that?"

"That's just crazy." He rocked forward. "Maybe someone found the knife I dropped and stabbed her."

His surprise seemed genuine, but he could be an accomplished liar. Most sociopaths were. "Tell us about the fire you set. What were you trying to hide?"

His eyes darted back and forth between them. "That wasn't me, I swear. I didn't get home until after midnight, and the fire trucks were already there."

"What were you trying to hide? Fingerprints? DNA?"

"Nothing! I didn't do it."

"The house didn't burn down. We'll still find whatever you were trying to destroy."

He swallowed hard. "Okay, I was in the house a few times. It was vacant for a long time, so I went over there sometimes just to—" He paused. "You know, to explore, like kids do."

Was it enough to get a warrant for a DNA comparison? Jackson pushed a little harder. "We'll search your house and find the accelerant you used. Tell us what happened and we can cut you a deal."

A knock on the door, then a voice through the intercom. "Mrs. Gilmore is here with a lawyer. They want to terminate the interrogation."

Crap! Jackson pressed the button. "We're done then. Please book Dylan into custody at the juvenile justice center and request a psych evaluation." Captain Ottovich could interview him there.

The task force meeting started late, and Jackson worried about making his flight. As they ate sandwiches, the other three detectives chatted about Dylan Gilmore's interrogation and the fire at the crime scene. Schak and Quince were convinced he'd committed the murder and set the fire. Evans was skeptical. Jackson let them hash it out, then said, "I think we need to keep looking at other suspects."

"I agree." Evans set half of her meal aside and stood to update the board. "Dylan might be a killer in the making, but he looked stunned when you lied to him about the knife wounds, then responded instantly. He didn't seem to know you were lying, which means he didn't see her body up close and didn't likely kill her."

"We can't just dismiss him," Quince argued. "We have to get a subpoena and search his house."

"Agreed. That's your next task." Jackson checked his watch. "I have a flight to Salt Lake City that leaves in two hours."

"What?" Evans spun from the board.

He summarized what he'd learned about the victim and where she was from. "We have to find the boy's father. He either needs to be reunited with his son or questioned in Andra's death."

Evans added the victim's real name to the board, then turned back. "If the father killed Andra and wants the boy, he's likely still here in Eugene."

"Maybe. But the Salt Lake flight is direct and short, and I'm hoping to gain information. We can't locate the father if we don't know who he is."

"I'll contact the airlines and see if the name Caiden was on any flights in the last week," Schak volunteered.

"Excellent." Feeling weary, Jackson took a long pull of coffee. What was he forgetting?

"What about the autopsy?" Evans asked.

That was it. "The victim's trachea and hyoid bones were crushed, so the pathologist thinks the assailant pressed down on her throat, while also cutting off her air with his other hand."

"Someone powerful?"

"Not necessarily," Jackson said. "If she was pinned down and losing oxygen, it may have been impossible to fight back."

A moment of quiet, before Quince said, "We have nothing new to go on?"

Jackson turned to Schak. "Did you learn anything in your neighborhood canvass?"

"I got confirmation of the light-blue truck being parked in front of the house Saturday afternoon sometime between three and five." Schak checked his notes. "She said it was a Nissan with a damaged tailgate. Probably a 2003 or 2004."

Evans jotted it on the board. "I'll follow up on that with the DMV."

"Here's the weird part," Schak added. "She saw the truck when she passed the house on her way home, and she's pretty sure the back was empty. Then later, she went out to her car to bring in something she forgot and she thinks the truck had furniture in the back. As if someone was moving out."

CHAPTER 23

Thursday, September 5, 2:45 p.m.

Sophie Speranza grew frustrated with the news story she was writing. A twenty-eight-year-old man had been hit by a driver, who'd refused a breathalyzer. Springfield police had withdrawn charges of manslaughter after discovering the victim was suicidal and had probably stepped in front of the car. She'd interviewed the victim's father, and he was distressed, claiming his son would never do that. In some ways, it was a great story with plenty of conflict. What frustrated her was the likelihood she would never know what had really happened. She hated stories with no closure.

She'd been working the crime-and-court beat for almost a year now, and she'd written about too many dead and troubled young people. The car-accident victim had only been a year older than her. And now she had Jackson's new homicide, a young woman. He'd contacted her this time, as well as given her exclusive details, so he was finally starting to trust her . . . a little. She'd run a layout that morning with a couple of paragraphs asking for the public's help identifying the victim. So far, no one had called, but she couldn't get Amanda out of her mind. An image of the victim lying dead in an empty house kept sliding into her head and begging her to explore it. What if it was a zombie house? So far, the abandoned homes were a problem for neighbors and home values, but had they become magnets for crime as well? She'd have to look into it.

"Hey, Sophie."

She turned to see her boss standing in her cube opening.

"I told you not to run that picture of the dead woman on the front page of the City section." Hoogstad, a Humpty Dumpty man with marginal hygiene, shook his head in an exaggerated gesture. "Two readers have already complained. You get to call them both and apologize."

Oh hell. The newspaper was at the point where it couldn't afford to lose a single paying subscription. "If I have to." She reached for the slip of paper in his hand. "Has anyone called to identify the victim?"

"No. Do we have a follow-up story?"

"Not yet." Sophie glanced at her cell phone. "I'll call again and see what else I can find out."

"While you're at it, see if you can get something on Logan Grayson's death. Coach Harper is holding a press conference today, but I want to know what the police have to say."

"What do we know so far?"

"Only that his roommate found him with blood on his face."

"I'll see what I can find out."

He waddled away, and she called Jackie Matthews, the EPD spokesperson. The officer gave her a quotable statement. "Logan Grayson died of a heart attack, but we won't know what caused the hypertensive event until we get the toxicology report."

"What about the blood on his face?"

"I don't have that information."

"What's the department's best guess? Drugs?" Sophie didn't expect an answer.

"We don't speculate."

"Who's handling the case?"

"Detective Lara Evans. But she gave me the information, so there's no point in calling her."

"Thanks." Sophie grinned as she hung up. She could use the info to bargain with the head sportswriter. He'd want the information, but what could he give her in exchange?

She hurried over to the corner where the three sports guys still had the best cubicles in the building. They no longer had the corner upstairs with the great view because the whole staff had been condensed into the first floor, but they still had two giant flat-screen TVs in their workspace.

As she approached, Marcus Sanyo stood to greet her. "Hey."

He didn't remember her name? That was sad. "I've got a statement from the EPD about Logan Grayson's death. Do you want it?"

"Hell yes." He sat back down. "I've been calling all day and couldn't get anyone to pick up."

"What have you got to trade?"

Marcus laughed. "Seriously? What do you want? Tickets to a Ducks game?"

Now she laughed. "No thanks. I want info. Tell me something about Grayson that's normally off the record."

"Why?" He crossed his arms. "You're not taking the story. Even if it turns out to be a crime, it's still my beat."

"I'm not trying to steal your story." She was bored with the conversation now. "Grayson had a heart attack."

"I knew that." Marcus was clearly disappointed. "Shit. What a week for the Ducks." He shook his head.

"What do you mean?"

"Trey Sandoval was in a car accident Tuesday and is still in the hospital."

Sophie didn't know the name, but she assumed he also played football. "That's a shitty break." But was it a coincidence? "Do you suppose the incidents are related? Like they were both taking steroids or something?" She couldn't help but think like an investigative reporter.

Marcus spun back to her. "If you don't have proof, don't say it. Don't print it."

Right. Sports section advertising kept the newspaper going. "It was just a thought. I'm going back to my space now." As she walked away, she called over her shoulder, "You're welcome."

The sports guys, deep in conversation, ignored her.

Back at her desk, Sophie called Detective Evans, who occasionally was willing to discuss her cases. Not today. She had to leave a message about Trey Sandoval's accident. She closed by asking Evans to call her. *Yeah, that would happen.*

Her desk phone rang and she took the call on headphones, in case she needed her hands free to type. The caller was worked up and sounded young. "I want you to write about a terrible scam that's going on. I called the police but they don't have time to investigate."

A rush of adrenaline. "Tell me your name." Sophie clicked open a Word doc and started taking notes. She lived for these moments.

CHAPTER 24

Thursday, September 5, 4:36 p.m.

Jackson rented a car from an airport terminal, keyed Christy Chadwell's address into the GPS, and headed into the unfamiliar city. His first impression: brown, dry, and flat, except for the massive mountains that loomed on the east side. Sure, the landscape had trees, but not the tall, lush, deep-green variety found in Oregon. But Salt Lake's downtown buildings were tall enough to form a skyline, something Eugene didn't have.

The GPS coordinates were a little off, and it took two circles around a looping subdivision to find the address. A nice middle-class home in a pleasant neighborhood, with a three-car garage and a sports boat parked alongside. Andra's friend from high school was doing much better financially than Andra had. No cars were in the driveway, and the house looked dark and quiet. Jackson parked on the street and rang the doorbell anyway. No answer.

He went back to his car to wait, hoping Christy would be home for dinner soon. He'd talked to her yesterday, so he was optimistic she was in town. Coming here was a long shot, but if he didn't get what he needed, he would visit City Hall and/or the hospital to look at birth records. Plus make a stop at the police department. He wouldn't be surprised to discover Andra had filed a restraining order, or that the baby's father had reported his son kidnapped. Some parents did whatever they could to protect and hang on to their children, even at the expense of the other parent.

While he waited, he checked in with his daughter. She was grilling hot dogs and corn-on-the-cob for herself, Benjie, and Derrick. They'd filled a wading pool earlier and made crazy bubbles with dish soap. Jackson yearned to be there. He had missed Katie so much and now that she was home, here he was, proving once again that work came first. Even though this trip was as much about finding Benjie's family as solving Andra's homicide, part of him hoped he wouldn't locate anyone. He'd become attached to the kid and hated the thought of handing him over to a stranger. Why had he bonded so quickly with the boy? Because he felt like he'd lost Katie as a child?

Kera didn't answer when he called, and he didn't leave a message. Was she with her ex-husband? Daniel Kollmorgan had wanted Kera back after she and Jackson started dating, and Jackson had almost let her go. At that point, he'd been trying to consider little Micah and how Kera and Daniel might have to raise their grandson themselves. They could be having the same discussion again now. Danette's parenting had always been questionable, and her bad choices seemed to have finally caught up with her.

Five minutes later, he called Kera again. This time she answered, sounding weary. "Okay, Wade. You have my attention. What now?"

Good question. "I want to apologize for not being there for you in the hospital yesterday. Things got a little crazy for me, and I didn't find anyone to take Benjie."

"I heard. Don't worry, I know you hate hospitals." Her voice had a detached quality that worried him.

"How is Danette?"

"They drilled into her skull to relieve the pressure on her brain, but it didn't go well. Her body is shutting down."

"Are you at the hospital now?"

"No. Her mother's there, and I had work this afternoon. A few days from now, they'll ask Maggie to pull the plug and donate her viable organs." Kera was a nurse who'd once volunteered with Doctors Without Borders. She'd experienced field trauma and knew what to expect.

"I'm so sorry." Jackson paused, trying to find the right words. He wanted to make an offer, but not go too far. "Will you adopt Micah?"

"Yes."

"When all this has settled down, we need to talk about our future." The sound of a car made him look up. A small SUV with a woman driving.

Kera hesitated. "I'm glad to hear we have a future. But I think you're still on the fence, and I worry that I don't have your full affection."

"What are you talking about?"

"You know what I mean. I saw Evans this morning."

That was weird. "Where?"

"At the hospital. What's important is that you make up your mind. We're at a critical point."

"I know. I love you, but we have to talk about the kids."

The SUV pulled into the Chadwells' driveway.

"I have to go. I'll call again later." Jackson hung up. Did Kera think he had feelings for Evans? Did he have feelings for Evans? Of course he did. He loved her the way he loved Schak and Quince and McCray, his retired partner.

Jackson slipped his phone into his pocket and watched a young woman climb out of the vehicle, carrying a paper bag. He didn't want to startle her, but he also didn't want her to get inside the house and ignore him.

He climbed from his sedan and strode up the driveway. "Can I help with your groceries?" A hundred-watt smile. "I'm Detective Jackson, Eugene Police." He reached for the bag, and she let him take it. Probably to free herself to run. "I called you yesterday about Andra Caiden. I'm trying to solve her murder, and I need your help."

Tears rolled down the pretty blonde's face. He really knew how to make women unhappy.

Jackson continued. "I'm sorry for your loss. Can we go inside and talk?"

"My husband doesn't allow men in the house when he's not home."

"I'm a police officer." Jackson reached for his badge.

"So is he." She gave him a rueful smile. "His job doesn't build faith in humanity."

She had that right. "Can we sit in the backyard?"

"Sure. I'll take the groceries in and meet you out there." She pointed at a side fence. "You can go through that gate."

As he headed around the house, he reflexively felt for his weapon. He didn't hear any dogs, but that didn't mean anything. He forced himself to relax. Shooting her dog wouldn't inspire Christy to open up to him.

He reached the patio area in their perfectly manicured yard and took a seat. A few minutes later, she came out with two glasses of iced lemonade and set them on the table. "Sorry to make you sit out here in the heat."

"I'm fine." He normally didn't drink anything strangers offered in an open container, but he was thirsty and she wasn't really a suspect. Jackson downed half the glass, wondering why he never made lemonade.

Christy stretched out on a chaise lounge, still dressed for office work in a black skirt and pink sweater. She pulled a tissue from her purse to wipe her eyes. "I can't believe Andra's dead. Yet, I'm not surprised."

"Who would want to kill her?"

"You mean besides her father, her ex-fiancé, and the baby's father?"

He suppressed a groan. Why did it have to be so complicated? He needed to get the unlikely scenarios out of the way. "Why would her father want to kill her?"

"She left the Mormon church." Christy made a face. "But Mr. Caiden's dead now, so he didn't kill her."

"And the fiancé?"

"Also Mormon and angry. He thought she cheated on him, so he dumped her. But Isaiah Bowen isn't really violent. Besides, he's engaged again."

That left the baby's daddy. "Who's Benjie's father?"

"I really don't know."

He didn't believe her. "What hospital was he born in?"

"St. Mark's. But Andra didn't stay long after Benjie was born."

"When did you see her last?"

"Three years ago. She stopped at my office with her newborn baby and said good-bye." Christy took a drink of lemonade and mulled something over.

He waited her out.

"Andra said she had to disappear and couldn't contact me ever again. I broke down and cried." A sad smile. "I do that a lot."

Jackson squeezed his hands into fists, then released his tension. "You don't know who she was dating? What about the ex-fiancé? Could it be his child?"

"No. They'd been split up for a year, and she wasn't seeing anyone. She said the baby was special and she planned to give it up for adoption."

He remembered the brand. "Was Andra ever a prostitute?"

Christy sat up, aghast. "No! She was homeless and broke after Isaiah dumped her, but she would never do that."

"Did you know anything about the brand on her hip?"

She pressed her lips together. "No, that's just weird." Christy leaned over to whisper. "I probably shouldn't tell you this, but the day she left town, Andra told me she'd been a surrogate mother and had signed a contract. Then after the baby was born, she couldn't give it up, so she took him and ran."

A surrogacy? How messy would it be to untangle the parental rights? "Any idea who the contract parents are? There's a little boy who needs a family."

Christy shivered, even in the heat. "Andra was afraid of the father. That's why she begged me to never tell anyone about the surrogacy and to never try to contact her."

Why would she be a surrogate for someone she was afraid of? "I need to talk to Andra's family. Are they here in town?"

Christy's lips trembled. "Her parents died in a plane crash two years ago, and her brother is in Uganda doing missionary work." She perked up. "But I think she has a grandmother in Oregon."

Not anymore. He didn't want to tell her about Lucille, afraid she'd start crying again. "Did Andra ever file a restraining order against the father?"

"Not that I know of." Christy shook her head, tears dripping. "But she didn't tell me anything the whole time she was pregnant. It hurt our friendship, and we didn't see each other much."

"Give me your best guess about who the father is."

"I really don't know. Maybe the police can help you. You should talk to my husband, Dan, at the department. He's a sergeant in Internal Affairs." She grabbed Jackson's hand. "Do you think the baby's father killed her?"

"It's very possible. And if he did, I need to find him and bring him to justice."

"What about the little boy? Who has him? And what happens now?"

"He's safe." Jackson instinctively held back the details. "He may end up in foster care." He stood to leave. "What day was he born? I need to find his birth certificate."

Christy had to give it some thought. "August seventeenth, three years ago."

At least he had a starting point.

CHAPTER 25

Friday, September 6, 7:55 a.m.

St. Mark's Hospital was smaller than Jackson expected, giving him hope the administrators would be flexible and want to assist him. But he was soon disabused of that notion. The silver-haired administrator looked soft and matronly, but she was reluctant to reveal birth information without a subpoena. "I'd like to help you, but I can't if you're not a family member or guardian." The expansive blue sky in the window behind her did little to soften her words.

"The boy is in my care."

"Show me your court papers."

Jackson wasn't giving up. "What if I was a parent who'd lost a birth certificate and needed a new one? How would I go about that?"

"You'd fill out a form, pay a fee, and wait a month."

He didn't have that long. "What if I was a parent, sitting right here, needing a birth certificate because I had to leave the country?"

"But you're not the child's parent. You already told me that."

"Call the Oregon state office for Children and Family Services." He remembered that he had Mariah Martin's number in his phone. "Better yet, I've got the number of the boy's caseworker." He located it and handed her the phone. "This child needs a family. And I need to know who his father is. You don't have to give me a copy of the certificate. I just need the information."

The administrator pressed her lips together and thought it over. "What's the child's name again?"

"Benjie Caiden." It was his best guess. Jackson gave her the date too.

After a few clicks and a moment of staring at her monitor, she said, "The father's name is John Doe."

Jackson clamped his jaws to keep from cursing.

His next stop was the Salt Lake Police Department, oddly located in the middle of a residential neighborhood. Its parking area was somewhat empty except for a few white patrol cars. The woman at the front desk wore civilian clothes and probably wouldn't be able to help him. Jackson introduced himself and showed his badge. "I need to talk to the sergeant or detective who handles custody dispute cases or parental kidnapping incidents."

She seemed stumped. "We don't have a specific department for that."

New strategy. Christy had said he should talk to her husband if no one else could help him. "Is Sergeant Dan Chadwell in?"

"I'll check."

"Thanks. This is important."

The woman made a call and shared Jackson's credentials. After a moment, she nodded, held her hand over the phone, and said, "What is this about? He only has a few minutes before a lunch meeting."

"A three-year-old boy and his dead mother. I called about this yesterday."

She relayed the information, then escorted Jackson down the hall. "I'm the one who took your call. I passed the information to the patrol sergeant, but apparently that wasn't the right decision. I'm sorry."

"No problem. It's a complex situation."

They stopped at a corner office. She knocked, then walked away.

A man in an expensive suit opened the door and held out his hand. "Sergeant Dan Chadwell. But call me Dan." Chadwell was shorter and heavier than Jackson and pale enough to look Icelandic.

Jackson introduced himself as they shook hands, then took a seat, noting the private office. Chadwell had rank for someone in his thirties. "Thanks for your time. I'm not even sure you can help, but I have to try."

Chadwell sat too. "I know you talked to my wife about this last night, but I'd like you to recap for me."

Jackson wondered if the other man knew Andra. But first, he summarized the case, then added, "If I can find the father, I can probably solve her homicide. As a bonus, I might be able to locate an aunt or cousin who'll take Benjie."

"Why do you think the boy's father killed her?"

"She had a threatening note from someone who thought she stole something. Plus, no other motivations have surfaced."

"I see why you're here." The sergeant cocked his head. "I met Andra a few times long ago, so I knew her name. And I would have noticed if she had been involved in any kind of domestic altercation." He reached for his keyboard. "But I'll search our database and see if we get a hit."

A few minutes later, he said, "She had a speeding ticket four years ago, but that's it. No complaints filed." Chadwell looked up from his monitor. "If anyone had accused her of kidnapping, I would know."

"Unless the father went to the FBI. Do they have an office here?"

"Of course. I'll call over there for you, but we would have heard about it."

The wait took a little longer this time, but the result was the same. "No kidnapping charges connected with either the mother or the child's name."

The custody dispute between Andra and the father had been kept private. Apparently, their surrogacy contract had been too.

Chadwell jumped up. "I have a lunch engagement. I'll walk you out."

On the way, Jackson asked for assistance in locating his murder suspect. "I know it's a long shot, but if you would keep this as a back burner project, I'd be grateful."

"I sure will."

As they stepped outside, a tall man with a buzz cut approached. Chadwell introduced him. "This is my friend, Carson Buckley, a retired police officer."

They shook hands. Buckley's grip matched his size.

"Andra Caiden was murdered, and Jackson is here to investigate," Chadwell said. "I guess she moved to Oregon."

"You think the perp fled to Salt Lake?" Buckley asked. "We're not exactly a haven for criminals."

"I think he's from this area. He may even be the father of her child." Jackson had to ask. "Did you know Andra?"

"I met her once, but I didn't know her."

Chadwell snapped his fingers. "What's the name of the couple from church who took Andra into their home when she was pregnant?" He turned to his friend.

"You mean Carl and Susan Wagner?"

The surrogacy parents? A tingle shot up Jackson's spine. He was closing in. "What can you tell me about them?" He grabbed his notepad and scribbled the names.

"They're friends of her mother's. God rest her soul." Dan Chadwell started down the steps and talked over his shoulder. "They're good people. They risked the scorn of church members by taking in an unmarried pregnant girl."

"The Mormon church?" Jackson asked.

Both men laughed. "It's the only church around here."

"Please tell me how to find them."

"They're probably in the phone book."

Jackson handed Chadwell a business card. "If you think of a family member, let me know."

CHAPTER 26

Friday, September 6, 1:05 p.m.

Evans called the Department of Motor Vehicles again and asked for Stacy Garrett. She was Jackson's contact, and Evans had been trying to reach her all morning. This time, the woman came on the line. "Who is this? I didn't catch your name."

"Detective Evans. I'm working a case with Jackson. He said to call, that you could help us."

"Why isn't Jackson calling?" A little worry in her voice.

"He's out of state, looking for a murder suspect."

"Huh. I didn't know he ever traveled."

"It's unusual." Evans grew impatient. "What we need is a list of owners of light-blue Nissan pickups from 2002 through 2005."

"Statewide?" The clerk's dismay was obvious.

"No, just Lane County." They might have to expand the search, but it made sense to start local.

"That's probably doable. But color information isn't in the database, so your list of owners will be huge. And all you'll get is a name and address, an address that might not be current."

"I understand. But we have to find this guy."

"You want male owners only?"

Evans hesitated. It would make the list more manageable, but it could also eliminate the suspect's car. Some people drove cars listed in their spouses' or parents' names. "No, I want them all."

"I'll get it to you as soon as I can."

"Thank you."

Now what? She needed to show some initiative on Andra Caiden's case while Jackson was gone. Without bank statements to peruse or coworkers to interview, the leads were hard to find. She hadn't taken a close look at any of the physical evidence, so the crime lab was a good place to start. As she stood to leave, her phone rang.

"This is Paula Grayson."

Logan's mother. Evans had called her yesterday to give an update, but the woman hadn't answered. "Did you listen to my message?"

"I did. But I still don't understand how a college senior could have a heart attack." She sounded a little slurred, as if she were medicated. "Did you ask his coach about steroids?"

"Yes, and I asked other players. They all denied it. We still have to wait for the state to analyze the blood sample." Evans didn't bring up the cocaine. It was still speculation.

"Will you call me when you get the report?"

"Of course." She remembered Catalina had asked about his funeral. "Will there be a service here in Eugene?"

"Yes, it's tomorrow at eleven at St. Mary's Church. Then we'll have a proper funeral at home in Iowa next week." A pause. "Will you be at the service tomorrow?" It was more of a request than a question.

"Yes, I'll go." She dreaded the thought, but it would give her one last chance to observe Grayson's acquaintances. Maybe she'd spot the man he'd fought with. "I have to get to work now. Bye."

She made a quick call to Catalina about the memorial service. After she hung up, she wondered if it had been a mistake. Would the pregnant girlfriend stir up some trouble? Evans let it go. The young woman deserved to mourn Grayson with everyone else.

Evans grabbed her coffee and headed toward the exit. As she passed Schak's cubicle, she saw him reclining in his chair with his eyes closed. She tiptoed over and conjured up her best imitation of Sergeant Lammers. "Schak! What the fuck?"

His eyes flew open and he slammed forward, nearly tumbling out of his chair.

She laughed so hard, she had to set down her coffee. "That was too good to pass up."

"You about gave me another heart attack!"

She'd forgotten his first one, which had happened while arresting a killer. "Sorry, pal. You okay?"

"I will be." He took a deep breath. "What's up?"

"How did you do out at the burned house this morning?"

"We didn't find anything, but Quince is still over at the Gilmores' rounding up his computer and personal things."

"I hope we can convict him of something. He needs to stay locked up for the next five or six years."

"Or life. If we didn't have the custody issue and the threaten-ing note, we would be all over this kid for the murder."

"True enough." That reminded her about the transportation issue. "How did you do with the airlines?"

He gestured with a thumbs-down. "Nobody named Caiden flew in or out of Eugene last week."

"Were there any repeat flyers to Salt Lake?"

"Shit. I didn't ask that."

"Better get on it."

"Will do." He gave her a mock salute. "Then I'm leaving early—in case we get called down to campus later for riot patrol."

"Oh right. This is crazy-student season." She remembered another memo from yesterday. "There's also a block party in the Whiteaker neighborhood tomorrow. This will be an overtime weekend for most patrol cops."

Schak groaned. "That means all hands on deck to deal with drunks. I'm getting too old for this shit."

She was having second thoughts about her plans for the evening, so she didn't share them. "I'm heading over to the crime lab. I'll see you tomorrow."

Evans flashed her ID card and waited for the gate to let her into the parking area. The gray-brick building that housed the crime lab also served as the evidence locker, where three officers had recently come under scrutiny for theft and mishandling of property, including a huge pile of cash. The chief had put the desk officers on leave of absence and was scrambling to establish new protocols. But the revelations not only made the whole department look bad, it made everyone nervous about their convictions being overturned by lawsuits.

As Evans parked, she noticed one of the big bay doors was open, and Joe Berloni was cleaning out the green Ford Focus from the Pershing house. The crime scene technicians were not at fault in the scandal, but they worked in the same building and also handled evidence, but a different kind. They too had trusted their coworkers to be accountable and were getting burned for it.

"Hey, Joe." She'd called him Berloni once and he'd corrected her.

"Hey, Evans. Are you on this case?" He looked up from his work as she stepped into the bay to get out of the sun. The processing area looked like a garage stuffed with things nobody used but couldn't throw away.

"Yep. What have you got? We need a break."

"I ran prints from the car this morning and didn't get any hits in the databases, so no help in identifying a suspect."

They had no reason to think the killer had been in her car, so she wasn't surprised. "We mostly need to figure out who's the father of the victim's child. Jackson flew to Salt Lake City yesterday because that's all we've got to go on."

Joe reached for a plastic evidence bag lying on a shelf, his compact, muscular body reminding her of a wrestler's. "You're welcome to look through this collection. I found it all stuffed down in the seats." He handed her the bag. "There's a ticket stub for the Maverick Center, which is in Salt Lake. And a few other odd items. Plus this pink breast-cancer-awareness bracelet. We found it on a doorknob in the Pershing house." He produced a clipboard and pen. "You have to sign for it. I'm covering my ass on everything."

She didn't blame him.

CHAPTER 27

Friday, September 6, 3:35 p.m.

Jackson hated hotel rooms. The small space and ugly colors were bad enough, but it was the stillness that bothered him most. He missed the sound of Katie chatting with friends in another room, Kera banging around the kitchen, or even the noisy birds in his backyard. And surprisingly, he missed Benjie. The little guy had really grown on him. Not finding his family was worrisome, yet also a surprising relief. He'd dreaded the moment when he would have to hand the boy over to strangers. Now he didn't think that would happen. Andra hadn't named a father on the birth certificate, so unless the other biological parent came forward with DNA proof and a court order, there was no one to claim Benjie. But was he the right person to raise the boy? His own daughter might disagree. His work schedule wasn't family friendly during the first few days of homicide cases, which seemed to happen more and more frequently.

Jackson paced the room, waiting for the Wagners to return his call. For the last hour, he'd been online, researching surrogacy and the contracts involved. Unless Andra and the father or couple had used a lawyer, or at least a notary, any contract would be meaningless. Assuming they even had a legal agreement. He wasn't sure what else he could accomplish in Salt Lake and felt anxious to get back to Eugene. He worried about how Benjie was handling his absence—and he had a homicide to solve. He owed it to Andra.

Another worry wormed deeper into his brain. If Benjie's father had killed Andra in an attempt to reclaim his son, then Benjie might still be at risk. Jackson had left his backup weapon with Derrick just as a precaution, but the only long-term solution was to put the assailant in jail.

His phone rang, startling him. "Jackson here."

"This is Susan Wagner, returning your call. How can I help you?"

"I need to talk about Andra Caiden. In person. Can we meet?"

"We're in our RV and just pulled into a campground near Boise, Idaho. Where are you?"

Well, damn. "I'm in Salt Lake City. When will you be back here?"

"Not for a few days. What's this about?"

"I'm sorry if you don't already know, but Andra was murdered."

She gasped, then let out a little cry. "Oh no." Her voice was suddenly distant. "Carl, will you come here?"

"Please put your husband on the phone. I'd like to ask him some questions."

"Let's do a Skype call instead. You said you wanted to talk in person. It's the next best thing."

Jackson started to reject the idea, then thought better. He wanted to watch Carl Wagner's face react to loaded questions. "Good idea." He spelled out his Skype ID, hung up, and opened the program on his laptop. He'd chatted with Katie this way a few times since she'd moved out. The big talking heads on the monitor were weird, but better than no visual at all.

For five long minutes he waited, wondering if the couple would call back. If Carl Wagner had fathered Andra's child—and/or murdered her—he might be more inclined to crank up the RV and hit the road. Finally, his computer pinged. When the dialogue box opened, a middle-aged couple appeared, their faces close together: Susan looking plump and sad and forty, while her husband seemed angular and worried and closer to fifty.

Carl Wagner led off. "We're quite upset to hear about Andra. She was special to us."

"How did you know her?" Jackson wanted to question them one at a time, but it seemed important to earn their trust first.

"Her mother and I worked together at the utility company for years," Susan said. "After Nadine and her husband died, Andra fell onto hard times. When we heard she was pregnant and homeless, we took her in."

"Who told you she was pregnant?"

A long pause. Finally, Susan said, "I don't remember. It was long ago, and we haven't seen or heard from Andra since she left with the baby."

"I need to speak with Carl alone for a minute. Can you give us some privacy?"

Susan's mouth set in a grim line. "We don't have any secrets from each other."

"This is standard police procedure."

Her face moved away and she disappeared from the screen.

"When was the last time you saw Andra?" Jackson had his recorder on. Proving a lie was sometimes the best way to get at the truth.

"The day we took her to the hospital," Carl said, his face dead-pan. "She didn't want us to stay with her during the birth."

That was a little odd. Time to mix it up, keep his suspect off guard. "Do you have any children?"

"No. Why?"

"Did you want children?"

"Of course. But the Lord didn't bless us." A pained expression.

"Did you try in vitro fertilization?"

His mouth dropped open. "That's none of your business."

"Andra needs justice. Please answer my questions."

Carl was silent.

Jackson took a gamble. "I already know you're the one who arranged for Andra to move in. Tell me how it came about."

His cautious eyes widened, but Carl didn't deny it. "Susan and I saw Andra panhandling at the mall. We talked about it on the way home, trying to figure out how to help her. I went back the next day, found her, and offered to let her stay with us."

"She wasn't pregnant then, was she?"

"What do you mean?"

"Andra's pregnancy was a surrogacy. She had the baby for another couple. Considering you and Susan took her in, I'm pretty sure it was your child."

Carl pulled back, startled and angry. "I did a good thing for that girl! I would never take advantage of her."

"I realize most surrogacies are mutual arrangements, and the pregnancy is an artificial insemination. How much did you pay her?"

"This is insulting!"

"You must have been quite upset when she took off with your son. Did Susan know?"

The wife was suddenly back in the room. "Did I know what?"

Jackson hesitated. What if he was wrong about her husband? He could ruin their marriage. "Do you know who the father of Andra's child is?"

"She never told us." Susan kept her expression neutral, seeming to realize they were under scrutiny. "I thought maybe she didn't know. She'd been on the streets for a while after her boyfriend dumped her."

"Did you talk about adopting her child?"

"We offered to, but Andra said no." Susan glanced to the side. Carl had moved out of Jackson's sight.

"What were her plans?"

"She was vague about that."

"Where were you guys camped on Monday night?"

"Outside Springfield, Oregon."

Eugene's sister city! A twenty-minute drive to the crime scene. "Do you tow your car behind the RV?"

"Why are you asking? I don't like your insinuations."

From the background, Carl shouted, "Just shut it down. He's barking up the wrong tree."

The screen in the dialogue box went black. Jackson flopped against the back of his chair. The couple's proximity to the crime scene made Carl—and/or Susan—viable suspects. But he needed a DNA sample to compare with the trace evidence on Andra's body. Or to Benjie's DNA. Could he get one? He had to try. Maybe even a handwriting sample to compare to the threatening note.

For the first time, he felt like they might bring Andra's killer to justice.

CHAPTER 28

Friday, September 6, 8:05 p.m.

Evans pulled on faded jeans and a tight black tank top with a red no-war symbol across the chest, a shirt she'd bought for plain-clothes work and hadn't worn in ages. The goal was to look young and blend in at the party. She was slim and had taken good care of her skin, but her job had worn some lines into her forehead. She brushed a few long bangs forward to cover them and pulled the rest of her hair into a high ponytail, then tied it into a spiky knot—a current style. She applied more makeup, then stuffed handcuffs into her black bag. The purse strapped across her chest so she didn't have to hold on to it. After a moment of internal debate, she slipped a small gun into an ankle holster. The thought of having the weapon in a crowded party with inebriated young people worried her. Not having it terrified her.

A look in the mirror to see if she could pass for a college student. Maybe. Her heart-shaped face, which she'd always hated, would work to her advantage this time. As a patrol cop, her *sweet* look had earned her verbal scorn from men she arrested, though she could take down suspects before they had time to blink in surprise. But tonight needed to go smoothly No altercations. She just wanted to find Marcos the dealer and buy a little coke from him for testing. Maybe take his picture when he wasn't looking, or filch his wallet to see if she could learn a last name. Or, if it worked out, lure him outside to be arrested.

What if the party got huge and out of control like they often did in the fall—when students were reconvening and the weather was still warm enough to be outside? A few years back, a drunken gathering of four-hundred-plus students had spilled into the streets to throw bottles at passing vehicles and turn over a few parked cars. The department had responded with riot gear and tear gas.

A knot of worry tightened in her stomach. Lammers had told her to drop the case. Even if Marcos ended up doing time for manslaughter because of tainted drugs, her boss might still be pissed. Lammers didn't give a shit about dealers. Unless they were also violent offenders. Marcos might not be violent, but if people were dying because of the coke he was distributing, he was a problem. Evans' gut told her Logan Grayson's death had been caused by someone's greed or negligence, and she owed it to the victim to pursue the truth. Jackson would. He would also do the investigation by the book. She wished he were in town for backup.

Bracing for an argument, she called Lammers' cell phone, but her boss didn't pick up. Relieved, Evans left a message explaining her theory about the toxic street drug and the tip about where to find the dealer. "I'll check out the party in plainclothes and have a backup outside," she added. Then Evans called dispatch, gave the location of the party, and asked for a patrol unit to hover in the vicinity for the next couple of hours.

At the last minute before leaving, she texted Schak: *I'm going to a campus party to look for a coke dealer in the Grayson case. If I find him, will you help me interrogate?*

Schak called as she pulled out of her West Eugene duplex.

"What's the address of the party?"

"Brown house on the corner of Fifteenth Alley and Hilyard. You could have just texted me back." She couldn't resist teasing him.

"You're hilarious. I can read the damn things, but I can barely type on the computer with these giant thumbs."

"Thanks for getting back to me. I've requested a patrol unit, so just hang tight."

"Will do."

The bass beat of the music reached her from three blocks away, where she finally found parking. Darkness had settled in, but the air was still warm—a rare evening in Oregon. She locked her car and strode up Hilyard, barely able to hear her own footsteps. Her shoes were a compromise, attractive flats she could run in.

The big house loomed ahead, with a deck full of students drinking and talking, and even more dancing in the yard below. Evans glanced up the street, hoping to see a patrol car. Not yet, but they would be in the area even if she hadn't called in the location. This was crazy-outdoor-party season at the university.

Up the steps and smiling at a young man who watched her approach. He held a red plastic cup, which meant a keg was open in the house. "Where's the brew?" she asked.

"In the kitchen." He grinned. "Nice shirt."

"Thanks." She kept moving. It was too soon to ask questions, and the drug activity would be inside, in a back bedroom.

Evans threaded her way through a thick crowd of young people, most with a plastic cup in hand and many with e-cigarettes. The room reeked of sour beer and sweat, and a cloud of sticky-sweet vapor hung in the air. The kitchen was packed even tighter, and the floor was wet with spilled beer. She wondered who owned the home. Landlords could be fined a thousand dollars if the police had to come out and break up a ruckus.

With a beer finally in hand, she drank half to keep it from spilling, then made her way to a flight of stairs. She struck up a conversation with two shorts-clad men perched at the bottom. Both held red cups and one had a fifth of Jack Daniel's between his feet. Neither looked old enough to drink. For a few minutes, they chatted about their college majors—she said marketing and they said business—then one of the guys brought up the two football players who wouldn't be in the starting lineup for the next game.

"Burning out after the first game of the season," the chubby one whined. "That's just lame."

"Dude, he's dead. Don't be an ass." The other guy punched his shoulder, sloshing beer into his lap. They both burst out laughing.

They didn't look like coke users, but they were on topic. "I heard Grayson was loaded on coke when he died," she gossiped.

"No surprise to me," chubby boy said. "Athletes aren't saints, even if we do worship them."

"Hey, I'm no saint either." Evans shrugged. "In fact, I'm hoping to score some C before I crash. Who do I talk to?"

Skinny boy gestured down the hall. "Go get in line. I'll be right here when you get back. I hope it makes you horny."

Evans made a kissing gesture and trotted into the hallway. At the end, two college-age women stood outside a bedroom door, chatting loudly about the next party they were headed to. After standing behind them for a minute, she learned they were only here to score cocaine, then would head to a frat party where *the cute guys* were. Evans tried to strike up a conversation but they weren't interested.

Waiting her turn made her nervous. She didn't even know if the dealer behind the door was Marcos. Or if he would be alone. Or what to expect. She'd only worked Vice for a few months before transferring to Violent Crimes, and she wasn't good at hiding and pretending. Her emotions tended to show up on her face, and it was her biggest weakness in interrogations. She just wasn't cut out for undercover work.

After another minute, a couple came out, both sniffing and wiping at their noses. The young women went in. Before the door closed, one of them said, "Hey, Marcos."

Yes. She was on target.

The college girls seemed to take forever. Evans bounced on her toes, adrenaline kicking in. A guy came up behind her and said, "Girl, you don't need any more. You're already flying."

She willed herself to relax, turn, and smile. "I intend to rock this night, and I'm just getting started."

He leaned in and kissed her. Evans fought the urge to punch him. She stepped back and joked, "Hey, you could have pretended to ask my name."

"So tell me."

The door opened behind her. "Too late."

Laughing, the college girls rushed by. Evans stepped into the bedroom and closed the door. Only a lamp by the bed was on, and the small, dark room with piles of clutter added to her stress. Marcos was alone, cross-legged on the floor, and not much bigger than she was. But she was a cop, with a gun, handcuffs, and years of self-defense training.

"Hey, what's your pleasure?" Marcos smiled, his blue eyes not matching his dark, Afro-curly hair.

Evans sat on the floor to be at his level. "I need some C to go. I'm meeting a guy later and I want to surprise him."

"My kind of surprise." He reached for a zippered case on the floor. "How much?"

"I've got sixty bucks on me. Whatever that will buy." Evans dug out her wallet and cash.

He laughed softly. "You're too old to be new at this. But I like you, and I'll give you a good deal." He handed her an inch-size plastic bag with a tiny Ziploc seal.

She slipped it into her pocket and passed him the cash. "Sweet. Where's this from? Mexico?"

"Why?" Suspicion in his voice.

"Because I'm a cop and I want to know." Evans pulled out her handcuffs. "Don't make this hard on yourself. I've got patrol units right outside."

"Oh fuck." He leaned back against the bed. "Why me? Who pointed the finger?"

"We'll talk at the department." Evans stood.

"I'll be out of jail and dealing again before the night is over."

The little fucker had a surprise coming. "Get up and turn around."

Moments later, he was cuffed and she had his product case tucked into the back of her pants. She read him his rights, then said, "Let's just get out of here quietly. I'll be right behind you and no one needs to know you're busted."

They were almost to the front door when a young man burst into the house and yelled, "Cops in the neighborhood! Let's show 'em who's in charge!"

Oh fuck! Evans' pulse raced and she pushed Marcos toward the door.

The student crowd behind her broke into a roar and moved in mass. Someone shoved her and she slammed into her detainee. They stumbled through the door and down the steps. The crowd kept pushing, and she and Marcos kept stumbling forward toward the sidewalk. Evans tried to catch herself but couldn't.

Another crowd of students surged up the street, yelling and smashing bottles on cars.

Marcos pulled free and yelled, "Get her! She's a cop."

No! A fist slammed into her back and she went down to her knees. As she landed, someone kicked her in the head. Flares of pain blinded her. Before she could react, more fists began to pummel her upper body. She tried to reach for her weapon, but the fists kept coming, paralyzing her arms. She heard sirens, then another blow smashed into her head and everything faded.

CHAPTER 29

Saturday, September 7, 1:05 a.m.

Jackson woke to the sound of his cell phone. He sat up, and for a moment had no idea where he was. The room came into focus. A hotel. Salt Lake City. What time was it? He glanced at the red digital numbers on the clock. Who was calling in the middle of the night? He grabbed his phone: *Schak*.

"What's going on?" He swung his legs to the floor, looking for pants.

"It's Evans. She's been hurt."

No! A sharp pain as he sucked in a breath. "What happened?"

"She was looking for a drug dealer and got caught up in one of those campus parties that turned into a riot."

A drug dealer? Why? The late hour of Schak's call told him the situation was probably worse than it sounded. "What kind of hurt? She's not dying, is she?" The words felt thick on his tongue, and he remembered the feel of her body next to his.

"No, but she's beat up pretty badly. I shouldn't have called, but I guess I'm upset. Another officer was hit with a bottle and might lose his eye."

"Oh no." They talked about the injured officer for a minute, but all he could think about was that Katie was safe in his house and not at one of those parties—and that Evans had been hurt. "Is the situation under control?" Jackson put in his earpiece and pulled on clothes as he talked.

"We ended up with sixty-plus officers out there and had to use tear gas again, but it's calm now. Two vehicles were torched."

"We need a curfew." Even as he said it, he knew that wasn't the answer. "Is Evans in the hospital?"

"Yeah, I just left. They medicated her to make her stay overnight."

"That sounds like Evans." He found his shoes. "I'll catch an early flight and be in town by eight." His voice sounded emotional even to himself, but he hoped Schak wouldn't notice. "Gotta go."

A call to the airlines put him on a standby flight in four hours. Jackson started packing.

His first impulse after leaving the Eugene airport was to drive straight to the hospital and see Evans. He hadn't stopped thinking about her on the flight—except to occasionally worry about Benjie. If the Wagners were connected to the boy, how long would it take them to get here from Boise in an RV? Ten hours? Or had they lied about where they were?

If Andra had been a surrogate mother for them, the child might not be biologically related to Andra. She could have stolen him from the Wagners. Which meant they were entitled to get Benjie back—unless Carl had killed Andra in his quest to reclaim his son. And if Susan knew about the crime and hadn't reported it, then she wasn't fit to be a parent either. So he drove home instead, just to lay eyes on the boy and give him and Katie a hug.

They were both at the table eating breakfast when he walked in.

"Hey, Dad." Katie sounded casual.

Just another morning for her—but having his daughter back in his kitchen made his world right again. He ruffled Benjie's hair and gave Katie a one-armed shoulder hug. "I have to see a friend in the hospital, so I'm taking off again after I shower. But stick around, I'll be back soon."

Katie rolled her eyes. "Where would we go? It's seven thirty in the morning."

After a shower, coffee, and toast, Jackson called Sergeant Dan Chadwell in Utah. "I need a favor. Can you get the license plate number and a description of the Wagners' RV? They're on the road right now, and I'd like to keep track of them for a while."

"It's Saturday, but I'll see what I can do. Have you thought about tracking their mobile phone?"

"Yes, but I'm sure I'll need a subpoena."

"I'll get back to you on the license plate as soon as I can."

On the drive to the hospital, Jackson called Schak and asked him to track down the Wagners' cell phone carrier to see if he could get a location on their phones. His partner made a mocking sound. "Fat chance. It's the weekend, so even if we had the paperwork, it would still be tough."

"We have to try."

"You think Wagner is the father?"

"Andra stayed with them when she was pregnant, and they were in the vicinity when she died."

"I think you've found our perp."

"I'll work on a subpoena for his DNA this afternoon." But that was a bigger long shot, with only circumstantial evidence to back it up.

"We need something solid," Schak said, echoing his thoughts. "Like a witness who saw him in the area."

"Then let's find Wagner's photo, and we'll get out to Pershing again this afternoon." His earlier sense of success was fading in the reality of building a convictable case.

Evans was arguing with a nurse when he entered her hospital room. The woman in scrubs turned to him. "Tell her she needs to stay until the doctor releases her."

Jackson nodded but wouldn't waste his breath. The nurse left and Jackson took in Evans' details. A dark abrasion on her forehead had swelled to a golf ball–size lump and her eyes were bloodshot, but otherwise, her face hadn't been beaten. A sense of relief washed over him. Yet seeing her in a hospital gown reminded him of how dangerous their job was.

"Hey, Jackson. You almost missed me. I'm getting out of here as soon as they bring my clothes."

He stepped over and held her hand for a moment. "Schak said you'd been badly beaten, and I've been worried."

"I got lucky they didn't ruin my face, but you should see my ribs and back. They kicked and stomped me until the tear gas rolled in. That's why my eyes are bloodshot."

"Did they arrest the bastards who did this?"

She gritted her teeth. "A few. After the tear gas, the crowd scattered pretty fast." Evans slid her legs over the side of the bed, as if preparing to get up.

"What can I do for you?"

"Help me up, then go find my clothes."

He knew he should encourage her to rest, but there was no point. She was even more driven than he was. Jackson held out his hands and she grabbed them, then pulled herself to her feet. She looked up and met his eyes. For a moment, they stood inches apart, holding on and understanding each other like no one else ever would. In that instant, Jackson knew they were more than just friends. He leaned over and kissed her injured forehead, aching for more. She pushed up on her toes and kissed his mouth.

Surprise. Intense pleasure. Guilt.

Jackson finally pulled back. What did it mean? What should he say? "Don't ever get hurt again, okay? I need you." Should he have said *love*? No. That wouldn't have been fair because he didn't know what he wanted. And loving someone wasn't the same as being in love.

"Thanks for being here."

He had to move. To think. And get back to work. "I'll have a nurse bring your clothes." He pulled her IV stand over so she would have something to hang on to, then let go of her hands.

Jackson took the stairs down, needing to keep moving. His mind raced as fast as his legs pounded. Why were these feelings surfacing now? Why hadn't he fallen for Evans when they had first worked together—before he met Kera? Because raising Katie had been his priority, and Evans didn't want that responsibility. She wouldn't want to be Benjie's mother either. Evans was a free bird—exciting and impulsive. Was that the real attraction? A relationship with no responsibilities? Did he really love Evans or just the idea of being with her?

His thoughts turned to Kera, who would gladly take him and all his baggage, because her heart just kept expanding to make room. She was the right woman for him. *Damn!* He shouldn't have kissed Evans. Or kissed her back, as he recalled. The act had been reckless and unfair, and he'd probably ruined their working relationship.

If he didn't get it together soon, he could lose everybody.

CHAPTER 30

Saturday, September 7, 8:35 a.m.

Katie found Benjie an unopened toothbrush and watched him in the mirror as he scrubbed. Such a sweet kid. She remembered her dad showing her to brush up and down instead of back and forth. He'd taught her almost everything she knew that was important. Her mother had read to her as a kid and had been there after school—often drunk, she came to realize—but her father had taught her how to analyze everything and get along with people. Not that she would ever tell him. He was so damn self-righteous and uptight. Or at least he used to be. Since she'd left home, he'd finally started treating her like a person with free will.

"Do you live here?" Benjie asked when he was done.

They'd been through this once already. "I used to. I'm just staying for a while this time."

"Jackson is your dad?"

"Yes." It was funny to hear the little boy call her father *Jackson*—even though everyone else did. It made Benjie sound like a grown-up.

He swung his arms in an excited gesture. "Can Jackson be my dad?"

Oh sweet. But uncomfortable. "I don't know. He's trying to see if anyone is looking for you and misses you."

"No. Just me."

Well, that was sad. She knew what it was like to lose a mother. Still, she couldn't let herself get caught up in it. She needed to get dressed, check her Facebook page, and text Trevor. "Let's go watch cartoons for a minute."

"Mom says no cartoons."

Oh boy. This kid was stricter than her dad. Benjie had refused to eat cereal for breakfast too. "Just for a minute while I get ready."

"I want the park."

Again? She didn't feel that great this morning. "Give me a minute, then we'll go for a while."

He scooted for the living room. "I like Discovery Channel."

She tried to imagine her dad raising this kid and laughed out loud. Boy, would they be a pair.

Half an hour later, with his little hand in hers, they walked down the front path. The day was bright and pretty, but the air was still a little cool. She needed a sweater. "We have to go back for a second."

She turned around, but Benjie resisted.

"I want the park!"

"We'll go, sweetie. I just need to get a sweater. And we should probably find something warmer for you too."

She started toward the house, but he pulled away from her and ran toward the street. "I go by myself."

What a pain. Katie turned and started after him. A dark car on the street next to their driveway caught her eye. The driver's door opened as she jogged down the footpath.

A tall man emerged from the car and she instinctively picked up her pace. "Benjie! Come back!"

The man—wearing a ski mask—charged toward the little boy.

No! Her heart felt like it would burst as she sprinted across the grass.

The abductor closed the gap in seconds, reaching Benjie just as she did. Katie scooped him up, but stumbled as she tried to stop. The man jerked her upright with one hand and grabbed Benjie with the other.

The boy screamed.

Katie yelled too. "Uncle Derrick! Help! Call 911!"

The man backhanded her face, stunning her. Tears welled, but she clung to Benjie with all her strength. For a moment, they engaged in a tug-of-war. But the abductor was too powerful. He pulled the boy free and ran toward his car.

Footsteps pounded and Derrick charged past. As the man neared his open car door, Derrick grabbed him by the back of his jacket. The man spun and swung wildly with his free hand.

She had to help! Katie rushed forward as the two men traded blows and Benjie struggled to get free.

Coming in low from the side, she grabbed the boy and pulled so hard she feared she would break his bones. But she had him in her arms! Katie sprinted for the house, her lungs feeling like they would burst.

She bolted through the open door and kicked it closed with her foot. She locked the door with one hand, then raced through the kitchen for the sliding door. Benjie wailed, but she held on. The back door was already locked. Good. What next?

Uncle Derrick could be in trouble. Where was her cell phone?

Arms aching from the weight of the child, she ran to her room. Her phone was on the bed. Katie put Benjie down, grabbed the cell, and dialed 911. She wanted to call her dad first, but she knew what he would say. While she waited for someone to answer, she stepped over to the window and yanked open the curtains.

The dark car was driving away, and Uncle Derrick was on the ground. *No! No! No!*

"What is your emergency?" The dispatcher was irritatingly calm.

Katie gulped in air and struggled to find her voice. "Someone just tried to kidnap a little boy. And my uncle is hurt. We might need an ambulance."

"Take a deep breath and tell me where you are."

She did her best to be calm and answer questions, but when the call taker asked for a description of the car, Katie fought back tears. Why hadn't she paid more attention? Or looked at the license plate? "It was a dark sedan. You know, like older people drive. And maybe some silver on it."

"Keep your doors locked and don't hang up. A police officer will be there in a minute."

Benjie bawled, "I want Jackson."

For the boy's sake, Katie wouldn't let herself cry, but she desperately wanted her dad to come home too.

CHAPTER 31

Jackson turned on his street and saw two patrol cars parked in front of his house. Holy shit! His heart missed a beat. He careened into the driveway and jumped from his car. Where was everyone? He rushed into the house and heard his brother talking. Katie's voice too. Thank god.

In the living room, Derrick lay in his recliner with an ice-pack on his nose, and Katie was on the couch with Benjie in her lap. Everyone accounted for! His heart settled into a steady pace. Two uniformed officers stood near the dining room. Officer Whitstone, a woman he'd worked a case with before, and Officer Anderson, who had taken his investigative class. Benjie rushed to Jackson with a plaintive cry. He scooped him up.

Katie spoke first. "I was going to call you, but the dispatcher made me stay on the line. Then the officers showed up and started asking questions."

"What happened?" Jackson didn't know who to focus on. He wanted to hear it from Katie, but instinct told him to get the official version.

His daughter moved in for a hug too. "Someone tried to take Benjie, but Uncle Derrick fought him off."

He should have seen that coming. Jackson held Katie for too long, but it felt so good to have her back.

"*We* fought him off, but you saved him." His brother sat up. "My nose may be broken, but I'm okay."

How had he let this happen? He'd been at the hospital, kissing Evans, instead of here, protecting his family. The pain in his gut made him flinch. He would never forgive himself. "Who was it? What did he look like?"

"He was tall and wore a black jacket," Katie answered. "But he had on a ski mask."

Was Carl Wagner still in the area? Had his wife lied about their location?

Officer Whitstone seemed to sense his concern. "What is it? Do you know the perp?"

"I have a possible lead. Carl Wagner of Salt Lake City. We need to call the Utah motor vehicles department and see what he drives. And put out an attempt-to-locate." He hugged Katie again. "Take Benjie into a bedroom so we can discuss the case for a minute."

But the boy cried and wouldn't let go of him, so Jackson resorted to putting the headphones on Benjie while he and the officers exchanged information. Katie headed for her room, and Jackson called after her, "Please don't post anything on Facebook or text your friends. This is an active case."

She shook her head and kept walking.

. . .

Once the patrol officers left, Jackson had to confront the issue of how to protect his family while they hunted down the assailant. Benjie couldn't stay here—that was clear. But this was *his* investigation, and he had to get out there and find the bastard. It wasn't in his nature to sit around and babysit while his team did the legwork. There had been too much of that already.

How the hell had the perp found his address? He wasn't listed in the white pages. No, his old home hadn't been listed. Derrick's address probably was. Still, there were other Jacksons in the phone book and it would have been guesswork. Had the father/perp been here in Eugene all along? Maybe following him around, waiting for an opportunity?

"We can keep Benjie right here," Derrick argued. "I didn't know he and Katie were leaving. I'll do better."

"I thought you had to get back on the road."

"I got the forklift job. I'm gonna be home this weekend and every evening in the future." His brother offered a hopeful smile.

Jackson tried to look happy for him, but everything in his own life was about to change again. "I appreciate your help, but we have to relocate Benjie, and I have another idea." The boy had finally let go, but he was sitting right next to him, wearing headphones, while he and Derrick drank coffee at the table. "Let me make a call."

Ed McCray, a retired detective and friend of twenty years, was near the top of his phone list. Jackson expected him to be out golfing on one of the last warm Saturdays of the season, but he picked up. "Hey, Jackson."

"Hey, pal. I need your help again." The ex-cop had found Katie for him when she first ran away.

"Good, cuz I'm bored out of my mind."

Jackson summed up the case and outlined Benjie's situation. "Can he stay with you for a few days until we nail this perp? We'll do a sting if we have to."

"Of course. The wife will be pleased to have a little one around."

Jackson knew Benjie wouldn't handle the transfer well, but he had no choice. "I'll bring him over soon."

"You have clothes and toys and things? Or do we need to go shopping?"

What a good friend. "He's set for now, but he may need new puzzles in a day or so. He loves them."

"He's three?"

"Yes. And he doesn't eat junk food."

Katie came into the room. "Or watch cartoons."

Jackson looked up, surprised. He finished his conversation with McCray. "Thanks. I'll be in touch." He called to Katie as she rummaged in the fridge. "Would you go with Benjie to Ed McCray's house? He could use a familiar face around."

"No. Sorry." She leaned into the archway. "I have a life and I'm going back to it very soon."

He tensed, but tried to sound calm. "I'd feel better if you stayed with me until we put this guy in jail."

"I'm not here to make you feel better, and the creep isn't after me." She grinned to soften the sting of her words.

Jackson didn't have time to argue, and he knew better than to push her when she was dug in. "I'll give you fifty dollars to stay for another day or so."

"Seriously?" She shrugged. "I'll take your money."

Relieved, Jackson pulled the cash out of his wallet. Katie had never gone back on a promise or deal. Also, patrol officers would swing by the house periodically, while he met with his team and gathered forces to track down the perp. Everyone was safe for the moment.

Katie grabbed an apple and went back to her room.

"How do we get the kid over to McCray's without the risk of being followed?" Derrick asked. "Shouldn't we wait until it's dark or something?"

"The perp is probably busy now, trying to switch cars and maybe get out of town until the pressure eases. This is the best time to act." Jackson finished his coffee and stood. "We'll switch cars and both leave at once, just in case he's watching and waiting for us to make a move."

"I assume you know how to lose a tail," Derrick joked.

"I think I'll manage."

Jackson gathered up Benjie's things into an overnight bag—vowing to buy him more clothes—and the four of them, including the patrol officer, huddled near the front door.

"You two go out first, blocking the view of Benjie," Jackson instructed. "I'll head between the cars, then duck into yours from the wrong side."

None of it was probably necessary. Only an idiot or a psychopath would hang around the neighborhood, waiting for another opportunity. But then, most criminals were one or the other. Still, he felt confident they would pull this off and Benjie would be safe—for a while. Police and sheriff departments around the state were looking for the Wagners' motorhome, a black midsize sedan with silver trim, and a light-blue Nissan truck. They would get him soon.

CHAPTER 32

Saturday, September 7, 10:25 a.m.

Evans stared at the clothes the nurse had brought her. The tank top she'd worn to the party had been cut open and the jeans were bloody and stained with scuff marks from her attackers' feet. *Bastards!* She dug in the front pocket and was relieved to find the little bag of cocaine she'd purchased from Marcos. At least she still had the sample. It could have disappeared so easily into a tired nurse's pocket. She'd drop off the drugs at the crime lab today for Joe to send to the state lab for analysis. Schak, who'd brought her to the hospital with lights and siren wailing, had reported that Marcos had been arrested. The handcuffs she'd put on the dealer had kept him from running too far or too fast. Of course, he'd probably be released this morning, but at least now he faced distribution charges, so she had some leverage.

The jeans she could wear, but she still needed a shirt. Her purse had stayed strapped across her chest when she went down, so she still had it too, but no car. She could have asked Jackson to wait and give her a ride, but he'd been spooked and had bolted. Worried that she had ruined their friendship, Evans regretted her part in the kiss. But what did it matter? Either Jackson would come around and want to be together or she would transfer out of his unit. At least now she knew he had feelings for her too. But would he act on them? Not likely. He was a family man, and she was a wild card. She fought the tears threatening to overwhelm her and shut down the train of thought. The physical pain she was dealing with was bad enough by itself. Why wallow and make it worse?

The sound of footsteps made her look up. Ben came in, carrying clean clothes, a vase filled with flowers, and a stack of magazines. Her first emotion was relief. She really needed the clothes. Then gratitude filled her heart. The gifts were thoughtful, reminding her that Ben was a good guy. Seconds later, guilt set in. If he was such a great guy, why couldn't she love him the way she loved Jackson?

"Why didn't you call me last night?" A frown creased Ben's brow, but it didn't detract from his sexy shaved-head look. "I had to hear about this through the grapevine." He kissed her gently as she stood up. "Why aren't you in bed?"

"I'm getting out of here, and your timing is perfect. After I'm dressed, will you give me a ride to my car?"

"Of course, but are you okay? I mean, you look better than I expected, based on the stories I heard about the campus riot."

"My head hurts, and I feel like someone beat me with a bat, but I'm functional." She reached for the clothes he'd laid on the bed. Jeans and a black sweater. Not work clothes, but they would be all right. "Thanks for making a trip to my place to get these. I have a funeral to attend."

"What?"

Evans pulled on the jeans. "Logan Grayson, the football player. I was assigned to investigate his death."

"I knew that. But why are you going to the service? You should rest." Ben grabbed her hands. "It's Saturday. You're injured. Your case is closed. Come to my place for the weekend and let me pamper you."

He was so sweet. Uncommitted, but really good to her . . . at times. "That is very tempting." She pulled her hands free. "But I told his mother I would go, and I still need some closure on the case." Evans peeled off the hospital gown and grabbed the black sweater. "I'll come over later."

"I'm glad I brought you something black." He smiled, but his eyes were worried.

"Me too." It suited her mood.

The memorial was being held at St. Mary's Church, a huge red-brick building in the downtown area. As late as she was, the parking lot was full and so were the streets around it. Evans finally parked at the Kiva and walked over, each step a painful reminder of the drunk students who had viciously assaulted her just for the hell of it. Maybe not all of them had been students. Campus parties attracted all kinds of young people, including addicts and lowlifes.

From the alley across the street, she could see the crowd filling the church steps and figured she wasn't getting inside. If this had been yesterday, Evans would have flashed her badge and pushed her way in. Today, she would keep her distance from the gathering of college students and football fans. All she really wanted to do was observe the crowd and see if anyone stood out as not belonging. Or if anyone had a black eye from a fistfight with Grayson. She could do that as people left the building in a half hour or so. She took a seat on a bench nearby, pulled out her cell phone, and called Schak.

"Evans! Did they kick you out of the hospital for being an obnoxious patient?"

"I didn't give 'em the chance. But I wanted to thank you for being my backup and bringing me in last night. You may have saved my life."

"A patrol officer reached you first. I was almost too late getting downtown." His voice shifted. "I should have been outside that party house ten minutes earlier."

"You were there and I'm fine. In fact, I'm sitting across from St. Mary's waiting for Grayson's memorial service to let out."

"You're working?" He let out a bitter laugh. "You're getting as bad as Jackson."

She took it as a compliment. "Aren't you working? What's happening with the Andra Caiden case?"

He hesitated for a long moment. "There's been a development." His tone was deadly serious.

A shiver of worry went up her neck. Evans reached for the sample pack of pain pills the nurse had given her. "What is it?"

"Someone tried to abduct Benjie from Jackson's house this morning. Jackson wasn't home but his brother was and intervened."

"Oh shit. Is everyone okay?"

"Yes, but the perp escaped. We've got a massive manhunt underway."

"Maybe this is the break we needed. If we catch him, we catch the killer. "

"That's what we're thinking. But I'll know more in a while."

"What do you mean?"

"There's a task force meeting at one."

"Why didn't anyone tell me?" She knew why, but it still pissed her off.

"I just told you, but you don't have to be there. We've got this."

"I'm still on this team. I'm moving slow, but I'll be there." She hung up and stared at the pain pill in her hand. If she took it, she would feel and move better. But it might dull her critical-thinking skills. Oh hell, not enough to make a difference. She worked up some spit and dry-swallowed it. She would have given just about anything for a kick-ass cup of coffee to wash it down with.

As the church bells tolled, the mourners spilled out the wide doors, moving like a slow-motion, weeping parade. Evans crossed the street to stand near the sidewalk and see faces up close. The crowd was overwhelming as people moved toward their cars and stood on the sidewalk talking. A tremor of fear shook her. *Goddamn*, she hated being afraid. Many of the mourners were big young men dressed in dark clothes, and she almost missed Jake Keener, who walked by with Danica Mercado. The cheerleader looked more upset today than she had earlier in the week.

Evans kept shifting her eyes, looking for anyone who seemed out of place or uncomfortable about being there. She caught sight of a young man who looked so much like Grayson she did a double take. His brother? Did he play football for the Ducks too? She jotted down *brother?* in her notebook, then went back to scanning the crowd.

After a few minutes, Catalina Morales came down the steps, accompanied by another woman who looked like her, but was a little older and a little heavier. Probably a sister. Catalina likely wouldn't have been notified about the service if Evans hadn't done it herself. She felt a little sorry for the woman and wondered if her presence had set off any sparks. Evans followed Catalina to the parking lot to observe who she interacted with, if anyone. Every step made her wince.

She lost the girl in the cluster of vehicles all trying to exit at once. Hobbling and cursing, she made her way through the cars. A light-blue Nissan pickup got in line to pull out onto Tenth Avenue. It took a moment to realize why the truck was important. The other homicide case. It matched the vehicle the neighbors had seen at the house the day before Andra Caiden moved in. *What the hell?* Who was driving it? Two people were in the front and they looked like long-haired women. She needed to get her car and follow them.

Evans turned and jogged for the Kiva parking lot, her ribs screaming and her head throbbing. Halfway there, she had to slow down, unable to take the jarring pain. She knew where Catalina lived and could find her there. But what if it hadn't been Catalina in the truck? She hadn't seen the their faces. The people in the Nissan could have been men. Some of the football players had long hair. But if the truck's occupants had been at the Pershing house, she had to find out who they were.

What if the driver was the killer? The man who'd tried to abduct Benjie and the perp everyone was looking for?

Evans picked up her pace, trotting down the alley in an awkward gait, unable to see the little blue truck, which was on the other side of the library now. She reached her car just as a meter maid was ticketing it. The health food store obviously monitored its parking lot.

"Police officer. Get away from my car." She didn't have her badge and couldn't show it.

The woman in the blue uniform looked up, startled.

"Move!"

The meter maid stepped aside and yelled, "I have your license number!"

Good for you. Evans climbed in, started the engine, and roared out of the parking, turning left toward Tenth Avenue. When she reached the corner, she eased into the intersection and spotted the truck traveling east toward Willamette. She turned right, pulling out in front of a yellow sports car. The driver honked, and she resisted the urge to flip him off, staying focused on the truck.

The Nissan turned right on Willamette and crossed Eleventh Avenue heading south. Toward Catalina's apartment? A few minutes later, the truck pulled into an apartment complex. Evans stopped in the parking lot next door and watched as a dark-haired woman got out of the truck on the passenger's side. The same one who'd been with Catalina at the funeral service. The passenger closed the door and walked upstairs as the truck turned around. Evans could see the driver now and she had platinum-blond hair. She made a mental note of the complex's name and location but stayed with the truck.

Five minutes later, Catalina pulled into her own complex and parked at the end of the lot behind a large black SUV that obscured the little truck. No wonder she hadn't seen the Nissan when she was here before. Evans parked on the street and watched Catalina head upstairs, her slim pregnant body swaying in a tight black dress.

She called Jackson but he didn't pick up. Frustrated, she didn't leave a message. The scenario for the Grayson case was too complicated to bog him down with. She climbed from her car and followed Catalina upstairs. Had Jackson ignored her call on purpose? Was it awkward for him already? The thought troubled her, but she couldn't focus on it. Pounding on the woman's door made her bruised back ache. The pain pill had been only marginally helpful.

From the other side, Catalina called out, "Who is it?"

"Detective Evans. I was just at the funeral." In no shape to give chase, she didn't want to make the suspect skittish.

The door opened, and Catalina stood with her hands on her hips. "What do you want? I'm tired and depressed." She sounded like she would cry at any moment.

Evans wouldn't let herself feel any sympathy; the woman could be a killer. But she wanted to take her to the interrogation room for questioning, so faking compassion was in order. "I know, and I'm sorry. But I have a sketch at the department I need you to look at."

"What are you talking about?"

Evans thought quickly. "A witness saw someone with Logan at his apartment right before he died. Our sketch artist made a drawing but I need you to see if you can identify the person." Kind of lame, but plausible.

"Right now?"

"Of course. Time is critical."

"Everyone at the service said Logan had a heart attack."

"But what caused it? I think somebody harmed him on purpose."

She looked skeptical.

"Don't you want me to solve this?" A loaded question, for sure, if she was guilty of anything.

"Well, yeah, but—"

"Let's go. Right now." Evans stepped through the door and gently grabbed her by the elbow. "I'll bring you right back when we're done." *Not likely.*

"Okay, but I told you, I don't know Logan's college friends." Catalina stepped outside and locked her door.

"The suspect isn't a student. He's older than that." She just needed to get Catalina into the car and to the department. The task force meeting would start soon, and she needed to confer with her teammates. Catalina could sit in the pit and worry for a few minutes.

The connection was still a puzzle. Why had Catalina been at the Pershing house on Saturday? Had she rented it to Andra Caiden in some kind of scam? Evans knew she was onto something important here, but she couldn't make it come into focus. It would, though, once Catalina started answering the important questions.

CHAPTER 33

Sophie checked her Gmail again and found the response she'd been waiting for all morning. It was from *Tessajones*, and read: *Meet me at house in hour. bing cash & we'll sign renal papers.*

Not only was Tessa probably a scammer, she couldn't spell, didn't use articles, and didn't proof her e-mails. Criminal! Sophie loved digital media but hated what it had done to the quality of communication. People didn't even use capital letters anymore. Still, her body hummed with excitement. She was going out on a sting!

Sophie turned to her lover, who was reading in bed. "Jasmine, I've got to leave. Are you going to stay and hang out?"

"No, I've got to work for a while this afternoon. We're behind, as usual." Jasmine stood, her long, lean frame topped by dark hair and an exotic face. The crime scene technician was scary smart, and Sophie thought she might be in love. Jasmine tossed her

Kindle in her shoulder bag and came over to where Sophie sat at the computer. "Be careful. This person is a scammer. You don't know how he or she will react when you expose them."

"I think it's a woman. But don't worry, a photographer will be there."

"I still think you should get the police involved." Jasmine sounded tired.

"They weren't interested in the case. That's why the victim called me."

"But since you think the scam could be connected to Amanda Carter's death, why not call Jackson?" Jasmine's tone was more rhetorical than pressuring. They'd been dating a while but didn't feel compelled to control each other.

"This one is probably a different scammer, and I need to see if I'm right about what's going on with these rentals. I'll call him later."

Jasmine kissed her good-bye and left. Sophie grabbed a bottle of water, her purse, and sunglasses, then followed her out. She'd taken the cash out of her account the night before, prepared to lose the money if necessary to get the story. And, of course, her recorder and cell phone were always with her.

Surprisingly enough, the rental was in southwest Eugene but located on a busy thoroughfare. After doing some research, she'd come to realize that zombie houses were everywhere, except the pricey subdivisions in the south hills. Banks were overwhelmed by defaults and often didn't have the personnel or systems in place to handle real estate, especially if it had little value.

Sophie had trouble finding the house at first, until she spotted the numbers on the curb and noticed an entrance between two fences. She turned in and cruised down the L-shaped driveway, thinking the panhandle lot was the only feature that made the place livable. Otherwise the street traffic and sports-crowd noise from a nearby high school would have been overwhelming. After Tessa had given her the address, she'd contacted county records and found the owners' names, but their telephone number was no longer in service, and they clearly no longer lived in the house. If her theory was correct, this house had been empty for a long time, and the woman she was about to meet didn't have permission to live there, let alone sublet to anyone. Like other digital innovations, Craigslist was both a blessing and a curse.

Sophie parked in the empty driveway. Good, she was first to arrive and could snoop around. She hoped Brian would arrive before the Craigslist "struggling tenant" showed up. Using her cell phone, she took pictures of the house: dirty white with faded green trim, weather-damaged siding, and dead grass in the front and side yards. Despite the large lot, the house looked small, maybe eleven hundred square feet and built in the sixties before anyone cared about vaulted ceilings. Peeking in the front window confirmed her preconceptions. Sophie pulled out her recorder and took verbal notes. She would need these details to set the scene for her readers. Though she rarely wished she worked in television, this story seemed suited to it. A bleak setting, a hidden camera, and a sting to catch the scammer. They could put the video on their website and boost digital subscriptions.

Around back, the blinds for both bedrooms were closed. *Darn.* She wanted to see if there was furniture in the house. Was that the sound of an engine in the driveway? With the nearby traffic, it was hard to tell, but she trotted around to the front. Her photographer climbed off his motorcycle, gave a small wave, then pulled a brown leather man-purse from his saddlebag.

"Hey, Brian. Have you got a camera in there?"

"Yep. Cool, huh?" He pointed to a brass button-like feature on the side. "This is the lens. Ahmed helped me set it up."

"I love tech guys. Hey, should I call you Brian or make up something fun?" A pretend boyfriend didn't bother her at all. She'd dated men before Jasmine, but found most to be either too distant or too needy.

"Stick with Brian. The public doesn't know me."

In her e-mails with the scammer, Sophie had used the name Monica, after her mother, which amused her. It wasn't likely the scammer was a newspaper reader, but why take the chance on someone recognizing her byline? She'd been involved in a hair-raising standoff with an eco-terrorist a few months earlier, and ever since, her job had seemed routine. This was just what she needed.

She and Brian talked about potential scenarios and how they would react to them. A small silver car drove up a few minutes into the discussion, and Sophie resisted the urge to snap a picture.

A woman stepped out. Or at least she looked more like a woman than a man. Tessa wore a bulky gray hoodie that covered her hair and hid her upper body. The black jeans and running shoes were androgynous too. She came toward them, moving with the fluidity of a female, and looking annoyed.

"Tessa? I'm Monica. And this is my boyfriend, Brian."

"I said I wouldn't rent to a couple." Her dark eyes glinted and her mouth tightened.

"Oh no, he's not moving in." Sophie laughed, as though it were a ridiculous idea. "We're just dating, and he has his own place."

"He can stay out here then." Tessa started toward the front door. "If you like the house, we'll fill out the paperwork and you can move in today."

Brian followed. "I need to use the bathroom."

Tessa didn't argue, unlocking the door with a key.

The living room had less furniture and less appeal than a hooker motel. Sophie smiled. "I like the uncluttered look."

"It's not on purpose," Tessa said. "My roommate just moved out and took half my stuff. She left me with the full rent though, and it's due on Monday."

Brian was in the room and had hopefully caught her back-story on film.

"That's a crappy deal." Sophie had read some of the setup during their e-mail exchanges. Tessa had also asked a lot of personal questions, such as: Do you have a good rental history? Proof of income? A criminal record? Sophie suspected the scammer wasn't looking for someone highly respectable, so she'd tailored her responses to make herself seem borderline, with an old drug conviction. In other words, someone desperate who couldn't access traditional housing, yet wouldn't call the police if she were ripped off. No surprise, Tessa had picked her, even though the scammer had probably received plenty of responses to her ad about a room for rent with only a small security deposit.

The dining room was completely empty.

"Don't worry," Tessa said. "I bought a table this morning at Goodwill. I'm just waiting for a friend to help me pick it up."

"Can I see the available bedroom?"

"Sure."

Brian came out of the bathroom, nodded at them in the hall, then stayed there—filming, she hoped. The other bedroom door was closed, and she could smell mold in the bathroom from the hallway.

A third door stood open and Sophie walked in. The empty bedroom was clean but had spider webs in the corners and smelled like stale perfume. She was ready to make the deal happen. "I'll take it. I need a place to stay ASAP. My friend needs me off her couch when her mother visits in a few days."

"I've got the paperwork in the kitchen." Tessa gestured for her to move along. "The owner doesn't care who I sublet to since I'm responsible for the whole rent."

Sophie read through the single-page agreement. Simple and standard. Tessa had probably downloaded it from the internet or created it herself. "Will my rent be due on the first?" She signed the paper.

Tessa scooped it up. "Sure. I'll pro-rate next month's."

Her cameraman moved in closer, pretending to examine the woodwork on the cabinets. Sophie wished he'd had a chance to aim the lens at the rental agreement, but it probably didn't matter. She pulled a rumpled envelope out of her purse and handed Tessa four hundred dollars, three for the rent and one for the security deposit. No legitimate rental owner would ever take in a tenant for that little cash—unless the homeowner happened to be your mother.

"Thanks." Tessa stuck the cash in her front pocket and handed Sophie a key. "It's such a relief to be able to pay the rent."

Time to pounce. "Who did you say owned the house?"

"An older woman. I think her name is Helen, but I can't ever remember. She pretty much leaves me alone."

"Can I see your rental agreement with the owner?"

"I don't have it with me." Tessa scowled. "Why do you ask now?"

"Because you don't have one. Nor do you live here. This house was owned by Tina and David Wilson, and it's been vacant for months."

"You don't know what you're talking about." Tessa spun and strode toward the door. "I have to go to work."

"Talk to me or talk to the police!" Sophie called after her.

Tessa kept moving. Brian followed and filmed the scammer climbing into her car, capturing her license plate too. Tessa flipped him off and squealed out of the driveway.

Sophie turned to the photographer and held out her hand for a fist bump. "Even if the police don't investigate, we can at least warn the public."

He shrugged. "Too bad people who would fall for this probably don't read the paper or online news."

"We do what we can." Maybe they would send the footage to a TV station after they broke the story. Sophie started toward her car. "Tessa must break into the house, then change out the front-door lock."

Brian nodded. "She probably has a couple of sets that she just keeps swapping."

"I wonder if others are doing this, or something like it." How did they get away with it? Victimizing people who had few choices and fewer resources was the lowest of the low. Sophie remembered that Amanda Carter, the homicide victim, had been found in a nearly empty house. It was time to call Jackson and tell him about the sting. She would text him too. He often didn't listen to her messages until much later. If he was interested in her scoop, he might give her more details about his murder investigation in exchange.

CHAPTER 34

Saturday, September 7, 11:25 a.m.

From the department, Jackson called Judge Cranston at home. His wife picked up and said the judge was about to leave for a golf game.

"This is critical," Jackson pleaded. "A young life is at stake."

"I'll get him." He heard her set down the phone, and it clunked like an old-style handheld.

After a long wait, the judge came on. "What is it, Jackson? I hope you haven't oversold your case."

"A young mother was murdered earlier this week, and her three-year-old son was almost abducted from my home this morning. I need a DNA sample of the only suspect we have."

"Who is he?"

"Carl Wagner. He lives in Salt Lake City, but he and his wife have a motor home and were in our area at the time of the murder."

"Why is he a suspect?"

"I think he's the boy's father."

A pause. "You can substantiate the connection?"

"I think so."

"Bring me the subpoena and I'll read it. No promises."

On the drive up to Cranston's home in the south hills, Jackson worried about everything. Benjie's safety. Whether Katie would take off again. But mostly about whether the judge would help them go after Wagner.

What did he really have on the Utah man? Not much other than Andra's presence in his home during her pregnancy and his trip to Lane County at the time of her murder. Was that enough? As a precaution, he'd had two subpoenas prepared. One asking for a DNA sample to compare to the trace evidence they'd found on Andra's body, and a second request for a handwriting sample to compare to the threatening note. He hoped the judge would sign both, but he suspected he might only come away with the handwriting demand. At least it would give him an excuse to confront and/or arrest Wagner. If they established a handwriting match, they would get the DNA next.

The house on Blanton Heights was a new two-story with pretentious columns in the front and a circular drive. It looked out of place among the older, modest homes that had been in the area when it was considered rural.

Cranston opened the door and gestured for him to sit in the dining room. Jackson laid his paperwork on the table. "I'd like a sample of his handwriting as well. The victim had a threatening note in her purse."

"We'll see." The judge started to skim, then stopped and looked up. "If Wagner isn't actually here in Oregon, this subpoena may not be valid in Utah. It depends on their state laws."

"I'm pretty sure he's here." Jackson expected a call, any minute, from a patrol officer or deputy. Or from Schak, who was checking with car rental companies. Quince was going door-to-door in Jackson's neighborhood, searching for a witness who might have seen the masked man's car or witnessed the botched abduction.

Jackson's leg vibrated under the table as he waited. A little too much coffee. Cranston finally looked up. "You don't have anything connecting him to the original murder scene."

"But Wagner is associated with the victim and the vicinity." Jackson knew it was weak. "What if his DNA matches the boy? What if it matches the hair on the victim? We can use it to pressure him into a confession and/or plea agreement."

"Can you connect him to the abduction? Does he own a dark sedan?" The judge peered over his glasses, obviously wanting to do the right thing.

Jackson's frustration mounted. "I'm waiting for the DMV in Utah to get back to me. A police officer in Salt Lake City is working on it too, but it's Saturday, so I'm not hopeful."

"I'm sorry, but I can't sign the DNA subpoena to compare to the homicide evidence. You haven't justified it, even though I trust your instincts." Cranston took off his glasses. "I shouldn't even sign the handwriting request, but I will. If it matches the threatening note, I'll give you the DNA."

Jackson wanted to argue, but he handed him a pen instead. "Thank you."

He drove too fast across town but had to slow down on Country Club Road, named after the golf course across the street from the department. A group of men were on the green, and he had a flash of guilt. The golfers had to hate it when officers discharged their weapons in the traps outside the building. It could ruin a guy's swing, for sure.

Schak was already in the conference room, wolfing down a sloppy sandwich. "I had to eat," he said between bites. "Sorry I didn't get you anything."

"I'm fine." Coffee and stress had killed his appetite. "Have you heard from Quince?"

"Not yet." Schak put down his meal. "Evans called and said she plans to make the meeting. She wants to help."

Jackson hadn't let himself think about Evans since leaving the hospital. It was too confusing. "That's crazy. She needed help standing up this morning. We can't let her work."

"You can't stop her either." Schak took his last bite and talked with his mouth full. "Give her phone calls to make. Something sedentary."

"All right." He didn't want to see Evans yet, but it was inevitable. They would have to work through this. Whatever it was.

Quince came in, looking sunburned and carrying a huge paper cup. "Man, it's hot out there. I forgot what it's like to be outside for hours in late summer."

"I thought you were a cycler."

"I go early in the morning." Quince took a seat and glanced over at Schak's sandwich wrapper. "You didn't think I'd be hungry too?"

"I'm not your mother." Schak rolled the trash into a ball and made a basketball shot to the can in the corner. "I should've eaten faster."

"Let's get started," Jackson said. "We have to nail this guy before he tries again or gets the hell out of town." Too hyper to sit, he took the board and summed up the subpoena situation. "It doesn't help us find him, but it gives us leverage when we do."

"I don't think the car was a rental," Schak said. "Five small-size black sedans were rented out yesterday. Two from the airport. But Wagner's name wasn't on any of them, and only one of the rentals went to a middle-aged couple." He looked at his notes and read their names. "I called and the couple is booked into the Hilton, so I stopped by. They're both forty-something, athletic, and don't match your description of the Wagners."

Jackson wasn't surprised. A rental was too easy to trace.

"He might have used his own car," Quince offered. "Can we find out what he owns?"

"I've made the calls. And Sergeant Chadwell is trying to find someone in the Utah state office who can access the vehicle database." It worried him that Quince hadn't offered any new information. "Any luck with witnesses?"

"Yes and no." Quince's pink forehead was sweating. "A woman down the street noticed the black car sitting there, but she didn't get a license number and has no idea what the make or model was."

"What about the driver?"

"She said he looked tall."

"We knew that." Exasperated, Jackson paced the room. "I wish Derrick or Katie had gotten a plate number."

"They were fighting off an abduction," Schak reminded him.

"I know." Jackson tried to plan their next moves. "We need a profile on this guy. He's obsessive about getting his son back, and he was audacious enough to try to abduct him from a police officer's home. So he must be ready to disappear with the boy and start over somewhere."

"How does his wife fit in?" Quince asked.

"I don't know. It could be her baby too, so she may be an accomplice."

"Andra stole their child?" Schak's tone held disgust. "That's damn cold. I kind of feel sorry for them." Schak had an adult son, but he didn't talk about him much.

"We don't know that," Quince argued. "The boy may not be related to the wife. Sometimes they use the surrogate mother's egg because the wife can't produce viable embryos."

Schak stared at Quince, mouth open. For once, he didn't say anything.

Quince continued. "If Andra is the biological mother, she might not have been able to give up the baby after it was born. The court sometimes sides with the surrogate."

Schak wasn't buying it. "But if Benjie is Wagner's kid, then isn't he entitled to custody too? Especially if he paid her? Don't fathers have rights?"

Jackson stepped in. "If he killed Andra, Wagner gave up his right to be Benjie's father. He should have taken her to court."

Schak held up his hands in surrender. "You're right. And he's obviously unstable. Benjie is better off without him."

"Society is better off without him," Quince added.

The door opened and Evans hobbled into the room. "You're not going to believe what I just discovered."

CHAPTER 35

Saturday, September 7, 12:32 p.m.

She was so bored. Now that Benjie was gone and Dad was working as usual, the house felt empty and she had nothing to do. Katie
picked up her phone and texted Trevor, her sort-of-boyfriend:
hey. what r u doing? I gotta get out of here.

While she waited to hear from him, Katie took a shower,
changed into shorts, then played Angry Birds on her phone.

Uncle Derrick knocked on her bedroom door. "Want to
watch a movie with me? Or play cards?"

He was trying to be nice, or maybe just trying to keep her
entertained so she didn't leave, but she didn't know Derrick that
well. For most of her life, he and her dad hadn't spoken to each
other, even though Derrick had only lived a mile away. She'd
heard they'd had a falling out over this house after their parents
were murdered. She and Dad had moved in here after selling her
childhood home—which still pissed her off—and she'd started to

get to know Uncle Derrick. Then her mother had been killed, and everything spun out of control.

Finally, she answered, "Thanks, but I'll pass." Was that rude? Sometimes she sounded unfriendly when she didn't mean to. It just took too much time to find pleasant ways of saying everything.

"I'll make popcorn," Derrick called out. "Come join me if you change your mind."

Popcorn? Oh, please. How old did he think she was? She opened the door and grinned. "Got any beer?"

"No. I don't drink much these days."

"Dad made you feel guilty about it, didn't he?" She made a mocking sound. "Don't let him turn you into a prude too."

Derrick looked a little sheepish. "I finally found a decent job, so being sober most of the time is working out for me."

She wanted to say *Whatever* but decided to be nice. "Glad to hear it." She didn't believe for a second that she was an alcoholic who could never drink again. That was manipulative crap. But she had to control it or she'd end up in jail. So she'd laid off the hard stuff and only drank beer now—and not every day. Just to prove to herself that she didn't need it. But she sure wanted a brew right now. This morning had been stressful.

Her phone beeped. "I gotta get that." She smiled at Derrick until he walked away.

The text was from Trevor: *Last weekend before school. Drink a beer by the river?*

She texted back: *Hell yes!* Then added: *Pick me up at Sundance in 30.*

Relieved to have a plan, Katie gathered up her clothes and makeup and shoved it into her backpack. The money in her pocket gave her a twinge of guilt. She'd promised Dad she would stay for another day. What difference did it make if she left now or later? She didn't live here anymore and he couldn't make her.

She heard the shower come on and decided it made sense to leave while Uncle Derrick was occupied. On the way out, she left the fifty bucks on the kitchen table. She wasn't a cheat. A moment later, she turned back and picked up the ten-dollar bill. If Dad were here, he'd loan her the money for food. He always did.

Outside, the blue-sky summer day brightened her mood. But only for a moment. The memory of the black car and the masked man made her shiver. He'd only wanted Benjie because the boy was his, and she couldn't really blame him for that. But he was still creepy. It was also kind of weird that her dad had brought the boy home from a crime scene. But his motives were always good. She gave him credit for that, even though having a cop for a father had turned out to be a pain in the ass.

As she started down the street, Katie glanced around. No black cars, no lurking strangers. Sheesh! Her dad was paranoid. But she kept up a good pace on her way to the market. She would get there before Trevor did, but that was fine. It was great to be outside. And in charge of her own life again. The only downside to her situation was lack of money. She planned to get a part-time job to fix that soon. Maybe in a clothing store or a movie theater.

She crossed Potter Street and decided to cut through the park, which took up an entire city block and had been her favorite place as a kid. Mom had brought her there all the time in the summer. Her mother had often sat and read—and drank, Katie realized later—while she played on the swings, but at least her mother had taken her. Today the gorgeous green open space was empty. Summer was mostly over and classes hadn't started yet. Everyone was in transition—out clothes shopping, registering for classes, or taking some last-minute vacation trip.

She reached the sidewalk on the other side and turned right. Sundance was another five blocks, on the corner of a busy street. It was a cool store where she liked to buy trail mix from the bulk bins. And Trevor lived not far away on Alder. She'd met him last spring in the store, where he had a part-time job. But they hadn't hooked up until recently.

Katie passed under a big oak tree that shaded the sidewalk and cooled the air. Parked nearby was a bright-yellow Volkswagen van. The rainbow on the side made her smile. Eugene was such a hippie town. She was dying to go to the Oregon Country Fair someday—hippies, art, music, beer, and pot—what more could you ask for?

The van's side door clanged open and she glanced over, expecting to see someone with dreadlocks.

The tall man with a mask rushed at her. As she opened her mouth to scream, his hand clamped over it. The cloth in his palm smelled like medicine. Katie grabbed his wrist with both hands, but she had no strength. She couldn't even think straight. Her mind clouded over and went dark.

CHAPTER 36

He lifted the girl and laid her in the cargo van. He would duct-tape her hands and wrists in a moment, but he had to get the hell away first, in case someone had witnessed the incident. He shut the sliding door and glanced around. A cyclist was coming down the street, but no one else seemed to be out and about. Still, some snoopy old lady could be watching from behind closed curtains in any of the houses on the block. He jumped in the driver's seat, fired up the engine, and got rolling. He'd stolen the van earlier from the little hippie market and had parked in an alley, watching and waiting.

When he cleared the neighborhood, he pulled off his ski mask, which would only draw attention to him at this point. For a few minutes, he drove west in a zigzag pattern, pushing the speed limit and making sudden turns. Now that he'd fooled the girl with the goofy van, he had to ditch it as soon as he could. The bright yellow was like a neon sign. First he had to make sure the girl wasn't going anywhere when she came to.

He pulled into an alley between two streets and spotted only a couple of houses on the gravel lane. The town seemed to have a bunch of these little tucked-away places. He parked, climbed into the back of the van, and grabbed the duct tape from his overnight bag. The girl was still unconscious, her pretty, pale face sprinkled with freckles. She'd better be Jackson's daughter. Otherwise, she wasn't much of a bargaining chip. For three years, ever since that cunt had stolen little Ben from the hospital, he'd searched and longed for his son. Now that he'd found the boy, he couldn't just give up and let someone else have him. The older Ben got, the less likely the boy would bond with him when they were reunited. It was now or never. He had to believe God had intervened and brought Ben back into his life.

Working quickly, he bound the girl's hands and ankles with duct tape, gave her another dose of chloroform, then stuck tape over her mouth. If she woke up, she could still be trouble, but he had to keep moving and get out of this damn neon van.

A few minutes later, he reached the alley where he'd left the green Tahoe he'd stolen from the airport. He'd grabbed the little black sedan just for the kidnapping, then abandoned it shortly after the botched attempt. *Fuck!* It had looked like it would be so easy. He'd watched Jackson drive away, then not long after, the teenage girl and his precious boy had come down the sidewalk, saving him the trouble of a home invasion. Then the other man had come out of nowhere. He hadn't expected another adult male to be in the house and was pissed at himself for not doing enough surveillance. But that was the past, and now he was doing the only thing he could to salvage the situation.

He transferred the limp girl into the backseat of the Tahoe and drove two blocks to a nearby motel. The low building stretched along a side street, looking dingy and neglected in the harsh sunlight. He'd used a phony name and paid cash for one night. The clerk, a washed-up man in his late forties, didn't even ask for ID.

He hurried into the sleazy motel room and grabbed a blanket. He wrapped it around the girl, leaving just her face showing, and pulled the tape off her mouth. Now she looked like a sleeping child, being carried into the room by her father. Or so he hoped.

Three or four seconds of exposure and they were inside. He laid the girl on the bed and cranked up the air-conditioning. After a long drink of water, he searched her backpack and found her phone in an outer pocket. Once he made initial contact with Jackson, he would toss the phone into a moving car as a distraction, then steal another one. Or buy a cheapie. No, that shouldn't be necessary. There would be no negotiation. Jackson had his kid and he had Jackson's. The fact that Jackson was a cop didn't matter. He was a father first, and he would act like a father and do whatever was necessary to get his daughter back.

CHAPTER 37

Jackson couldn't believe Evans had come to the meeting, but he was eager to hear her news. "Please sit. Can I get you anything?"

She laughed. "I could use about five more pain pills, but I'll settle for water to wash down the one I have."

Schak jumped up and hurried from the room, moving fast for someone with a barrel chest and short legs. While they waited for him to return, Evans answered Quince's questions about her assault. Schak hurried back in, Evans took her pain pill, then started to give her update.

Jackson's phone beeped, indicating he had a text. Everyone waited while he pulled the phone from his pocket and looked at the ID. "It's Katie. Just a second."

He pressed the icon to open the text. Cold fingers of fear dug into his heart as he read the message: *You have my son. Now I have your daughter. Let's trade. No cops. No FBI. No waiting. Just 2 fathers doing the right thing.*

"Motherfucker!" He slammed the phone into the table.

His teammates jerked in surprise.

Jackson fought for control, but his chest hurt, and his voice sounded like a dying man. "The perp has Katie. He wants to trade for Benjie."

"Holy shit!" Schak was on his feet. "Should we get the feds? They have more resources."

"Not yet." Jackson wasn't sure how he would handle it, but instinct told him to keep it simple.

He couldn't believe he was dealing with this again. Only it was Katie this time. He couldn't bear to lose her. If he did, he just might become one of those cops who put their gun in their mouth and said good-bye to the pain and darkness.

"What are the instructions?" Evans struggled to stand and move toward him.

"I don't have any yet." He handed her the phone, knowing she would want to see the message. They all would. It's how they did their jobs. Looking for clues, idiosyncrasies, any piece of information that could help. "Why the hell haven't they found his car yet? Why hasn't the damn cell phone company called?" He had to blow off some frustration before he could focus.

"He probably switched vehicles. I would have," Schak said.

"How did he grab her?" Evans passed the phone and its deadly message to her teammates. "I thought she was at your home."

"She was, and she promised she wouldn't leave." *Pigheaded girl!* Why did she have to be so damn independent? He had to call Derrick and find out what had happened. Jackson pressed speed dial three, and his brother answered. "Hey, Wade. Everything okay?"

Jackson turned away from his crew. "No, everything is not okay! The son of a bitch has Katie. What the hell happened?"

"Oh fuck. I didn't even know she was gone."

"How is that possible?" Jackson wanted to berate him, but what was the point? Katie wasn't his brother's responsibility. She was his. And he had failed her again. "Never mind." He hung up.

"What now?" Schak asked.

"Call Wagner's cell phone provider again. Now that someone has been kidnapped, maybe they'll locate his phone for us." It wasn't typically his nature to be sarcastic, but he didn't feel like himself right now. Jackson started to pace. "I'll call our company and get a trace on Katie's phone. If he's stupid enough to hang on to it, we might be able to nail him."

No one said anything.

Quince offered, "I'll check the logs and see if anyone has reported a vehicle stolen."

"Good." Jackson turned to Evans.

She had a peculiar look on her face. "I want to help, but I have a suspect in the interrogation room."

"What?" Confusion and anger fused with his anguish. "Who is he? Why didn't you say something?"

"*Her* name is Catalina Morales. She drives a light-blue Nissan pickup, which may have been parked at the Pershing house the day before Andra Caiden died."

Jackson couldn't see the connection. "How did you find her? And why was she at the house?"

"Catalina had a relationship with Logan Grayson, the football player who died. I went to his memorial service this morning and saw her leaving in the blue truck." Evans looked pained and lowered herself back into the chair. "So I brought her in for questioning. I thought you might want to take the lead. But then you got the text . . ."

Yesterday, it would have felt like a breakthrough. Right now, it annoyed him. But the woman had to be questioned. What if she knew Wagner? Or the freaky teenager next door? Or whoever the hell they were dealing with? "Let's go talk to her. We can't do much until we hear from the kidnapper again." He strode toward the door, then turned back. "Quince, call Sprint and get them to track Katie's phone."

The woman behind the table in the stark windowless room looked young and scared. And pregnant. Jackson took a seat, and Evans joined him, easing into the hard chair. He didn't have time for niceties. "My daughter is missing, and I'm in a foul mood. So don't lie to me and don't waste my time."

Her lips trembled. "I don't know what you're talking about."

He needed to locate the kidnapper first, then figure out what had happened at the Pershing house after he had Katie back. "How do you know Carl Wagner?"

"I don't. Really!"

"Have you ever lived in Salt Lake City?"

"No. I moved here from Sacramento with my sister five years ago, and I've never lived anywhere else."

"How do you know Andra Caiden?"

"Who?"

The suspect might not know her real name. "Amanda Carter."

A pause. "I don't know her either."

He slammed the table. "Don't lie to me! She was murdered, and you're the only person I can connect to the crime. Tell me what happened."

She blinked rapidly, color draining from her rosy cheeks. "When was she killed?"

"You tell me!"

"I don't know. I never met her."

"But you know who she is."

Catalina burst into tears, then began to sob. And didn't stop. Frustrated, Jackson stood. "Would you like some water?"

She didn't answer.

His phone beeped. Another text. He left the room, opening it as he went. The message was from Sophie Speranza. *Not now,* he thought. But he read it anyway, amazed at her timing: *Call me ASAP. A rental scammer may have killed Amanda Carter.* He'd never told Sophie the victim's real name. Now he had to call her. Maybe the reporter had details that could help him crack open Catalina's story.

As he dialed, Evans stepped out of the room. "I'm getting her a soda. Want one?"

"Please."

Sophie answered, sounding more tightly wound than usual. "You mentioned the victim, Amanda Carter, was found in a nearly empty house. And I just conducted a sting on a rental scammer who calls herself Tessa. A similar setup. Want to hear about it?"

A sting? She was too much. "Tell me." He knew Sophie expected something in exchange, and he was pressed for time. "And yes, I'll give you more information."

"Great. Here's the short version. Tessa advertised on Craigslist for a roommate to share a house, then gave me a story about how her last roommate moved out, took all her stuff, and left her without rent money. After I had the address, I found the owner's name and concluded the house had been abandoned. So I met her there, signed her phony rental agreement, and gave her cash. A cameraman who was with me filmed the whole thing."

What the hell? Had Andra been the victim of a rental scam gone wrong? Or had she been victimized twice by different assholes?

Sophie kept talking. "Maybe something similar happened to Amanda. Maybe even the same scammer or group of scammers."

"What do you know about Tessa?"

"Not much. I'm sure the name is fake, and she wore a hooded sweatshirt and sunglasses. But she's driving a silver Toyota, and I have her license plate."

"Tell me."

Jackson wrote it down as she talked. He cut her off. "I have to go. This case is bigger now. But the victim's real name is Andra Caiden. She's from Salt Lake City and she has a three-year-old boy who survived the incident." He hung up before she could ask more questions. The father/kidnapper already knew Benjie was here. Releasing info about him now might bring a legitimate family member forward.

While he waited for Evans, he hurried upstairs to their work area, the building strangely quiet. He called out to Schak and Quince, "Got anything yet?"

Quince stood and talked over the cubical wall. "A yellow Volkswagen van was stolen this morning from the Sundance Market."

"That's a half mile from my house. Get a bulletin on the vehicle now."

"Yes, sir."

Schak stepped out of his cube. "Nothing yet from Wagner's phone company, but they've prioritized it and promised to call back within the hour."

Jackson had second thoughts about calling the feds. Would the FBI be able to apply more pressure? Should he get Agent River involved? They'd worked a kidnapping together before, but she'd had to bring tech people down from Portland, a two-hour drive. He wanted to have the bastard in custody before then. "Let me know as soon as you have it. I'm going back to the interrogation room."

CHAPTER 38

Catalina had stopped crying and was drinking a Pepsi. Evans sat next to her, coaxing the suspect to make a deal so her baby wouldn't be born to a prisoner.

Jackson stayed on his feet. "We know the Pershing house was a scam. You went there to meet Amanda Carter, take her rent money, then disappear. What happened to her?"

"I never met her."

Evasive, but maybe not a lie. "Who are your partners? What is Tessa's real name?"

She blinked rapidly but didn't speak.

Jackson raised his voice. "We're going to hit you with a murder charge if you don't tell us everything you know about the Pershing house and Amanda's death." Considering the rape/strangulation theory, it didn't seem likely Catalina had committed the crime, but he couldn't rule it out either.

"Yes, we used the house to make some cash. We ran an ad on Craigslist and picked Amanda to rent to."

Evans cut in, "You and Logan Grayson?"

"Yes. He was trying to help me get money together so I could see a doctor. I've been having pain from my pregnancy."

Please don't let her miscarry in this room. Jackson pressed ahead. "When and where did the money change hands?"

"At the rental house, Sunday afternoon."

"You were there?"

"No. Logan handled this one."

"This wasn't the first?"

"I want a deal. I won't incriminate myself unless you promise I'm not going to jail."

"That's up to the district attorney. But I'll work with him to get you probation only. Unless you killed Amanda and your DNA turns up on the murder weapon."

"I never met her! I swear." Catalina hiccupped in the middle, then held her breath.

"You participated in other rental scams, correct? Composed e-mails? Spent the money?"

"Yes." Another hiccup.

Pregnancy did weird things to the diaphragm, and he wanted to wrap this up before she started puking. "Did you go to the Pershing house on Monday?"

"No."

"Quit wasting my time and tell me who did."

"I don't know. Logan was at my apartment for most of the evening, but after he did the coke, he took off. He said he had to run an errand."

Evans leaned forward. "You lied to me. You said he was with you all evening."

"I know. I'm sorry."

"Why did you lie?" Evans pressed.

"To protect him. Logan's a good guy." A pause for more hiccups. "He was under a lot of pressure, and some of it's my fault for getting pregnant."

Jackson turned to Evans. "Do we have his DNA?"

"In blood samples at the state lab."

"Let's get a comparison to Andra Caiden's trace evidence." He turned back to the suspect. "Did Logan know Amanda?"

A crease appeared between her eyebrows. "Why would he? She was just a loser who answered the rental ad."

Jackson wanted to shake her up. "Logan had sex with Amanda before she died. He probably killed her too." Jackson wasn't convinced, but it was starting to seem possible.

"No!" She jumped up and kicked her chair. "He wouldn't cheat on me. And he didn't kill anybody."

Evans was on her feet now too. "What about Danica? Logan was still seeing the cheerleader, and she's got bruises. Logan had a mean, violent streak, didn't he?"

"No." So soft they barely heard it.

Jackson wished he knew more about Evans' case. And he still needed to tell Evans about Sophie's sting and the other scammer named Tessa.

Catalina was crying again and still hiccupping.

Evans started toward the door. "I'll get you some water." The new building had a drinking faucet right outside.

Jackson didn't have the luxury of giving the suspect a break. "What time did Logan come back to your place?"

"He didn't. He called me later and said he didn't feel well and needed to go home."

"What time did he call?"

"I'm not sure." Another hiccup.

"Look in your phone."

"I don't have it. The lady cop took it."

Evans came into the room with the water, and Jackson turned to her. "Do you have Catalina's phone on you? She needs to check the time of a call." He needed to know if Logan Grayson had the opportunity to kill Andra. His motive was still unclear. And if he hadn't killed her, then Wagner or the teenage sociopath probably had.

"I have it, but drink this first." She handed Catalina the glass. "Drink it all at once while I cover your ears with my hands. It'll get rid of your hiccups."

Jackson watched the process, his impatience growing. The kidnapper still had Katie, and they were not any closer to figuring out who or where he was.

The suspect choked at the end and couldn't finish the water, but her hiccups stopped anyway. She scrolled back in her phone and found the log from nearly a week before.

"Logan called at nine thirty-six. He was driving, I could tell."

Andra had been killed between eight and ten, so Grayson could have done it. But why?

Evans asked, "When he took cocaine, did it make him angry?"

She shrugged. "Mostly hyper. Sometimes impatient."

Evans had the lead now. "Sexually aggressive?"

"Sometimes."

"Were the two of you still sexually active or did your pregnancy interfere?"

Catalina picked at a fingernail. "I told you. I've been having pain and needed to see a doctor. So we hadn't had sex in a while." More tears. "That doesn't mean he cheated on me with a stranger."

Jackson had to get out of the room. "We'll be back." He bolted for the door. Knowing more about the circumstances of Andra's death was a relief, but it wasn't helping him find Katie. He wanted to be out there, searching. Even driving around would feel better than waiting.

As he and Evans conferred in the space outside the holding cell, keeping some distance between themselves, Schak thundered down the nearby stairs. "They located Wagner's phone. He's in Pocatello, Idaho."

What the hell?

CHAPTER 39

They were back in the conference room, and Jackson couldn't sit still, so he paced and speculated. "Just because Wagner's phone is in Idaho, doesn't mean he is."

"True." Schak nodded. "He could have left the phone in the RV just to throw us off."

"How did he get here?" Evans stood at the board, asking for suggestions.

"He probably drove. It's only ten or twelve hours from Idaho." Jackson had called Susan Wagner's number at least five times that morning, hoping for some cooperation, but she had ignored him. Now he suspected she wanted Benjie back too. She probably wouldn't believe her husband had killed the surrogate mother. Jackson wasn't sure *he* still believed Wagner had killed Andra. But the father was the only one with motive. Evans suspected Logan Grayson had snorted tainted cocaine, then died of a heart attack. But whether the football player stopped at the Pershing house to rape and/or kill Andra between those two occurrences was still an unknown. Grayson and Andra could have had consensual sex, then Benjie's father, also still an unknown, could have shown up later.

He turned back to the group, which had gone quiet. "We need to call the state lab and get our DNA work prioritized."

"It's Saturday," Evans reminded him.

Jackson bit back another outburst. "Why hasn't the kidnapper contacted us again?" A pointless question.

Quince's phone rang and they all jumped. He answered it, then was silent. Jackson held his breath. Finally, Quince said, "Sprint tracked Katie's phone to a shopping center at Fortieth and Donald."

"Let's get a patrol car out there."

"Would he be stupid enough to hold on to her phone after using it?" Evans' tone indicated she didn't think so.

"He's acting irrationally on some levels," Jackson responded. "But he's also clever enough to steal vehicles and avoid detection." A headache had been building, and now it felt like a vice grip was pressing into his temples. He looked in his carryall for aspirin. "The perp probably ditched the phone or tossed it into the back of a truck or something."

"He'll have to arrange a meet," Evans said. "We can close in when he does."

The desk officer barged in. "A patrol unit spotted a black Malibu with silver details in the parking lot at the Hilyard Community Center. The vehicle was empty, but he called in the license, and it belongs to Eleanor Marsh. He's trying to contact her."

Damn. Probably stolen. The community center was also near his home. "Thanks. Do you have the plate number?"

The clerk handed him the registration information and left.

"He stole a vehicle to conduct the first attempt this morning," Schak said. "Then stole another one for the second abduction. He's cautious."

"Only on some levels," Jackson argued. "Kidnapping a child from a police officer's home is irrational."

"And audacious," Evans added. "What do we do with Catalina? We can't leave her in the pit indefinitely."

"Get her something to eat, then put her in the soft room. She can lay down on the couch."

Evans locked eyes with him. "I don't think she knows Wagner or had anything to do with the murder or kidnapping."

"I'm inclined to agree. But what if we're wrong? What if she gave up Andra's location to Wagner? What if she knows how to contact the perp? Katie's life is at stake."

"We'll get your daughter back soon," she promised. "He wants the boy and won't just go away."

His phone rang and he snatched it from the table. "Jackson here."

"Is Benjie with you?"

The kidnapper! "He will be soon."

"Not good enough. I want to hear him speak. And you need to send a time-stamped picture of him from your phone." The kidnapper's voice was low and scratchy.

Had he heard it somewhere before?

"Do it quickly," the man continued. "I'll be gone before the feds can set up. But if I leave town without my son, you'll never see your daughter again."

Bastard! Jackson locked his jaw to keep from responding. He'd heard the perp's voice somewhere, but he didn't associate it with Carl Wagner. Whoever he was, they needed to build rapport. "I haven't called the FBI, and I have no reason to keep your son from you. Benjie should be with his family. But I have to know that Katie is alive. Let me talk to her."

The perp had hung up.

Jackson forced himself to breathe deeply. No more outbursts. No more emotional blindness. He had to stay focused. To be as cold and calculating as his adversary.

"Should we get Agent River?" Quince said. "The FBI can trace phone calls and put a chopper in the air if we need it."

Jackson knew it was the right thing. It was also pointless. "Go ahead and call the bureau, but I'm not waiting two hours for their tech people to get here. The kidnapper wants to hear from Benjie, so I'm heading over to McCray's."

"We need a damn plan!" Schak sounded rattled.

"We can't plan until we know when and how he wants to do the exchange." Jackson clapped his partner's shoulder. "He's calling the shots, for now. We have to play it out."

"I'm coming with you." Schak pushed to his feet.

"Thanks." Jackson turned to Quince and held out his phone with the latest call displaying. "Try to track down this phone number." To Evans, he said, "You're not going out in the field today. You're injured."

She didn't argue, but that didn't mean she would go along. "Have McCray bring Benjie here," Evans suggested. "That way we can all network and plan."

It made sense but it worried him. "What if the perp intercepts Benjie? He could be sitting in a vehicle across the street, watching us."

"He doesn't know where Benjie is. That's why he took Katie. We just have to meet McCray outside to protect him." Evans looked pale and pained, but her eyes were on fire. "We're a fucking police department. He's not going to grab him from our parking lot. If he does, we'll crush him."

Jackson almost smiled. He loved her fierceness. "Good plan. I'll call McCray now. Go move Catalina and tell her no deal until she gives up all her conspirators, including Tessa. If she won't talk, we'll have an officer book her into jail after we have eyes on the perp."

Evans gave him a warning look—one that meant he'd better not do anything stupid while she was gone.

CHAPTER 40

Evans escorted Catalina to the bathroom, then took her to a larger interrogation room with a comfortable couch and chair. They typically used it for underage suspects and their parents or witness/suspects that needed a gentle, coercive touch.

"Why are you keeping me here?" she complained. "I've told you everything I know."

"You committed fraud, so your next stop is jail. Enjoy the couch while you can."

"I thought I was getting a deal."

"You haven't told us who Tessa is."

"I don't know Tessa." Catalina looked away as she flopped on the couch.

Probably a lie. "We will find her too, and whoever talks first gets the best deal." Evans didn't know who Tessa was, but Jackson seemed to think the woman was involved in another rental scam. Which meant she might be connected to Logan Grayson or Carl Wagner. Not knowing where or how Jackson had received the information bothered her, but his daughter's kidnapping had taken precedence over everything.

"I'm hungry. My baby needs to eat."

"I'll get you a protein bar." Evans headed toward her cubicle, then remembered she didn't have her shoulder bag with its wide assortment of work tools and emergency supplies. She'd left it home when she went undercover to the party the night before. *Damn.* She felt a little worthless without it. But with Jackson's daughter in the hands of a kidnapper, she didn't have time to go home for it. Or the willpower. With the pain she was experiencing, she couldn't bear the idea of going up and down the stairs and across the parking lot twice.

Yet her shoulder bag also had the evidence she'd picked up from the crime lab the day before. Items that had been in the car seat folds of Andra's vehicle, including a tube of lip gloss, a baby's pacifier, and a ticket stub. She'd called the Maverick Center in Salt Lake City, hoping to identify the event on the stub, but the phone had rung unanswered until she finally hung up. Later, she'd gone to the party and ended up in the hospital and hadn't been home since. How important could a ticket from an event four years earlier be? The pink cancer-awareness bracelet from the Pershing house might be important though. She assumed Joe had scraped the inside of it for skin-cell DNA.

Evans bought a bag of chips and some peanut M&M's from the vending machine in the break room and took them to Catalina.

She scowled. "My baby needs real food."

"I know, but this is the best I could do for now. Tell me who Tessa is, and we'll order in whatever you want."

Catalina silently opened the bag of M&M's. Evans started toward the door.

"She's my sister." Her voice was quiet, almost ashamed. "Her name is Angelina Morales. The whole thing was her idea."

Evans turned back, wishing she had her recorder. "Was she in the car with you when you left the memorial?"

"Yes."

Then she knew where to find her. She'd watched Catalina drop her off. "We'll need a detailed statement of the scams you pulled with Angelina's involvement. I'll get someone in here soon to process you."

"Can I have my phone? I'm bored."

"Not yet."

Evans hurried out, happy to pass off the fraud case to the Financial Crimes Unit. She had to call Sergeant Lammers, who would call her own boss, and then the captain would contact another detective who specialized in fraud cases. The rental scams were minor crimes, but Angelina might link to bigger criminals. Evans hoped to question the sister about Logan Grayson and cocaine at some point too, but it wasn't a priority today. But turning in the coke she'd bought from Marcos at the party was critical. She would do it on her way home. Or maybe call Joe or Parker and ask them to pick it up.

She stopped at her desk to make those calls and check her e-mail. As soon as she pressed Lammers' name in her phone, she regretted it. What if the boss asked about Andra's case? Jackson might not want Lammers to know anything about Katie's kidnapping until it was over. *Please don't answer!*

"What have you got, Evans?"

Shit! She couldn't lie. "A case of fraud I need to pass to Financial Crimes. It developed out of Logan Grayson's case." Another bad move. Were the pain pills making her stupid?

"I thought I told you to let that one go and help Jackson with his investigation." Lammers wasn't yelling, so Evans held hope it wouldn't get ugly.

"I attended his memorial. You know the victim's family appreciates it."

"I thought you were in the hospital. Schak said you were badly injured." Now her boss sounded confused.

"I've got two cracked ribs and a lot of bruises, but I'm functional." She wanted to wrap it up and get back to the conference room. "Anyway, I've got a young woman in the soft pit who wants to give a full statement, naming her conspirators, in exchange for leniency. I thought Financial Crimes should handle it."

"I'll get someone, but how did this come up?"

Evans was desperate to hang up, and she had to keep this simple. "I discovered that Grayson and his girlfriend were involved in a rental scam.

"Is this connected to Jackson's case?" Lammers was getting loud. "He won't answer my calls. What's really going on here?"

Oh hell. "We had a new development this morning involving the victim's son." Evans couldn't continue, afraid for Jackson's career if she said too much and afraid for herself if she lied to her boss. "I have to go. The fraud suspect is pregnant, and I have to check on her. Please get another detective in here soon." She hung up before Lammers could respond.

On her way back to the team, she racked her brain for ideas to help identify Benjie's kidnapper and wrap up the case. Carl Wagner, a fifty-year-old married man traveling with his wife, didn't seem to fit the profile of a sociopath obsessed with taking custody of his biological son. She hoped to steer Jackson in a new direction, but she didn't have anything better.

Evans scanned through her phone log, looking for the Utah call she'd made the day before. She stepped into the conference room, where the team was discussing possible exchange scenarios involving Katie and Benjie.

"Anything new?" she asked.

"No. We're waiting for McCray to get here with Benjie, so I can prove to the kidnapper I intend to cooperate." Jackson's skin had a grayish tint, and his eyes were tight with stress. He seemed to have aged significantly in the two years she'd known him.

"What about the number he called from?" she asked.

"Probably a stolen phone. Verizon is tracking it, but no word yet. And Katie's phone was tucked into a cyclist's bike pack. This guy is very careful."

Evans hesitated, then gave the update on Catalina, including her call to Lammers. "I didn't tell her about the Nissan truck, the kidnapping, or that these cases overlapped. I'll let you handle that."

Jackson grimaced. "Updating the boss will have to wait. This is developing too quickly to handle any other way." He looked at each of them. "You don't have to go along. I'm not asking you to do anything you're uncomfortable with."

"We're on board," Schak said, before she could.

Jackson's phone rang, and it was McCray, announcing he was in the front parking lot with Benjie. Jackson and Schak went down to open the gate and let him into the back lot where they could come upstairs without being seen from the street. Evans stayed, not wanting to push herself physically until she had to. While they were gone, Quince stepped out to make a call, and she redialed the Maverick Center in Salt Lake City.

The number rang eight times, and just as she was about to hang up again, a young person answered, sounding rattled. "Ticket counter. Can you hold?"

"No. I'm with the police," Evans said in a rush.

A startled gasp. "What do you want?"

"I need to know what event was held at the Maverick Center on January thirteenth, 2010."

"I don't have time to find that. I'm not even sure I can."

"This is a murder investigation. I'm staying on the line until you get me the information."

The clerk whimpered a little. "I'll have to call my boss."

"Write down my phone number!" Loud and aggressive seemed necessary for the situation. If the clerk hung up, the lead went back to being a dead end. Evans gave her the number and made her read it back. After they hung up, she told herself to let the detail go. The clerk probably wouldn't call back, and the information probably didn't matter. If things went their way this afternoon, they would have the perp in custody soon anyway.

The guys came back with Jackson carrying Benjie, who clung to him like a boy whose father was back from deployment. What would happen when this was over? Did Jackson have a plan for the kid?

"Hey, McCray, good to see you." Evans squeezed his arm. He still wore brown corduroy and looked like he hadn't eaten in a week. She'd heard he was volunteering on cold case files with other retired detectives, but they hadn't crossed paths in a while.

"Thanks." He looked around at the big wall monitor and comfortable chairs. "The city finally came through. For twenty-five years I broke my ass on one of those metal fold-up pieces of crap."

"You just need more padding," Schak said with a laugh.

"I'm calling the perp now," Jackson announced. "But I'm not optimistic he still has the phone."

They all went quiet. Evans thought about the last time the five of them had been together. A triple homicide. Right before the worst of the budget cuts. Right before McCray got hit with a stray bullet during a takedown.

After a long wait, Jackson clicked off. "It went to voicemail. A woman's message. The last phone he used must have been stolen." He set Benjie down, got him started on a puzzle, then paced the room. "We have to wait for him to contact us." He turned to Quince. "Did you call the FBI?"

"Yes. They're pulling together a team now. You need to update Sergeant Lammers."

Jackson nodded but kept pacing.

Evans' phone rang, and it was the rattled clerk at the ticket office. "The event the night you asked about was a fundraiser for the Salt Lake City Police Department."

The unexpected report gave her a prickly sensation. "Thanks." She clicked off and glanced up. Everyone was looking at her. "I don't know if it's relevant, but I picked up some items Joe found in Andra's car seats. One was a ticket stub from four years ago. I just learned that the event was a fundraiser for the Salt Lake police."

Jackson mulled it over. "Andra's friend who told me about the surrogacy is married to a police sergeant, so I'm not surprised to hear she attended a police function."

Evans voiced her concerns. "I don't think Wagner is our perp. He's older and married and traveling around in a motor home. He doesn't seem to fit the profile of a custody-issue stalker."

"I know that, dammit," Jackson said, rubbing his temples. "But Wagner has means and motive. And we don't have anyone else."

The prickly sensation again. "What if the perp is a police officer? You know the profession attracts control freaks and egomaniacs. Plus you talked to people in the Salt Lake department, alerting them to the case."

Schak nodded. "That would explain why he's confident, yet careful."

Jackson's eyes widened and his jaw tightened. "I think I know who he is."

CHAPTER 41

Buckley left the girl duct-taped to a chair and went out to search for a place to make the exchange. His brain had been firing on all cylinders since he'd grabbed the girl, and now his nerves were jumping too. He had so much riding on this and so little time. Knowing almost nothing about Eugene made it even harder. But if he was smart and played this right, he'd finally get his boy back and they could move somewhere, start over, and be a family. If he mishandled it, he would end up dead. Suicide by cop, if that's the way it had to go down. He wasn't going to prison.

He drove toward the center of town, thinking he needed a public place where he could disappear into a crowd, then steal another car. He didn't intend to bring the girl to the exchange. The logistics were too challenging. Plus, she was a police officer's kid. She probably wouldn't come along quietly just because he put a gun to her side. He had something a little more extreme in mind— a plan that could prove fatal for her if Jackson double-crossed him. He was counting on the other father to value his own child more than someone else's. That was human nature.

His window was down and music played in the distance. Buckley made a left turn on an angled street and drove toward the sound. A few blocks later, he entered a neighborhood with crowded sidewalks. Hordes of people wandered in and out of shops, galleries, and restaurants. The music grew louder, and he followed a group of young people down a side street. Cars lined both sides and dozens of people of all ages gathered in front of a large house where a band played in the yard. These people weren't from Utah or any middle-class neighborhood he'd ever seen. It was a block party for hippies and hoodlums.

Which could be perfect. He drove past the crowd, moving slowly, as people wandered into the street without looking. At the corner, a couple performed gymnastics on their front lawn for another crowd of onlookers. Another band played in the distance and he turned left, eventually coming to a large gated lot where vendors had set up booths. Every parking space was taken and he moved slowly past, craning through the metal fence to see what the attractions were. Food booths, a tattoo station, and jewelry vendors mostly. It was hard to see through the thick crowds.

A group in front moved, and he noticed the main booth. An information center with a door that opened into a gated court. Perfect.

The car behind him honked, and he pulled forward, nearly hitting a naked man with dreadlocks riding a bicycle. *For Pete's sake!* Why didn't someone arrest the pervert? He couldn't wait to get out of this crazy town and back to a quiet, rural, God-fearing place where he could raise his boy to be the kind of man he should be.

It took ten minutes to drive clear of all the crowds, which included another party at a huge brewery. He stopped at the

7-Eleven on the corner and waited for two young boys to come out of the store. They both had cell phones in their hands. Irritated and impatient, he grabbed one of their phones, held up his old badge, and said, "Don't fuck up this operation. Just keep moving, and I'll get it back to you."

One teenager started to protest, but Buckley grabbed him by the shirt. "Shut the fuck up." He jumped into the stolen SUV he was driving and gunned it into the street. Even if the kids called the local police, it would be hours or maybe days before anyone took their statement.

When he was headed back toward the motel, his nerves started to settle down. Three years later, and he still couldn't believe Andra had stolen baby Ben from the hospital and disappeared. That bitch had signed a contract! A private contract they'd all kept secret, but still, they'd paid her well and Ben was his son.

What heartbreak they'd been through, especially Melissa. Even after spending a fortune on fertility treatments, the eggs they'd created at the clinic hadn't implanted. His wife's uterus wasn't geared toward a pregnancy. Then through his friend and fellow police officer, they'd met Andra, and learned that she'd been abandoned by her family, church, and fiancé, and needed money to move away and start over. One night after they'd mentioned their fertility issues, she'd half-jokingly offered to carry a child for them. Melissa had hesitated, but he'd wanted to go for it. The surrogacy had seemed like a win for everyone.

He drove west, barely noticing traffic, lost in the memory of what had brought him to this fucked-up situation.

Halfway through Andra's pregnancy, his wife had been shot dead in a carjacking outside their home. While he was stunned and grieving, a detective in his department—a coworker—had hauled him in for questioning. Melissa's mother had apparently told investigators she thought he'd done it. *The bitch!* Buckley slammed his hands against the steering wheel. She'd started this whole fucking thing.

The next month had turned into a nightmare. A witness had come forward and described someone who looked like him. Before long, he was hounded by the press, arrested by his department, and subjected to a search of his home. Eventually, the charges had been dropped because they had no case. By then, his life was ruined. Not only had he lost his wife, but his job, his reputation, and thousands in defense lawyer fees. All he had left was his unborn son. Then the cunt had stolen baby Ben. He'd gone a little insane that day.

Now it was time to reclaim his boy and salvage what he could of his life.

Buckley parked across the street from the motel, knowing he needed to ditch the vehicle and steal another one. But first he had to call Jackson again. He needed to hear Ben's voice and see his sweet little face. He knew how cops functioned and that Jackson would try to trick him, so he had to stay a step ahead. He was counting on Jackson's emotional identity as a father to override his duty as a police officer. Today, at the exchange, they would just be two dads, each reuniting with their child, the person they loved most in the world. Jackson might not come alone, but the other cop wouldn't risk his daughter by bringing in the feds or refusing to give up the boy—a child he wasn't connected to.

He reached for the stolen cell phone, asking God to get him through the final act of this tragic episode.

Buckley had tracked Andra to Bremerton in the first few months, but once he arrived in town, she'd been gone. He blamed Christy Chadwell for tipping her off. In the meantime, the trail had gone cold. Andra seemed to have disappeared. Eventually, he'd learned that Andra's grandmother lived in Drain, Oregon. Last summer, he'd driven down and watched the house for a while.

It had quickly become obvious that Andra and Ben weren't living with her. Then last week, he'd asked his friends, Carl and Susan Wagner, to check on Lucille Caiden when they passed through Lane County on their road trip. Again, he'd been disappointed to learn that Andra and Ben still weren't with her.

Having Jackson show up at the Salt Lake department looking for Ben's family had been an answered prayer. God wanted him to get his son back. He'd believed that from the beginning and had never given up hope. He'd taken the same flight to Eugene as Jackson, keeping his hat over his face and sleeping for most of it. Once they landed, he'd stolen the Tahoe, followed Jackson home, and waited for him to leave again.

He resented that he'd been forced to become a criminal just to claim his rightful child. But he couldn't trust the court system. His contract with Andra had not been notarized, he'd been investigated for murder, and he'd had some anger issues after Melissa died. The courts also favored mothers, even if they were a surrogate. And he'd never been able to get close enough to Ben to get a DNA sample that would prove his paternity. A judge would never give him custody. This was his only chance to be a father. The system had left him with no other choice.

Buckley pressed the number he'd memorized from the business card Jackson had given Dan Chadwell, then keyed in a message: *Send Ben's pic with proof then get ready.* Jackson would know what he meant. He regretted calling earlier and talking to Jackson in person, but the other cop obviously hadn't recognized his voice. He'd only spoken a few words that day outside the Utah department, but since then his joy and excitement had been hard to contain. He was so close now. In a few hours, he would have his son, and they would be on the road to their new life together.

CHAPTER 42

Two weeks earlier

Andra Caiden put down her phone and burst into tears. Another property management company had turned her down. How could she ever develop a decent rental history if she had to keep moving and changing her name?

"Mommy?" Benjie looked up from where he worked a puzzle on the floor.

"I'm fine, sweetie." She gave him a bright smile. "How's the new puzzle?"

"It's fine."

He often mimicked whatever she'd just said, so she tried not to swear. But she had to get out of this shitty little quad unit. It was no place for a child. The guy who had just moved in next door—and shared a kitchen with her and two others—showed way too much interest in Benjie. The creep was a pedophile, for sure. She'd already given the manager notice, but with a limited amount of cash and no long-term rental history, she couldn't find an apart-ment she could get into. Frustrating! She liked Eugene and didn't want to leave. Such a pretty town, and the community college had a nursing school, which she wanted to attend someday. But it would never happen. Staying that long was a risk.

"I'll find a new place soon." She went to the fridge for a beer. Her one indulgence, and only on days off.

"With a yard and a swing?" Benjie said, his little voice full of hope.

"Maybe."

More than anything, she wanted Benjie to live in a real home with his own bedroom and a yard. It broke her heart to see him cooped up in this little studio. Had she done the right thing three years ago? She had no doubt that keeping him from his violent contract father was the right decision. After Carson Buckley had killed his wife, she knew she couldn't honor their agreement. But she'd needed the money to leave Utah and start over, so she couldn't bring herself to give it back. She'd also been too afraid to even confront him about it. After the shooting, he'd become angry and hostile and she'd worried about what Benjie's life would be like with him.

She couldn't let her baby grow up like she had, with a domi-neering man who treated his children like possessions. The tattoo had covered her father's brand, but the scar went much deeper. The more she'd learned about Buckley, the more controlling he'd seemed. For a while, she'd considered finding another couple to adopt the baby, so he could have a real family and a secure life. But once Benjie was born and she'd seen his little face, she'd fallen hopelessly in love.

Andra scooted to the floor to help Benjie with his puzzle for a few minutes. Maybe this time she needed to find a roommate. Another woman who already had a house and wanted to rent out a couple of bedrooms. It wouldn't be ideal, but it would be a better environment than this tiny space where they shared a bed. It might even be nice to have an adult housemate as well. Benjie and her caregiver work kept her busy during the day, but her nights were lonely. She'd been alone for years, and a boyfriend seemed out of the question. She had to be ready to pick up and move on a moment's notice. But Benjie was worth it. She loved her son more than life itself.

After the puzzle, Andra went back to scanning Craigslist for rooms and found a surprising offer. A young couple wanted to share their house and didn't require a deposit. She responded to the ad, saying she wanted both bedrooms, if they were okay with having a child in the house. Then she crossed her fingers. Maybe this would turn out well. Maybe her luck was about to change.

CHAPTER 43

While they waited to hear from the kidnapper again, Jackson googled Carson Buckley and learned the ex-cop had been charged with murder. Based on the date of his wife's death and the news stories about the investigation, the incident had taken place during Andra's pregnancy. Jackson looked up at his team, who were either on their laptops or their phones, digging for leads. "No wonder Andra took the baby and ran. Buckley was charged with killing his wife."

"I see that," Evans said. "But the charges were dropped."

"Let's get his name and description out to patrol units. When we're sure, we'll notify the state police." Jackson visualized Buckley standing in front of the Utah police department, a big guy with brutally short gray hair, icy-gray eyes, and a scratchy voice that he now realized matched the kidnapper's. Buckley, the sergeant's friend, was one of five people in Salt Lake he'd spoken to about Andra. Jackson felt pretty damn sure he was their man.

Yet Buckley didn't know they were onto him—or he wouldn't have risked making a call instead of sending another text.

"We shouldn't let him know we've identified him," Evans said. "We don't want him wearing a disguise or going to ground."

"I was just thinking that. It's the only edge we've got."

Jackson's phone beeped and he checked his messages. But it wasn't a text. A photo of Katie, duct-taped to a chair, filled his screen. Her mouth was covered with tape, and her eyes were wide with terror. A black satchel leaned against the chair legs.

He sucked in a long breath, and his lungs seemed to fill with hot oil. For a moment he couldn't speak.

"What is it?" Evans reached for the phone. He didn't want anyone to see the photo of Katie, but that was emotional and foolish. He let Evans take the phone, then pass it to the others.

"We'll get the bastard," she promised. "Let's get this photo up on the monitor and see if we can locate where it was taken." She plugged his phone into the room's computer and started working the keyboard.

Jackson remembered that some cell phone pictures had embedded codes. "Let's get a tech guy in here too. The photo might have a GPS location."

Another text came in: *Send Ben's pic with proof then get ready.*

"It's time." Pulse escalating, Jackson stepped out of the room and into the open space by the windows, where Schak was playing trucks with the boy.

"Hey, Benjie, let's take a picture."

The boy stood. "With my truck!" He held up the toy and smiled.

Jackson walked over and kneeled next to Benjie. He put their faces together, held out his phone, and took a selfie, as Katie would call it. *Please let her be okay*, he pleaded, no longer sure who he was asking for help.

"Anything new?" Schak asked.

"The perp has a new cell phone and asked to see a photo of Benjie." Jackson sent the picture, and a wave of shame washed over him. He had no choice. He kept telling himself that—so he could move forward. "Quince is calling phone companies, trying to track the number, but I'm sure the perp will ditch the phone soon."

"Knowing he's an ex-cop should make this easier," Schak said, grunting as he got up from the floor. "But it doesn't. It makes him smart and unpredictable."

"And sadistic. He sent a photo of Katie. She's taped to a chair and looks terrified."

The return text came back in a minute: *Bring Ben to the info booth at the block party. Tell him it's a game, then walk away. Katie will be nearby. Now!*

"What block party?" He showed the text to Schak, his hand twitching from too much coffee and not enough sleep.

"In the Whiteaker neighborhood. We've got units out there."

"We have to go now." To Benjie, he said, "I'll be back in a moment and we'll get a snack."

"I want grapes!" His face lit up. The boy was finally coming around.

And he was about to abandon him again. "I think you'll have to settle for popcorn or something." It was probably the healthiest thing in the snack case.

"I like popcorn." Benjie took a little hop of excitement, and Jackson's heart lurched. Despite being on the run and dirt poor, Andra had raised Benjie to be good-natured and polite. Jackson vowed, again, to find and punish her killer. Which was probably an ex-cop named Carson Buckley—who had also murdered his own wife. He may have killed Andra's grandmother too, when she wouldn't reveal their location. Jackson couldn't believe he was about to hand Benjie over to the psychopath.

Footsteps thundered up the stairs, and his gut clenched.

"What the fuck is going on?" Sergeant Lammers shouted from the landing.

Benjie grabbed Jackson's leg and whined.

"Can we take this into the conference room?" Jackson extracted the boy and tried to soothe him. "Everything is fine. Will you play with your truck for another minute so I can talk to my boss?"

Benjie's little brow furrowed into worry. "Is she mean?"

"Sort of," he whispered.

Benjie whispered back, "Maybe she needs a hug."

Jackson almost laughed. That would be a good way to get a knee in the balls. "Be right back," he said to the boy.

He and Schak followed Lammers into the meeting room, leaving the door open so he could see Benjie.

Their boss stood near the door, arms crossed.

Jackson gave the short version first. "Someone tried to abduct Benjie from my house this morning, but he failed. This afternoon, the perp took my daughter hostage, and now he wants to trade." He showed Lammers the photo of Katie duct-taped to a chair.

"For fuck's sake!" Lammers' expression went from stunned, to sympathetic, to angry. "Why didn't you call me? Why isn't the FBI involved? What the fuck are you thinking?"

"It all happened fast, and we think we know who took him." He glossed over his focus on the Wagners. "The perp wants to meet and exchange—" Jackson paused, struggling with what to call their respective children. Katie was a hostage, but Benjie wasn't. "He wants to exchange the kids. My daughter for his son."

"Who is he and what is your plan?" She stared at Jackson, her eyes drilling into him.

"We think he's an ex-cop from Salt Lake City named Carson Buckley. Patrol units have his description, and we're heading out to meet him now."

"Meet him where and do what?"

"The information booth at the Whiteaker block party." The next part was harder to articulate. "I plan to make the exchange. Katie is a hostage and her life is at stake. We have to give him Benjie to save Katie."

Lammers started to shout, but he cut her off.

"We will not let him get away! We'll have four of us out there, plus patrol units. And we know what he looks like."

"That's a dangerous proposition. We don't negotiate with hostage takers."

"It's not a negotiation. It's a ransom. And we have to pay it to get Katie back."

Lammers slammed a hand on the table. "You can't pay with another's person's life!"

He knew that! The thought of handing Benjie over crushed him. But he had no other choice. "Buckley won't hurt the boy! He just wants custody. He'll grab him and run, but we'll stop him."

Lammers sat down and drummed the table with her fingers. "We need the feds involved."

"We called them, and they're pulling together a team. But you know how long it takes to get tech and surveillance people down from Portland." Jackson started for the door. "He wants this to happen now."

"So stall him."

"She's my daughter and I'm getting her back!" Jackson strode out and his team followed.

Benjie stood near the door, his cheeks dimpled with pleasure. "Where are we going?"

CHAPTER 44

McCray and Benjie rode with Jackson, while Schak, Quince, and Lammers each took their own car. The boss had come along in case important decisions—such as barricading streets—needed to be made. Lammers hadn't wanted McCray to go along, because he was no longer officially with the department, but he'd climbed in the backseat with Benjie, and Jackson had taken off.

They took the expressway to Sixth and Washington, which was only a short distance from the Whiteaker neighborhood. Jackson didn't know where the information booth was located within the eight-by-eight-block gathering, but instinct told him it would be on the north side, probably along Second or Third Avenue, the only areas with open spaces. As he approached the turn on Blair, he thought about the small, sleazy motels a few blocks farther out. Was Katie in one of them? That's where he would hole up if he were a criminal from out of town. Too bad they couldn't just bust open doors until they found her.

"I'll bet he stayed nearby in one of the hooker hangouts," McCray said, echoing his thoughts.

"Do you think Lammers would authorize a room-by-room search?"

"For six or seven motels? It would take too long, and the lawsuits would bankrupt the city." McCray sounded worried. "They're probably not there now anyway. He's got to be here in the neighborhood, waiting in a parked car."

"I'm sure you're right." The one thing they had going for them was that Buckley—with his height and military-short haircut—would stand out in the crowd. "He can't walk around with Katie being duct-taped, so he has to keep her down and out of sight." It was bizarre to talk about his daughter as a victim in a case he was handling. Keeping his emotions in check was duplicitous and exhausting. No way in hell could he purposely stall this encounter. He was desperate to get it over with.

The orange ball of sun was sinking toward the horizon, reminding him they only had an hour of daylight left. A few blocks later, he had to slow down. The boulevard was crammed with cars, street performers, and spectators milling around. *Goddammit!* The crowd could make their job impossible. Buckley had chosen a good location—and lucked out with his timing.

"What are they doing?" Benjie asked, excited by the activity.

"It's a street party," McCray said. "Like a birthday for the neighborhood."

While waiting for traffic to move and pedestrians to cross, Jackson scanned the side streets, looking for a tall man in a parked car. It took five minutes to drive three blocks, and his upper body broke into a sweat. Knowing that patrol units were also searching the area gave him little comfort. Cars lined every inch of every street and filled every driveway, and the crowds were thicker than he'd ever seen at any neighborhood event, including campus parties.

The perp could be wearing a hooded sweatshirt or one of the wild party hats being sold by corner vendors. Or he could have stolen a tie-dyed shirt to make himself blend with the subculture crowd. A wave of panic washed over him. What if Buckley had already killed Katie to simplify things for himself? What if he took Benjie and got away? Jackson couldn't imagine his life without either of them.

A group of drunk young men stood in the road near the brewery. He honked and gestured for them to move. They ignored him.

"Want me to get out and use my powers of persuasion?" McCray asked.

A cop joke for drawing a weapon. "Not yet."

Jackson honked again, and a young man flipped him off. The others laughed. He let off the brake, inched forward, and honked again. They sauntered slowly off the road, and he was finally able to turn down Second Avenue.

An even thicker crowd greeted them, and the music was overwhelming. On the left, a band played in an open lot, but he couldn't see the musicians because of the large audience. On the right, shops lined the street—but only halfway. He stopped near a large corner lot with metal fencing and a ticket-taker at the gate. Select vendors were inside, and an information booth butted up against the fence in front. This was the drop spot.

Jackson radioed his team, which now included patrol units: "The information booth is on Second between Van Buren and Jackson Streets. North side." The department had recently started using a scrambler that kept people with CB radios from listening in. The public wasn't happy about it, but the change gave operations like this one a better chance of success. Especially since

Buckley was an ex-cop who would know how to monitor their activities.

A car behind him honked. *Damn!* He needed a moment to check things out, but there was nowhere to park. He also didn't have time for a confrontation with an asshole driver. For now, he had to circle the block and let the cars behind him clear out. He radioed Lammers and asked for blockades at both ends of the street. As soon as he visualized the setup, he worried that the perp would see the blockade and know he'd brought reinforcements. Jackson almost radioed again to tell the patrol units to wait, then decided to let it stand. Buckley wanted his son more than he wanted anything else, and he'd already demonstrated recklessness and impatience. He wouldn't be able to resist an opportunity to grab the boy and run.

He put his car in gear and rolled slowly forward. The great, terrifying unknown was Katie. Where the hell was she? And how did Buckley plan to release her? His daughter could be sitting in the information booth right now, thirty feet from him, not moving or speaking under the threat of violence.

Reluctantly, he turned the corner and began to circle. The side streets had less traffic, and it took less time than he thought it would. In the rearview mirror, he caught sight of Schak's sedan. He hoped Quince and Lammers were hanging back and keeping spread out. He was anxious to hear the radio crackle and someone to announce they'd seen Buckley.

"Why haven't we heard from him?" McCray wondered from the backseat.

"I think he's waiting for me to tell him Benjie is at the drop spot. Or he's watching the spot and waiting for me to show up."

A patrol unit was moving into place at the Blair intersection when he completed his circle around the block. The officer backed up and let him through, and Schak's car followed. His phone rang and he jerked his hand up to his earpiece. "Jackson here."

"I said no backup!" Buckley yelled.

"My partner insisted on following me. I couldn't stop him." Jackson parked in the street near the information booth, noticing only a woman behind the front counter. Thirty-something with a loose colorful dress, she didn't look like a kidnap collaborator.

"Bullshit! I saw two squad cars earlier. I will kill her if you fuck with me!"

Jackson's pulse raced and he scrambled for the right response. "The patrol units are here to keep an eye on this crowd. Standard department procedure. They don't know anything about our exchange." Nerves jumping, he wanted to get out of the car, but the damn music was deafening even from inside. "Do you have Katie? I want to hear her voice." Jackson switched his phone to speaker and turned on the radio transmitter. He wanted his team to hear everything as it happened. He turned and gestured for McCray to cover the boy's ears.

"You blew that chance." Buckley said. "If you want your daughter to live, you'll do exactly as I say."

CHAPTER 45

Jackson fought to stay calm. "Where is she?"

Buckley ignored him. "Bring Ben to the information booth. Lift him over the counter, so he's inside. Tell him it's a game so he doesn't get upset. Then get back in your car and drive away. Take your cop buddies with you. I'll be watching."

"What about Katie? When do I get my daughter?" Jackson's heart pounded so hard, he thought it would burst. Had he blown this operation?

"She's in the trunk of a car and that vehicle is about to leave. If you want to know which car to follow, you'll do what you're told. If I get shot or arrested, you won't find her until someone smells her dead body."

Son of a bitch! Jackson wanted to smash the phone against the dashboard. The crafty bastard! He bit down until he tasted blood. He had to work through this new development, but all he could think about was Katie in the trunk of a car—where she might die a slow, horrible death if Buckley didn't call again.

Time to fight back. "I know who you are! And if I don't get my daughter, every law enforcement officer in this country will be looking for you. You'll never get the chance to raise your son."

Buckley hung up.

Jackson willed his pounding blood to slow before he had an aneurysm.

Over the radio, Lammers said, "I'll get the state police to put up roadblocks at every access point out of town. No one will leave this area without their vehicle searched. We'll find Katie."

"She could be in transit right now. I have to do what he says." Jackson climbed from the car and opened the back door. "Come on, Benjie. We've got to visit somebody."

"Who?" His little voice was so innocent.

Nausea filled Jackson's stomach. How could he do this? Benjie trusted him. The boy wouldn't understand what was happening. Even after they arrested Buckley and rescued Benjie, the episode might scar him emotionally.

There was no other choice. Katie trusted him too, and she was counting on him to rescue her. He couldn't risk his own child's life to spare the boy a few minutes of distress. He vowed to make it up to Benjie by adopting him and giving him the best family life he could—whatever choices that meant.

Sick with guilt, he took the boy's hand and walked toward the sidewalk. A family crossed in front, with the father holding the hand of a boy about five years old.

Benjie looked up at him. "Jackson? Will you be my daddy?"

His chest contracted, crushing his heart. This kid needed him, and he was about to betray him. But could he become Benjie's father? If he made a verbal commitment, there was no backing out.

A dark thought gave him a moment of panic. Benjie's biological father was, at best, a sociopath who'd kidnapped a young woman, and, at worst, a psychopath who'd killed his wife and the mother of his child. What if that nature was embedded in Benjie's genes? What if he grew up to be like Carson Buckley? Oh no, why had he allowed the boy to bond with him?

Jackson pushed aside his fear. He had to do the right thing.

They were on the sidewalk now, directly in front of the information booth. Jackson squatted to look directly in Benjie's eyes. "If the authorities will let me, I'll be your dad. But we have to do something first. It's like a game." Jackson had to pause, so filled with disgust and worry he choked on his words. "I'm going to leave you in this booth with a nice lady for a minute. Then another man will pick you up. He's your uncle, even though you don't know him. I need you to hang out with your uncle for a minute. Then I'll get you right back. Okay?" Buckley would probably confuse the boy by telling him he was his father, but Jackson had no control over that. They would just have to work quickly to intercept him.

The boy shook his head. "I don't like this game."

"Me neither, son. But this will help Katie, and she needs our help." Jackson couldn't bring himself to say more.

He waited for a young man at the booth to leave, then lifted Benjie up to the counter and spoke to the staff woman. "I'm a police officer, and I need you to watch this boy until his uncle gets here. Please just go along. A life is at stake." Jackson kissed Benjie's forehead and lowered him to the floor on the other side of the counter. He scanned the back wall, noting the door leading into the gated area. Buckley was probably right outside, listening. Should he vault over the counter, charge through the door, and grab the perp by the throat? Jackson touched his weapon under his jacket. He could put the gun to Buckley's head and demand the information about Katie.

Risky and stupid. If Buckley lost his chance with Benjie, he might not care about his own life. Or Katie's. He might even punish Jackson by keeping silent and letting her die in the trunk. Some killers never revealed their victims' locations, leaving their families with no closure.

"Sir, I'll need to see some identification." The woman looked confused and worried.

Anxiety mounting, Jackson turned and walked away. McCray stood in the street, watching the booth. Jackson couldn't bear to look back and see Benjie disappear. He loved that kid. Back in his car, he grabbed the radio mic and said. "Benjie is in the booth, and Buckley has to be nearby. Probably on foot. He'll grab the boy and take off, any second now. I hope you've got this corner surrounded."

Lammers came back with, "Schak and Quince are on foot on the back side of the buildings. Two patrol officers are on Blair and another is on the corner of Third and Jackson. We'll get him."

A small measure of relief. "I still don't know where Katie is, so get eyes on the perp, but don't move in yet." Jackson grabbed his cell phone and hit redial. After ten rings, he clicked off and called again. Had Buckley tossed the phone? Or was the son of a bitch going to screw him over?

"Benjie just went out the back door, but I didn't see the perp!" McCray shouted to be heard over the loud music.

Jackson's call finally connected, and Buckley said in a rush, "She's in an older white Buick that just headed west from Fourth and Tyler." The call cut off.

Finally! Every fiber in his body wanted to jump in his car and go after the Buick. He needed to see Katie, to know she was alive. He grabbed the mic and relayed the information.

Lammers came back: "Schak and unit fifty-seven will go after him. Jackson, stay in the area. You're closest to the perp." A pause. "Anyone have eyes on him?"

Quince and two patrol officers checked in with negative responses. Jackson was silent. He wanted to be the one to rescue Katie, but others were closer to Sixth Avenue, the main artery heading west. He'd also made Benjie a promise.

"Buckley doesn't know me," McCray said. "So I'll follow him." He rushed toward the booth and pushed aside a couple. The skinny, fifty-something ex-cop hopped up, sat on the counter, and swung his legs to the other side in a single smooth motion. He was out the back door in a matter of seconds.

The music stopped, and some of the tension drained from Jackson's body. The street vibrated under him, and a train whistle sounded. He turned to see slow-moving freight cars a block away. He hadn't realized how close the tracks were. The noise wasn't as loud as the band had been, but it was still overwhelming.

Feeling more focused, he tried to put himself into Buckley's head. The perp knew they had his identity, but he also probably thought he'd cleared his pursuers out of the area by sending them after the Buick. Buckley would be looking to steal a car and get out of the state as quickly as possible. Or maybe a motorcycle. Something unexpected.

Jackson had to move. Instinctively, he headed west, jogging in the same direction the train was moving. He scanned the area for someone tall, with a toddler on his back, running.

The train picked up a little speed. The engine was probably pulling out of the track-switching station a half mile ahead—an area where homeless people hopped off after spending the winter in warmer cities down south. *The train!* Would Buckley try to board the damn train to avoid roadblocks?

CHAPTER 46

Buckley hugged his son, holding back tears of joy. He'd prayed for this moment for so long! It filled him with pride and pleasure to know his family line would continue. His mother would be so happy. Even though he couldn't risk visiting her in the nursing home for a while. If Jackson really did know his identity, he would have to change his name and stay the hell out of Utah. He hated the idea, but Ben was worth it.

From under the poncho, the boy squirmed to get free. "I don't like this game."

"You will," Buckley promised. He slid Ben around to his back and secured him with a bungee cord he'd taken off the back of a bicycle. "Hang on, we're going to have a lot of fun." He pulled on the colorful striped poncho he'd bought from a street vendor. "We have to hide you from the bad guys for a few minutes, so keep quiet."

The boy started to cry.

"I've got candy if you'll be quiet."

Ben didn't answer, but he settled down. Buckley slipped him a bag of M&M's, then trotted into the crowd milling around inside the gated parking lot. He moved quickly, nudging people aside, and strode into the art gallery that he'd cut through to enter the gated area. He followed its maze of small rooms to the exit.

The back door led into a narrow walkway between the gallery and the metal building that faced the other street. He hit the weed-covered path and ran straight for the street ahead. Logic and survival instinct told him to turn left, hot-wire the first unlocked vehicle he came to, and get out of the area as quickly as possible. But that's what they expected him to do. Instead, he turned right on a side street and ran for the train tracks that bordered the far side of the busy neighborhood. Once he crossed the tracks, he'd be out of their visual scope and could run west through the grassy strip along the railroad. After he cleared the police units' patrol area, it would be easier to steal a car, or maybe a work van, and head out of town.

He talked to Ben as he ran, trying to soothe the boy. In an earlier time, it would have attracted attention, but now people just assumed he was talking to someone on a cell phone. He spotted a dark-blue sedan cruising down the street and turned into a private yard. Pulse throbbing in his throat, he sprinted alongside the quirky yellow-and-purple house and ducked into the backyard. A built-up, homemade pond filled most of the space, and he charged past it to the fence on the other side.

"I need breath," Ben complained.

Did he have time to stop and be nice? Yes. Building rapport with the scared child who'd never known him seemed worth a moment. Ten seconds wouldn't matter now that he was away from the drop site and Jackson was racing after a dummy car. He lifted the poncho, unstrapped Benjie, and pulled him around front. The boy was stressed and panting like a dog.

"Take some deep breaths. You're gonna be fine." He bounced the boy a little, hoping to soothe him. "We'll soon be in a car, heading home, like a family." Buckley didn't know much about taking care of kids. His own father had only been around on weekends to take him hunting and fishing and scavenging for things to resell. They hadn't talked much. "We have to go." He slid the boy around to his back and hooked the ends of the stretch cord. "We're off!"

His first awkward attempt at fatherhood both excited and embarrassed him. He would get better.

Buckley climbed over the fence into the next yard and did the same for two more houses. At the last perimeter, he scanned the street for cop vehicles. None that he could see.

As he hopped the fence, the deafening music shut down. His first thought was *Thank goodness.* But the quiet made him feel suddenly more visible. He ran toward the intersection, head down, with Ben bouncing against his back. As he weaved through the crowd, the ground below him trembled, as if a minor earthquake were happening. What was that noise? He looked up and saw the train.

Fuck! What now? He couldn't cross the tracks, and he couldn't stand there and wait.

Then he saw it. Another gift from God. Fast-moving transportation out of town and out of the state—with no one following or stopping him. *Thank you!* He vowed to go back to church and take Ben, as soon as they settled into their new life.

Could he jump on a moving train? Why not? Teenagers and old drunks could manage it. He sprinted down the street, passing the vehicles that were stuck, waiting for the train. He kept his eyes on the freight cars as they rolled by and tried to observe details. Most seemed to be closed boxcars, but some looked like V-shaped container units. Those had metal rungs to climb on and hollowed out spaces across the back, with a platform to sit on.

Twenty feet from the train, he turned left and started running parallel with the moving giant. Buckley kept sprinting, watching the color and shapes beside him.

There! Now! "Hang on, Ben!"

He leaped and grabbed for a metal rung above his head. His hands made good contact, and he pulled up with his arms and lifted his legs at the same time. His feet found a bottom rung. He was on board. Buckley reached around to the back of the metal frame and grabbed another rung. He swung his feet again, praying the strap around his chest wouldn't slip and that Benjie would be safe. After another awkward maneuver, he stepped onto the narrow platform. He pulled off the poncho and strap and set Benjie down. With a tight grip on the metal frame, Buckley leaned out to see if anyone had followed him.

Fifty yards back, Jackson sprinted next to the train. Fuck! Time for plan B.

CHAPTER 47

Evans stood and stretched, needing a break. She'd already stared at the damn picture until her eyes watered. Before that, she'd been on the phone with a department tech expert, who'd coached her on how to check the photo's metadata for location, only to discover the information wasn't there. She'd learned that savvy users, who wanted to protect their privacy, could download an app that helped them disable the location technology. So far, the image was a bust.

As were her phone calls to every crappy little motel in the West Eugene area. They either hadn't rented to anyone matching Buckley's name and/or description, or the evening clerk had just come on shift and couldn't be helpful. She'd accomplished nothing and had let down the team.

She hated being left behind! But Evans didn't feel competent to join a takedown. She was moving too slowly, hurt too badly, and didn't feel right about being in a scenario where she might need to use her gun or protect her teammates. Maybe when the pain meds wore off . . .

The SWAT physical on Monday. *Damn!* She'd have to wait for the next one, which could be a month to another six weeks before they set up for it again. *More time to train,* she told herself, trying not to feel disappointed. Evans walked around the table just to keep from getting stiff, but it hurt like hell and she sat back down. Why hadn't anyone called with an update? She checked the clock. They'd been gone forty-six minutes. That was too long. Something wasn't right. *Please don't let it be Katie.* Jackson couldn't take another personal blow.

Evans turned back to the sixty-inch screen and stared at the image of Katie taped to a chair with her mouth and ankles bound as well. Her eyes were wide, but not only with fear. The girl was angry too, and that would work in her favor if she had an opportunity to escape. Starting in the upper left corner, Evans worked her way through the image again, chunk by chunk. The photo had been taken only a few feet from the chair, so not much of the room was visible. Ugly green carpet showed under the chair, but the wall behind Katie was blank. Buckley, thinking like a cop, had been careful not to give away his location. What was in the satchel on the floor? It worried her. But so far, Buckley hadn't mentioned it.

A tiny dark spot on the right caught her eye. Was it the corner of something? Like a TV? Clicking the magnify icon, she enlarged the image to the point where it was blurry and she had to scroll over to see the dark object. Yes, in fact, it was the corner of a TV screen, and it contained a curved line, something etched into the hard plastic. Probably a manufacturer's logo.

She grabbed a pen and paper and drew the curved line in a bigger size, then tried to visualize the rest of the pattern. When it didn't come to her, she opened her browser and scrolled through the list of motels again. No help. Most of the hooker/heroin crash pads didn't even have websites to peruse. Evans looked at the image again. The green carpet caught her attention. An unusual choice. Most motel carpeting was brown or beige or some ugly print. She clicked back to her browser and scanned the list again. The Shamrock. Would it use green carpeting? She picked up the pen and added to the curved line, drawing a four-leaf clover from a single corner. *Hot damn!* That was probably it. She started to call the motel again, but remembered that the clerk had said she'd just come on duty.

Evans called Jackson but he didn't pick up. Not good. Unless he was in the middle of something. She tried Lammers, who also didn't answer. Something was going down, and they were all focused. She didn't want to bother Schak or Quince, but instead texted Lammers the information about the motel. Her next step was to get out there herself and start opening doors. She didn't have a warrant, but the picture of Katie as a hostage should convince any reasonable human being to cooperate. Evans e-mailed the JPEG to herself, so it would show up on her phone, then grabbed her keys and headed out.

A fool's errand, she thought, painfully making her way downstairs. Buckley would have Katie with him for the exchange. But maybe if she found his motel room, she'd find a clue that would help them nail the bastard.

CHAPTER 48

Jackson ran toward the main boulevard, panic mounting. Lammers and the patrol units were still searching the side streets, but he hadn't seen McCray since he'd gone over the counter. It was too soon to hear from Schak about the white Buick carrying Katie, but he had to assume they'd stop the vehicle and rescue her. The driver was likely an unwitting participant and wouldn't flee unless he had another reason to run from the law.

He passed the patrol car blocking Third Avenue and ran toward the swarming crowd in the intersection. People of all ages and dress, but few small children. This group was spillover from the party at the nearby brewery. He scanned the crowd, moving slowly left, thinking Buckley would be coming from that direction. He heard the train whistle again and spun around. Jogging toward the tracks was a tall man wearing a hooded poncho—and carrying what looked like a large backpack under the fabric. Was that Buckley and Benjie? Jackson broke into a run, pushing people aside.

"Move!" He didn't have time for politeness or explanations.

Going on instinct, Jackson sprinted after the tall man. Ahead, the train crossed the boulevard, blocking the exit from the neighborhood. The perp had nowhere to go, except left, into the mostly empty acreage around the train-switching yard. Was Buckley planning to hop on the train? *Please no!* Jackson pushed himself, a jarring pain pinching his gut. If Buckley had been alone, he would have pulled his weapon and commanded him to stop. But Benjie was on the perp's back, so all he could do was try to close the gap and take him down. He hoped like hell a patrol officer was behind him.

As the man in the poncho neared the train, he turned left and moved in close to the passing freight cars. He was going to make the leap! Jackson raced after him, making the same turn. The massive train thundered along, moving slowly but still creating a wind. He was close enough to reach out and touch the freight cars, and his heart pounded as loudly as the wheels on the tracks. Should he stay with the perp and get on the damn train, or keep his feet on the ground and call for help?

He couldn't let Buckley out of his sight. What if he jumped back off a mile down the track and disappeared?

The perp turned his head to watch the cars, so Jackson glanced over too. Boxcars with no open doors and nothing to grab. He snapped his head forward again.

Fifty feet ahead, Buckley leapt and caught a metal rung on the back of a V-shaped container. He was getting away! Jackson kept running and turned to watch the train again. Two boxcars went by, then another V-shaped car was right there. He braced for the leap. The metal rungs came into sight. Jackson sucked in a breath and jumped.

He caught the rung with both hands, but his feet dangled and he ached with fear. Jackson pulled his legs up and groped for a rung. His toe caught one, and he jerked both feet into place. He was on the train, but it was picking up speed and he couldn't stay like this. Still gulping air after his sprint, Jackson leaned toward the rear of the car to see if it offered a safer place.

A two-foot-wide platform crossed the back, tucked under the slanting shape of the freight car. Carefully, he worked his way around to the back of the metal structure and climbed through the rungs. He landed on all fours and stayed like that until he could breathe normally.

When his fear subsided, he sat on his rear and scooted back against the big steel container. He couldn't see Buckley from this position, but he had to make calls. Hands trembling, he connected with Lammers first.

"It's Jackson. The perp hopped a train."

She swore loud and long. "I'll call the railroad. Do you see a number on any of the boxcars?"

"Not at the moment. I'm on the back of a freight container."

"You jumped on a moving train?" Her disbelief was like a slap. "Are you out of your mind?"

"Maybe. But I made Benjie a promise. What about Katie?"

A pause. "I'm sorry, but she wasn't in the Buick."

No! His heart dropped into his stomach. "The fucker lied to get me out of the area."

"We'll find her. I called the chief and he authorized off-duty officers to join the search."

Was Katie dead? Or had Buckley just ditched her? "We need to search sleazy motels in the area."

"I'll check in with Evans. Get me a number from one of those train cars."

"I'll try."

"And be careful!" She hung up.

Jackson grabbed his cell phone and called Buckley.

The perp answered immediately, screaming to be heard over the engine's roar. "Get off the train or your daughter dies!"

"Where is she?"

"That black bag at her feet contains an explosive. And a cell phone that will detonate it. Get off the train and let us go, or I'll kill her before you can find her." He hung up.

Fuck! For a moment Jackson was too freaked out to think straight. He sucked in oxygen, then called Lammers again. "Buckley says the black bag has an explosive. We need to find her!"

"I'll get the bomb unit out to the area. What does he want?"

"For me to get off the train and let him go."

"Get the train's number first. We'll find her." She hung up before he could argue.

Jackson was torn. He couldn't let Buckley get away with Benjie. But would the bastard blow up Katie? Would he know if Jackson stayed on the train?

He needed to stand up, lean out, and get Lammers what she needed. His body resisted, not wanting to move. The noise and sway of the train was terrifying and hypnotic at the same time. But the sky was nearly dark now, and he had to move quickly if he wanted to see markings on the freight cars.

Jackson pushed to his feet and grabbed the metal piping. He leaned out and tried to read the number on the side of the boxcar. He could only see part of it, but he texted the information to Lammers. Now what? Did Buckley know he was still back here? The perp hadn't called again with another threat. Was Katie already dead? He couldn't let himself think that.

Suddenly, the train lost speed again. Jackson sensed he was in West Eugene, near the wetlands. Lammers hadn't had time to orchestrate the slowdown, so the train was stopping for some other reason. Jackson didn't care. He just hoped Buckley would take the opportunity to get off.

Brakes squealed, and the massive metal cars slowed even more. Would Buckley exit on the same side he'd climbed on? Jackson stepped across the platform to the other side and saw open grasslands. What if Buckley didn't exit at all?

Jackson had no intention of staying on the train for a long ride into the night. Maneuvering back to the other side, he climbed out onto the metal rungs and prepared to jump down. The risk intimidated him. He could twist an ankle, or fall and break an arm. Jackson calmed his mind and formulated a plan. Buckley was only two boxcars away. Now that the train was moving much slower, he could close the gap on the ground. He would be on him before Buckley knew he was coming.

He held on, waiting for a safer moment. What if the train picked up speed again? Sometimes they slowed briefly for crossings or other trains. Sometimes they backed up, then started forward again. He had no idea where this one was headed or why.

It was time.

He let go with one hand and foot and swung out, watching the ground and looking for a safe landing area. A flat spot! Jackson jumped for the clearing, throwing himself as far from the moving train as he could. He landed on his feet but stumbled forward and went down on one knee. After scrambling to get up, Jackson sprinted alongside the train. His Sig Sauer bumped against his side, a small comfort.

He expected Buckley to be carrying a weapon—he was an ex-cop—but not to have it in his hand. The perp would be holding on to Benjie. It might come down to a physical confrontation. The only edge he had was surprise and two free hands.

As Jackson reached the back of the other V-shaped container car, Buckley and Benjie came into sight. The kidnapper was sitting cross-legged with Benjie in his lap. The train slowed, and it seemed it would stop at any moment. Jackson pulled his weapon and charged up to the freight car, prepared to leap on if he had to.

"Let Benjie go!"

The man and boy both looked up, startled.

The train screeched to a stop.

Benjie cried out, "Jackson!" and bolted out of Buckley's lap. He took two little steps across the platform, then leaped through the opening.

Jackson lurched forward and caught him with his free hand. He stumbled in the gravel but managed to stay upright, his heart beating like a flock of wild birds. Weapon still trained on Buckley, he set Benjie down and stepped in front of the boy. "Hands in the air!"

Buckley was on his feet now, and he grabbed a small handgun from an ankle holster.

"Freeze or I'll shoot!" Jackson yelled.

For a moment, Buckley was still.

"Where is Katie?" Jackson screamed.

"It doesn't matter now." The perp brought up his gun and pointed it at Jackson's head.

He had no choice. Jackson fired, and Buckley fell back against the steel car.

The train started forward again.

From behind him, Benjie clung to his leg, saying "Daddy" over and over again. Jackson kept his eyes on the perp, who still held a weapon. Buckley lowered his arm and collapsed to the floor of the platform. Jackson ran alongside for a moment, shouting at the bleeding man. "Where is Katie? Tell me! Where is she?" But Buckley was either dead or unconscious. The train picked up speed, and Jackson had to let it go.

• • •

With Benjie on his shoulders, Jackson hurried along the tracks, dodging chuckholes and weed clumps. His legs hurt from sprinting, but all he could think about was Katie. The street-party crowd was even thicker in the growing darkness. He pushed through the crowd until he reached his car and put Benjie safely inside. Grabbing the radio, he pleaded, "Give me an update! Does anyone have Katie?"

"Negative," two officers responded.

Despair filled his veins like wet cement, threatening to drown him with its weight. Had he given up his daughter for Benjie? How was he supposed to live with that? Jackson climbed in his car and stared at his phone.

Lammers came on the radio. "Where's Buckley?"

"On the back of a freight car, wounded and possibly dead. But I have the boy."

"Great news. We'll get units out to find the perp when the train stops, which should be soon."

"We need to find Katie first!" Jackson shouted, too distressed to think straight.

On the seat beside him, Benjie whimpered. "Did the bad man take her?"

"Yes." Jackson gave him a quick hug. "But we'll find her."

His phone rang. *Evans!* "Tell me something good, please."

"I just found Katie at the Shamrock Motel on Fillmore. She's rattled but unhurt. The satchel was empty."

"Thank god! Thank you. I'm on my way." Sweet relief washed over him, and he struggled to keep his composure. "Update the team, please. Lammers called in off-duty officers to search and they need to go home."

"I'm on it."

Jackson turned to Benjie. "They found Katie. Your sister's okay." It was the first time he'd ever said *your sister*, but it felt right.

His family had grown and Benjie was here to stay. He started the car and turned it around in the now empty, blocked street. Later he would go back over this day step-by-step, and question every decision. But not yet. For now he could only rejoice.

CHAPTER 49

Sunday, September 8, 7:15 a.m.

Jackson entered the elevator, aware that Kera might be in the building somewhere, dealing with the grief and trauma of watching someone she cared about die. He was on his way up to see Carson Buckley, who hadn't died. The relief of not having that death on his conscience barely outweighed the guilt of not being there for Kera. Yet this had to be done. Andra deserved justice, and he still didn't know if Buckley had killed her. They had two other viable suspects. In the coming weeks, his team would trace Buckley's movements and attempt to build a case against him. Questioning him now, while he was wounded and medicated, might elicit a slipup or maybe even a confession.

A patrol officer stood watch outside Buckley's hospital room. Jackson nodded as he passed but didn't stop to chat. He wanted to get this done and get home before his kids got up. The thought almost stopped him. Kids. Plural. He'd never used the expression before.

Shackled to the bed railing at both wrists, Buckley had his eyes closed but the TV was on. Gauze covered his left shoulder.

Jackson moved in closer. "Buckley. I have some questions."

The kidnapper opened his eyes but didn't focus for a minute. Jackson said his name again and waited.

"You're like a dog with a bone," Buckley mumbled.

Jackson considered it a compliment. He wanted to get to the heart of questioning but knew he needed to ease into it to get Buckley to cooperate. "How did you finally find Andra?"

"What do you mean?"

"How did you track her to Eugene?"

"I didn't. You led me here." Buckley's voice was even scratchier than he remembered.

"We'll dig through your credit card expenses and phone records and track your whereabouts all last week. Lying to me will only work against you."

"The paperwork will prove I never set foot in Eugene until yesterday morning." Buckley looked over at his tray table. "I need some water." The shackles kept him from reaching for it.

Jackson didn't believe him. Buckley could have driven here from Utah, used cash, and never showed his ID to anyone. The man was careful. "Why did you kill Andra? Because you couldn't find Benjie?"

"Water."

Grudgingly, Jackson held the plastic bottle and straw to his lips. He hated the man for what he'd done to Katie, but he needed information. Closure for his case.

Buckley took only a few sips. "I didn't kill her. I wanted to sometimes when I thought I would never see my son again, but I'm not a violent man."

Jackson made a scoffing sound. "You threatened to kill my daughter. And the Salt Lake City police think you killed your wife."

"I didn't!" The outburst made him grimace in pain. "Innocent people are accused all the time. You're a cop; you know it happens."

Innocent? "You kidnapped my daughter, so you don't have any credibility."

"I only used her as leverage for Ben. She wasn't hurt."

Rage flared in Jackson's veins. "She was traumatized! And she could have died in that motel room before we got to her."

The perp blinked. "I knew someone would find her. I never meant to hurt anyone."

In Buckley's twisted mind that might even be true. "What about Lucille Caiden? Did you traumatize her too?"

"What are you talking about? My friends the Wagners stopped in to see if Andra and Benjie were living there, but they didn't threaten her. They're nice people."

Jackson made a mental note to call the sheriff's office and see how Lucille Caiden's autopsy had come out. But he leaned toward thinking the old lady had died of natural causes—perhaps brought on by stress. But was Buckley telling the truth about Andra? He didn't seem inclined to confess.

"We'll compare your DNA to trace evidence found on Andra's body. This is your last chance to tell me what happened and get a plea deal that will let you out of prison someday."

Buckley shook his head. "I just wanted my boy." He closed his eyes. "I need to rest."

Jackson left, resisting the urge to punch him as a parting gesture. Buckley's DNA had already been sent to the state lab, and Jackson hoped they still had enough blood sample from Logan Grayson to run a comparison against Andra's trace evidence. He wanted to know who had killed her. But he would find out tomorrow. Today, he would spend with his family.

Later, while he was putting together a puzzle with Benjie, his phone beeped with a text from Kera: *They're taking Danette off life support. Heading to the hospital.*

Oh no. That meant she would die soon. He texted back: *On my way.* Jackson gathered up the puzzle pieces. "I have to go to the hospital and see a friend."

"With the baby?" Benjie asked.

The boy remembered visiting Kera and Micah in the hospital. "Yes. Would you like to go?" As if the kid had a choice. This was his and Benjie's life now. "Put on your shoes, please."

Jackson padded down the hall to Katie's room. He and his daughter had watched a movie together—a comedy—the night before, and it had felt like old times. Cautiously optimistic that Katie would stay with him for a while, he knocked on her door. "I'm headed to the hospital to see Kera. I'd like you to come."

She opened the door halfway, still in her pajamas. "Is Danette dying?"

"Yes."

"Then no. I can't handle that right now. I'm sorry."

"I can't handle leaving you alone. Not yet."

"Sorry, but you have to. Derrick is here and I'll be fine."

Why did she have to be so difficult? "I need to keep you close by for a few days. Humor me." The department would make him take some time off. Even though the perp hadn't died, Jackson had still been involved in another on-the-job shooting. Downtime was mandatory.

"I have something I have to do today," Katie insisted, "but I'm not going anywhere."

He felt himself give in. He couldn't smother her or she would take off again. "Okay. I'm taking Benjie with me. Keep the doors locked." Derrick was home, and she would be fine, he told himself. The threat was over.

"Give Kera a hug for me. Tell her I just can't leave the house yet."

Kera would understand. She was an incredible woman, who deserved someone better than him. Jackson wondered if her ex would be at the hospital too. He hoped not. He and Kera had important issues to discuss.

Benjie waited by the door, looking so cute and cooperative, it made his heart melt. *Please let it last until he's at least thirteen.*

Jackson stopped in the small waiting room on the ICU floor and called Kera to let her know he was there. She joined him a minute later, carrying a sleepy little Micah. When he saw her and the baby—who'd lost both his parents before he could talk—Jackson knew what he had to do.

First, he hugged Kera tightly. "I love you. I'm so sorry this is happening." Kera had only known her daughter-in-law for a few years, but she loved everyone in her life fiercely.

"Danette took her last breath a few minutes ago. Her mother is still in there with her."

"What can I do? Make calls or help plan a service for her?"

"Just tell me we're okay. That you're not leaving me for someone else."

"We're more than okay." Jackson plunged in. "Let's move in together and raise these boys as a family. Micah needs a father, and Benjie needs a mother."

She stepped back and gave him a long, uncertain look. "That's not a good reason to be together."

"That's not the main reason. We love each other and we're good together. Why should we each do this alone?" It wasn't a romantic proposal, but it was heartfelt. He'd already made a commitment to Benjie, but Kera deserved it more.

She smiled. "We do love each other, and we'll talk about it. But right now, I just need some time at home alone. Will you take Micah for a while this afternoon? I'll drop him by later with all his things."

She was testing him to see if he could handle two little boys. "I'm happy to. I'll cook dinner for all of us tonight as well."

Kera gave a soft laugh. "I'm not sure that's a good idea, but suit yourself."

On the way home, instead of nodding off for a nap, Benjie began to cry. "I want Tuffy."

"Who's Tuffy?" Jackson looked over his shoulder.

"My co-ah bear."

"What's a co-ah bear?" He didn't get the *co-ah* part.

In the rearview mirror, Benjie rubbed his eyes. "He's snuggly."

A stuffed toy. It was probably still at the Pershing house. Jackson didn't want to drive over there. "We'll get you a new bear."

"I want Tuffy."

He changed his mind. Benjie probably had more clothes and things he should pick up too, if they weren't too damaged from the smoke or fire.

The Pershing house looked more dilapidated every time he saw it. Someone had broken a front window and tagged the side with spray paint. He wondered how long it would sit like that— vacant, partially burned, and abandoned by both the owners and the bank. Would the neighbors force the city to condemn it? As he walked through the door, Benjie let out a whimper. Jackson picked him up, hating to bring him in, yet unwilling to leave him in the car, even with the doors locked.

He headed for the small room where Benjie's things had been. It smelled like smoke, but was mostly unscathed. All that remained was a basket of dirty clothes and some coloring books. No stuffed bear. "It's not here." He kissed the boy's cheek. "Sorry. Did you leave it outside?"

The boy pointed at the closet where Jackson had lifted him through the trapdoor.

Was the toy under the house? He started to tell him no, then changed his mind and headed back to his car for a flashlight. Was this how he would be with Benjie? Unable to tell him no because of what he'd been through?

Back in the bedroom, Jackson lay on the floor in front of the opening in the closet floor. The trapdoor had never been closed. He scooted forward and stuck his head and one arm down into the hole. Scanning back and forth with the flashlight, he quickly spotted the little toy. A koala bear. Now he understood what Benjie had been saying. Inching forward, he set the flashlight down and grabbed the toy.

Under it was a small cylinder with a yellow cap on one end. He reached for the item and brought it out. A medical device?

Jackson backed out of the opening and handed the bear to Benjie, who hugged the toy with a delighted grin. Jackson held up the device. "Is this yours?"

Benjie nodded and his lips trembled. "My EpiPen."

Epinephrine, to prevent anaphylactic shock. What was the boy allergic to? He had so much to learn about this child and no one to consult.

CHAPTER 50

A week earlier

Logan closed the textbook and went to the fridge for a beer. Political science was so boring. How was he supposed to remember all that stuff for a test when he didn't understand it? He just wanted to play football—and make real money—but he had to get through college before he could become an NFL player. His skills brought in a shitload of money for the college, but all he got out of it was tuition and room and board. He couldn't even take cash for autographs without getting into trouble. And Catalina needed money for the doctor and the baby. Being a student was such an inconvenience.

He tried again to read the assigned pages but couldn't concentrate. He wished his depression meds would make him more focused, like ADHD medicine did for his smart friend Nate. A little coke could help. He'd been keeping it mostly straight since the season started, and he deserved to party a little. Maybe Trey could hook him up. He'd stop by Trey's apartment, then head over to Catalina's. She always made him feel better.

Trey's girlfriend was at their apartment, so Logan waited until he reached Catalina's place to do a couple lines. He hoped the coke would bring back some of the juice in their relationship. When they'd first gotten together, Cat had been so hot—an amazing sexual partner. But the pregnancy had made her cautious and had taken some of the sizzle out of their romps.

After he kissed her neck and rubbed her breasts the way she liked, Catalina pushed him away. "Sorry, babe, but I can't do this right now. I'm too worried."

Oh fuck. He needed some release. "Worried about what? We got your rent money from the Pershing place."

"I've been having pain again. I told you I need to see a doctor."

Logan's erection disappeared. But his need didn't. "I've got one of those fake jobs coming up next month, and I'll make a thousand for it. I'll get the money to you then." Alumni and wealthy football fans sometimes offered one-day, overpaid no-show jobs to help players make extra cash, but they didn't happen often enough, and the team had nearly a hundred players. But as quarterback, he'd scored some of them over the years.

"I can't wait that long," Cat whined. "We should do another zombie-house scam."

"We don't want to push our luck." Still, they needed the money. Logan fingered a sore spot on the back of his head. He owed another player nearly a thousand dollars, and the asshole had jumped him the other night and pounded him over it. Not many men were big enough to take him—except a linebacker.

"Nobody reports the house deals, because the cops don't care." Catalina went to the kitchen and poured herself some chocolate milk.

The woman they'd rented to popped into his head. Strawberry blonde, slim and pretty. She'd kept touching his hand when they'd signed the papers. He wondered what she was up to.

"Do you want to watch a movie?"

No, he wanted to get laid. "I'm too hyper. Want to go for a walk instead?"

Cat shook her head, then grabbed his wrist. "Why aren't you wearing your pink breast-cancer bracelet? I thought the team was supposed to wear them all week."

Logan looked at his wrist. "Oh shit. I think I left it at the rental house." He hated the fucking pink wristbands and helmets, but the team wore them once a year as part of a fundraiser. It was good publicity for the team and the school.

They were both quiet for a moment. Worried, Logan said, "I think I have to go get it. If that girl finds it and realizes she's been scammed by a UO football player, she might go public."

"I don't know. I think it's riskier to go back," Catalina argued. "She's probably already figured out that we don't really live there." They'd picked up a couch and a TV off a street corner for free. And they'd moved a few of their own personal things in just long enough to make it look real and get the money.

"I doubt that. It's only been a couple of days. I'll be back in a bit." Logan grabbed his keys and hurried out. The coke had made him wired and restless and he needed to blow off some energy anyway.

On the drive over, he took the long way, speeding down the back roads and loving the warm wind on his face as daylight faded. For a few minutes, he felt free, just a young man with no responsibilities, enjoying one of the last evenings of summer.

The tenant's car was in the driveway, and at first it irritated him. He'd hoped to just get in and out without her knowing he'd been there. He'd driven Cat's little truck when he'd come before, worried that someone might recognize or remember his sports car. But when he saw Amanda sitting on the couch, wearing a halter top with her slim brown legs dangling, he remembered how attractive she was. And how she'd flirted with him, even though she'd believed he and his girlfriend would both be living there.

"Hi, Logan." Such a sweet smile.

"Hey, Amanda." A flash of guilt for scamming her. But the house was abandoned, so she might live there free for months, or even years. They might have done her a favor. He went to the dining area where they'd filled out the phony rental papers and looked around for his wristband. He didn't see it and tried to remember where he might have taken it off.

She came into the kitchen, her sun-kissed skin glowing on her pretty face. "Where's your girlfriend?"

He hesitated. "I don't know. I think we broke up." This girl would be the perfect casual fuck.

Amanda opened the fridge, brushing against him as she did. "Let's have a beer and get to know each other."

She was into him. "I'm down for that."

They moved to the couch.

One beer turned into two, and they had a few good laughs. But he was too hyped and too horny to sit around talking. Either they were going to fuck or he would move on. He leaned in and kissed her, grabbing the back of her head. She pressed her tongue into his mouth, tasting like beer and watermelon and summer sex. His erection came back fast.

After a minute of making out, he scooped her up and carried her into her bedroom.

"Hey, not so fast." Her tone was light and she gave a little laugh.

The bareness of her room, with only a mattress on the floor, was a strange turn-on, making the whole scenario seedy and sexy. Logan kicked the door shut and dropped down to the mattress, pulling down his shorts in a quick movement.

"Hey, stop. I'm not—"

He pressed his mouth against hers to silence her. She wanted it, he could tell.

Amanda struggled under him, but it was pointless. He was twice her size and the coke made him more powerful.

"Don't fight it. Let it happen." He kept his mouth against hers and pinned her wrists above her head with one of his oversize hands.

After he penetrated her, the girl started to get loud, so he pressed his other hand over her mouth. It wasn't right to tease him like that, then change her mind. Not today. He'd taken enough shit from his coach, from Danica, and from Catalina. At the moment, he hated them all.

After a while, the girl stopped fighting and grew quiet. As much of a horndog as he was, he didn't climax easily, and his frustration grew. The door squeaked behind him. *What?* He looked back over his shoulder and saw a little boy. *Oh shit.* "Get out!"

The boy came at him, his little fist gripped around something yellow and cylindrical. Logan's penis went limp and he cursed. Something hard and pointed shoved into his shoulder. He rolled off the girl and grabbed for his shorts.

His heart began to race and he felt light-headed. "What the fuck?" He struggled to his feet and shouted at the boy. But the kid scampered away. Nausea filled his belly and he nearly fainted. Logan glanced over at Amanda, who wasn't moving. Had he hurt her?

Holy shit, he was sick. He had to go home. Maybe he would call the team doctor. Logan stumbled out of the room, pulling in deep breaths. Where were his keys? He felt for his pockets. Yes. Keys, phone, and wallet. Heart racing like overworked pistons, he left the house and staggered to his car. Thank god it was dark and no one could see him. The team couldn't afford any more scandals.

The drive home was a nightmare. Whatever was in his system was worse than being drunk. And his chest hurt. But he finally made it. Alone in his apartment, he vomited, then the effects started to subside a little. But anxiety set in. What if he had done something bad to Amanda and people found out? He could lose everything.

Logan went to the bathroom and took one of his mood stabilizers. He wanted to lie down, but knew he should walk it off instead. Pacing the apartment seemed to help. After a while, the beers ran through him and he needed to pee. Heart still pounding, he stood in front of the toilet and urinated. A moment later, a searing pain ripped into his chest, and he couldn't think straight. What the fuck was happening now? He tried to walk and felt blood gush from his nose. Logan lay down on the floor and prayed. His team needed him.

The pain worsened and his brain shut down.

CHAPTER 51

Evans took a seat in the conference room, grateful to be moving around a little better now. Not being able to work out was making her hyper and irritated. She'd finally done water aerobics at the YMCA that morning just to burn off some energy. The exercise had hurt but was worth it.

Schak and Quince were already in the room, and Lammers came in behind her.

"Where the hell is Jackson? I want to make this fast." The sergeant plopped into a chair, making it creak. "I have to testify in the damn evidence clusterfuck this afternoon. Those lazy, corrupt fuckers have tarnished everyone in this department, and I hope they end up in jail."

They all felt the same, but no one responded because they were tired of hashing it out.

Jackson came in—without his little sidekick.

"Where's Benjie?" Schak asked.

"With Kera. They're bonding over health food and trampolines at Bounce." Jackson sat down, glanced over at her, then pulled out his casebook.

"How's Danette?" Evans asked, wanting to know so much more.

"She died Sunday, and Sandoval, the driver, is being charged with manslaughter. It was a rough weekend for the whole family."

So Jackson and Kera and the two little boys were one big family now. The news was crushing, yet strangely liberating. She had no future with Jackson—which meant she had to request a transfer so she could finally move on. Once she made the SWAT unit, she could start training as a crisis negotiator. Mentally ill people with guns made it a busy, high-profile job.

"Let's get started," Lammers said. "I have new cases to assign." She opened her file book. "But first, let's wrap up Caiden and Grayson. Evans, you worked both cases; tell me what I don't know yet."

Evans looked at the notes she'd prepared for the meeting. "Grayson's DNA matches the hair fiber we found on Andra Caiden's body, as well as the sperm inside her, so he's the one who raped and strangled her. But he's dead so there's no one to question or prosecute. And his toxicology indicates he snorted cocaine before he showed up at the rental." Evans paused, still stunned by what a scumbag her victim turned out to be. "The same house where he and his girlfriend had scammed Andra out of four hundred dollars. Grayson then drove back to his apartment and had a heart attack. The cocaine he took was potent, but it wasn't laced or poisoned, so maybe the heart attack was karmic justice."

Lammers' mouth dropped open in surprise. "Buckley didn't kill the woman who took his son?"

"He came here after I made the trip to Utah," Jackson explained. "I think he followed me home from the airport. He may have even been on the same plane." Jackson turned to Evans. "But Grayson's heart attack wasn't karma. It was probably triggered by epinephrine."

"How? When?"

"At the Pershing rental. Benjie had been having nightmares and asking for a toy he lost. So I went to the crime scene and looked around underneath the house where he'd been hiding. I found his stuffed bear and this." Jackson held up a yellow-and-gray cylinder.

"An EpiPen?"

"Yes. I asked Benjie if it was his, and he said yes. For bee stings. Eventually, I got the story. He jabbed Grayson with the device when the jackass was assaulting his mother, then ran and hid. The adrenaline probably made Grayson sick and dysfunctional. But it was a child's dose, so he was able to drive himself home."

Schak shook his head. "That's wild. So the cocaine and epi stuff caused a reaction that gave him a heart attack?"

Evans remembered the antidepressant in Grayson's cabinet and what the ME had said. "No, it was the epinephrine reacting with his depression medication. It caused a hypertensive event."

"So Benjie killed him," Lammers said.

"Don't say that," Jackson warned. "He just tried to help his mother. He's a brave and sweet kid."

"What is the death report going to say?" Lammers pressed.

Evans summed it up. "A heart attack brought on by contraindicated medications."

"Have we heard anything about the fire investigation?" Schak wanted to know.

Jackson nodded. "Captain Ottovich called this morning. A witness saw a dark-blue Ford truck in the neighborhood the night of the fire. The same vehicle the owners' son drives. We think they were trying to collect the insurance, get out from under their debt, and be rid of the house. Proving it will be challenging."

His phone rang, and they all waited while he checked the caller. "It's the state lab." He took the call and switched over to speaker. "Jackson here. And the whole task force. What have you got for us?"

"We rushed the DNA comparisons for the child in question. The woman, Andra Caiden, is the boy's mother, but the man, Carson Buckley, is no relation."

A moment of stunned silence.

"Andra duped him," Schak said, shaking his head. "She took Buckley's money for a child that wasn't even his. And now he's going to prison."

"How did she get away with that?" Lammers asked.

Jackson gave it some thought. "If the implanted embryo didn't take, she would have known she wasn't pregnant. But rather than give up the money, she went out and got pregnant, intending to pass off the kid as theirs."

Evans didn't see it that way. "Andra might not have known it wasn't his child. And it doesn't matter. He's a kidnapper and needs to be locked away."

Jackson spoke softly. "It's a tragedy for everyone, but Benjie especially."

"Anything else on this case?" Lammers asked.

"The state pathologist said Lucille Caiden died of natural causes," Jackson added.

"Let's move on then. Jackson, you can get out of here and get back to your time off. But the rest of you have new assignments. No homicides this time, just some old-fashioned beat-downs and a crazy lady driving her car into her neighbor's living room. He says she wanted to kill him. Who wants it?"

What the hell? Evans thought she might as well take one more case while she waited for her transfer. "I'm on it."

. . .

Later at home, Jackson attempted to make lunch while supervising Benjie and Micah. It took twenty minutes to make grilled cheese sandwiches between answering questions and keeping Micah out of the drawers. How did women do this? Katie came into the kitchen just as he shut off the stove. She was starting school tomorrow, and he was afraid to let her leave.

"Nice timing. Lunch is ready."

"Dad, I have something important to tell you."

Her tone indicated it was serious. He hoped she didn't plan to drop out of school. He turned and braced himself. "What is it?"

"Remember when I said I had something important to do Sunday morning?"

He didn't, so he joked with her. "You went out and got another tattoo? A belly-button piercing? Just tell me."

She held out a white plastic tube. "I'm pregnant."

Blood rushed out of his head, and for a moment, he couldn't think . . . or hear.

"Dad? I'm sorry. If I keep the baby, will you help me?"

A baby? A third little one to care for? He couldn't handle it. His chest ached, and he realized he'd been holding his breath. He wanted to yell. To rant about how she never listened to him. How a child would change her life forever. But the look on her face stopped him. She was terrified and asking for his help.

Jackson opened his arms, and Katie stepped in.

"We're family. I'll always help you."

ABOUT THE AUTHOR

L.J. Sellers is a native of Eugene, Oregon, the setting of her thrillers. She's an award-winning journalist and a two-time Readers' Favorite Award winner—as well as a cyclist, social networker, and thrill-seeker. A long-standing fan of police procedurals, she counts John Sandford, Michael Connelly, Ridley Pearson, and Lawrence Sanders among her favorites. Her own novels featuring Detective Jackson include *The Sex Club*; *Secrets to Die For*; *Thrilled to Death*; *Passions of the Dead*; *Dying for Justice*; *Liars, Cheaters, & Thieves*; *Rules of Crime*; *Crimes of Memory*; and *Deadly Bonds*. In addition, she's penned three stand-alone thrillers—*The Baby Thief*, *The Gauntlet Assassin*, and *The Lethal Effect*—as well as two books in a new series about FBI Agent Jamie Dallas, *The Trigger* and *The Target*. When not plotting crime, L.J. has been known to perform stand-up comedy and jump out of airplanes.